A WINTER'S KISS

"I have always thought you one of the loveliest ladies of my acquaintance, beautiful of face, elegant of countenance, witty, lively, and generous to a fault."

Grace swallowed hard, for he had drawn close to her and his voice had dropped to a whisper. "Is this indeed what you think of me?" she murmured.

"Would you permit me to kiss you?" he asked gently.

Her mouth fell agape. "Kiss me?" she responded. "B-but, whatever for?"

He shrugged and smiled softly. "Just a friendly salute as a pledge that I shall never speak crossly to you again."

Grace felt very strange as her gaze fell to his lips. He moved closer still. She felt certain she should put out her hands and prevent him from—too late! She was in his arms, and his lips were on hers.

Oh, what a joy, she thought. She had truly forgotten what it was to be kissed by Cheriton. She felt as though summer had suddenly begun to pour in through the windows, for she grew warm all through. Seven years was a dreadfully long time to have been without his embraces. . . .

—from "Much Ado About Kittens" by Valerie King

BOOK YOUR PLACE ON OUR WEBSITE AND MAKE THE READING CONNECTION!

We've created a customized website just for our very special readers, where you can get the inside scoop on everything that's going on with Zebra, Pinnacle and Kensington books.

When you come online, you'll have the exciting opportunity to:

- View covers of upcoming books
- Read sample chapters
- Learn about our future publishing schedule (listed by publication month *and author*)
- Find out when your favorite authors will be visiting a city near you
- Search for and order backlist books from our online catalog
- Check out author bios and background information
- Send e-mail to your favorite authors
- Meet the Kensington staff online
- Join us in weekly chats with authors, readers and other guests
- Get writing guidelines
- AND MUCH MORE!

**Visit our website at
http://www.zebrabooks.com**

SNOWFLAKE KITTENS

CAROLA DUNN
MONA GEDNEY
VALERIE KING

Zebra Books
Kensington Publishing Corp.

http://www.zebrabooks.com

ZEBRA BOOKS are published by

Kensington Publishing Corp.
850 Third Avenue
New York, NY 10022

First Printing: December, 1999
10 9 8 7 6 5 4 3 2 1

Printed in the United States of America

CONTENTS

A KISS
AND A KITTEN

by

Carola Dunn

ONE

Hearing hoofbeats in the lane, Mariana straightened, leaning on her spade. She resisted the impulse to press one muddily gloved hand to the small of her back.

Above the beech hedge, still thick with wrinkled brown leaves, appeared the head of a black horse, followed by the upper half of its rider. They moved slowly, at a steady walk. The gentleman wore a military uniform, blue with silver lace and gleaming buttons, neat as a new pin.

Mariana was not familiar with the regiment, but she recognized the insignia of a lieutenant colonel. She did not recognize the gentleman, hardly surprising considering she had resided in the village for no more than two months.

He sat bolt upright and poker stiff in the saddle, his gaze fixed straight ahead between the horse's ears. His rigid posture reinforced the impression of tiredness, perhaps of pain, which she observed in his thin face, as if he held himself on his mount's back by a vast effort of will. The very sight of him reminded Mariana of the ache in her back.

Time to stop digging, though she hated to waste the cloudy but mild and dry day, rare enough in mid November. She would just finish pulling up the weeds from the last patch she had turned.

As she stooped to move the oilcloth-covered pad she had been kneeling on, a lock of greying hair escaped its pins and fell into her eyes. Forgetting the mud on her gloves, she poked it back into place.

At that moment, Lyuba howled. Poor pup! She hated being shut in the house while Mariana was outside, but the sight and smell of the rich, damp earth being dug was always too much temptation for her. If she was allowed out, in no time she would be mud-coloured all over, instead of her usual pretty pale yellow.

Her howl attracted the soldier's attention. He glanced over the hedge at Mariana. His indifferent gaze moved from her hatless head and disheveled dark hair, touched with frost, past her shabby though well-cut midnight blue dress, mired at the hem, to her muddy boots.

As his eyes returned to her face, his mouth twisted in distaste and disapproval.

She must have mud in her hair, Mariana realized, as well as on her skirts. Too bad! One could not work in the garden and stay as spotless as the critical lieutenant colonel appeared to be.

It was none of his affair. Obviously what she had taken for weariness and discomfort was nothing but the odious inflexibility of a certain type of military officer. Her sympathy and interest waned, and without sparing him another glance, she sank to her knees on the pad, reaching for her trowel.

All the same, her interest was not quite banished.

Mariana possessed a lively curiosity about her fellow beings. Since her sphere had contracted to this small Hertfordshire village, none of its limited number of inhabitants could be dismissed without a second thought.

She had exchanged many a "Good day" across the hedge since settling at Merriman's Cottage. She had exchanged remarks about the weather with Mrs. Bradley, who kept the tiny village shop. The elderly rector had called to welcome her to the parish. In vain she had awaited other callers.

The truth was, she suspected, they simply did not know what to make of her.

Miss Mariana Duckworth's manner was ladylike, yet she lived alone and dabbled in the soil like any farmer's wife. She hired a village woman, Mrs. Plunkett, to do heavy cleaning and laundry, but her cook-maid, Hetta, her only live-in servant, was from London.

Perhaps she should not have gone to the domestic agency in Town, Mariana reflected, yanking up a dandelion by the roots. A local girl might have helped her integration into village society. At the time, to arrive in a strange place entirely alone, and then to have look about in an unfamiliar neighbourhood to find a maid, had seemed as disagreeable a prospect as it was impractical.

Hetta, though competent, was dour and uncompanionable. Hence the impulsive acquisition, on a visit to the nearby market town, of a small, wriggly, yellow puppy.

Lyuba howled again.

A mullioned casement window opened, and Hetta's head poked out.

"She's scratching the door to pieces, miss!"

"You may let her out now," Mariana called. "I have finished digging."

Gathering the weeds, piled on an old sack, from the ground beside her, she rose to her feet. Involuntarily she surveyed the lane, staring after the recent passerby. He was gone.

Lyuba bounced up to her and launched herself into the air. Laughing, Mariana fended off the puppy's attempt to kiss her nose.

"Down, girl!"

Setting off around the cottage with the bundle of weeds, Mariana glanced back to see Lyuba sniffing at the newly turned earth. She called the pup to her. Lyuba picked something up and came trotting to lay it at her mistress's feet.

"My trowel! I had forgot it. Good dog."

With a big, toothy grin, Lyuba followed her to the compost heap and watched with great interest as she dumped the weeds on top.

"I shall just wash, and then we will go for a walk in the woods." Was talking to the dog a sign of incipient madness? Mariana wondered.

Lyuba did not think so. Ears pricked, she caught the only important word and gave a happy yip.

Mariana headed for the cottage. Her new home was a small, two-story dwelling, built of rosy brick, with a tile roof. While the garden had been neglected of late—the lawyer had told her the previous tenant, Mr. Foster, had departed to live with his daughter at the age of eighty-three—the house had been put in order before it was advertized for rent. The doors and window frames gleamed with new primrose yellow paint.

Though it did not belong to her, Mariana felt a proprietorial pride in her cottage. For the first time in many years, she had a place to call home.

When she stopped on the back step to scrape her boots, Lyuba caught up with her—and proudly laid a large dandelion, root and all, at her feet.

"Oh, dear!" Mariana shook her head with a rueful smile. "I am going to have to teach you what to retrieve and what to leave be! Wait out here a minute now. I shall be back in two shakes of a lamb's tail."

Madness? No, loneliness, she acknowledged. Perhaps it had been a mistake to settle in the country. Yet, country born and bred, it was for the English countryside she had yearned during those long years of exile.

She had forgotten the clannishness of rural folk, their

slowness to accept outsiders. Somehow she must worm her way into the closed society.

Being seen in her present state was not the best way to go about it, she thought wryly, but she did so enjoy gardening. After the punctilious observance of every nuance of propriety for so many years, she refused to let herself be hemmed in still by other people's pettifogging notions of decorum.

In the little mirror nailed above the kitchen sink, she regarded the streak of mud across her brow which had so shocked the recent passerby. She frowned. Assuming he was not just passing through but lived in or near Wycherlea, she wanted to know: Who was the disdainful soldier?

TWO

Who was the slattern working in the garden of Merriman's Cottage? wondered Lieutenant Colonel Damian Perrincourt as he rode slowly on. Had the long, painful struggle against Napoleon consumed so many men that their womenfolk must now be hired as outdoor servants?

She had looked at him boldly, with what might have been the beginnings of a friendly smile. Something in his face had wiped the smile from her expressive mouth.

Just as well. Her figure was good, enticing even, despite the grey streaks Damian had noted in the dark, untidy hair exposed by her indecorous lack of a head covering. He had to admit to himself he actually felt a twinge of desire, and it simply would not do.

Quite apart from the aversion to fouling his own nest instilled in him by his father, he was in no physical shape for passion. Fortunately, the sight of a smear of mud on her forehead had dissipated the meagre trace of desire in his loins. No gentleman could possibly be attracted to so ramshackle a female.

He had been too far from her to see the colour of her eyes, he thought irrelevantly.

His mother might know who was renting Merriman's Cottage now, and whom the tenant had taken on as gardener. Mrs. Perrincourt had always taken a great interest in the welfare of dependents and villagers. Last time

Damian had come home on leave, she had bemoaned the increasing frailty that curtailed her visits to the poor.

A fine pair they would make, he and Mama, a couple of semi-invalids doing their best to run the estate and to bring up Jack's children.

At the thought of his much loved younger brother's demise, a pang of sorrow shot through Damian's breast. Jack was four months dead, but the immediacy of Damian's grief had had no chance to soften. His mother's letter had followed him to Spain and back, to catch up with him just a few days since, when he left the military hospital and found the news awaiting him at regimental headquarters.

He would have had to sell out then, of course, even if the wound to his back had not put paid to his military career. After two decades in uniform, twenty years with an ever-advancing rank before his name, as soon as the necessary papers found their way through the proper channels, he would be plain Damian Perrincourt, Esquire.

With heels and reins, he turned Saladin's head toward the gates of Wych Court. The slight motion, like the puff of bellows on smouldering embers, reignited the fire in his back. He braced himself, suppressing a groan. No more than a lieutenant colonel in Wellington's army could the master of Wych Court allow himself to appear a weakling.

He dared not allow himself to slump in the saddle. To bend his backbone was to invite agony. Tired as he was, he sat straight as a ramrod as he rode up the carriage drive.

"Uncle Damian! Uncle Damian!"

A small, fair-haired boy, liberally bespattered with mud, dashed out from behind one of the great oaks lining the avenue. One dirt-caked hand waved a vigorous greeting. With the other, he hauled his still smaller, equally grubby sister behind him. The little girl had a tiny kitten, remarkably white, draped on her shoulder.

"Halt!" Damian barked, as the heedless children scampered towards him.

Saladin was too well mannered to rear. The great black charger sidled, sending fresh spasms of pain radiating from the spot, horribly close to Damian's spine, where the ricocheting bullet had lodged. Half an inch over, the doctors said, and he would have been dead or crippled for life.

Sometimes death seemed desirable.

"Don't you know better than to run at a horse?" he demanded harshly.

"But Papa said you are a famous horseman," the boy argued, then added with deep suspicion, "I say, you *are* our uncle Damian, aren't you?"

At his last leave, three years ago, Thomas and Lucinda had been tots in the nursery. Uninterested in children, Damian had duly—and briefly—admired his brother's offspring. Most of his time had been spent examining and gratefully admiring Jack's excellent stewardship of the Wych Court estate since their father's death.

His niece and nephew must be five and seven years old now, or thereabouts. They were quite old enough, at any rate, to behave themselves with propriety, to have learnt a modicum of self-discipline.

"Yes, I am your uncle, though I confess myself ashamed to admit so close a relationship to two such disgraceful ragamuffins. You are both filthy."

"It's all right, we are wearing old clothes," Thomas said cheerfully.

Damian's brows drew together in a frown. "What is your governess about to let you run wild like this?" he queried in an ominous tone.

"Oh, we have no governess at present, Uncle. Miss

Robinson had to leave to nurse her sick sister. Gran'mama and Nurse make us do our lessons, but anyway, we both like reading, don't we, Lucy?"

"Yeth." Lucinda nodded, her beaming smile revealing the absence of two front teeth from the lower set. "Can I ride on your horth, Uncle Damian? He'th pretty. Here, Tommy, hold Pirate for me."

She handed the kitten—a black patch over one eye explaining the name—to her brother and held up her arms, in obvious expectation of being swept into the saddle before her uncle. Her innocent trustfulness touched his heart, but the very notion of bending to lift her was painful.

He must not admit his debility.

"Certainly not!" he snapped. "You cannot suppose I wish to arrive home with mud all over my uniform."

"Why not? Gran'mama says you are not going to be in the army anymore," said Thomas, with interest, not impertinence, as far as Damian could tell.

"Because the only excuse for a uniform not to be immaculate is exposure to battle," he said coldly. "Nor ought a gentleman ever to be seen in soiled clothing."

"But . . . ," said Lucinda.

"Nor a lady." Damian crushed her. "Pray excuse me now. I am eager to reach the house."

As he set Saladin to a fast walk, less jarring than a trot, he heard the child's plaintive voice behind him.

"I wath jutht going to tell him Papa uthed to get dirty quite often, out in the fieldth. Papa wath a gentleman. I wish Papa and Mama didn't die."

Guilt pricked him. He had not considered their loss, only his own. Of course they must miss their parents, but all the more reason why they should be sitting clean and quiet in the schoolroom conning their lessons, not haring about the park like wretched guttersnipes.

Apparently his mother was too feeble now to control

her grandchildren, or to find someone to control them. He would have to take them in hand himself, until a new governess, a strict disciplinarian, could be procured.

The avenue opened out into a wide carriage sweep before the house. As always, his heart leapt at the sight of the rosy brick and dark brown timbers of the Elizabethan manor. As squires of Wych Court, the Perrincourts stretched back in an unbroken line to the sixteenth century. Damian was merely the latest in the long succession.

He would soon have the place as smoothly running as he had left his regiment in Spain. And the doctors had promised the pain in his back would lessen, if never quite disappear.

In spite of everything, it was good to be home.

A groom was on the lookout for the master and came running to take his reins. Damian waved him away.

"I shall ride around to the stables," he growled.

He was afraid his mother might be watching from the windows. He did not want her to observe the dreaded, torturous and sometimes humiliating process of dismounting.

It was bad enough that the stable hands must witness his disability. There was no way to avoid that.

A brief trial of riding in a carriage had convinced him that the enforced immobility was even worse than the strain of riding on horseback. His coachman and his batman had had to lift him out, and it had been half an hour before he was capable of taking a step without their support.

Mounting Saladin—with their help—he had left them to follow with his baggage. Thank heaven Wycherlea was not far from London.

The groom raced ahead of him, round the corner of

the house. When Damian reached the stable yard, all the grooms and stable boys were lined up to greet him, cap in hand. His gaze swiftly scanned their rank, noting tarnished buttons here and a couple missing there, mucky boots without laces, sagging pockets, a torn sleeve, a lad with hay in his hair and another actually chewing on a straw.

This was not the army, Damian reminded himself. But by the same token, these men had not the excuse of battle or even weary marches to mitigate their appalling untidiness. Order must be restored.

Tomorrow, he decided wearily.

Old Benson, the head groom, stepped forward with his snaggle-toothed, tobacco-stained grin. "Welcome home, sir!" he exclaimed.

"Huzzah for the squire!" cried one of the fellows, and caps flew into the air as the old walls resounded with their enthusiastic cheers.

Damian could not help but smile in response. He felt himself relaxing, and quickly stiffened. Aware that his smile at once became strained, unnatural, he stopped smiling.

He ought to let the head groom present each man to him, but at present the effort required was too great.

"Thank you," he said. "I am glad to be home. Benson, I should like a word with you. The rest of you may go about your duties."

While the others scattered, a trifle bewildered by this abrupt dismissal after their spirited welcome, Benson came to Saladin's head and took the reins. Nearly forty years ago, Benson had set Damian on his first pony. Having so often been picked up and dusted off, he did not mind now accepting the old man's assistance to dismount.

"You need not hold him," he said gruffly. "He will stand still. I need a hand down."

Despite his gnarled appearance, the head groom was still a powerful man, as Damian soon gratefully discovered. He dismounted gingerly, with the greatest care. Nonetheless, so violent was the pain that darkness closed in on his vision, his ears rang, and his knees started to buckle.

Benson propped him up. He clung to the saddle, leaning his forehead against the great black, motionless gelding who had not long since borne his unconscious body from certain death on the battlefield.

The groom's anxious voice seemed to come from far off. "Ye're hurt, Master Damian!"

"Healing," he gasped. "Just a little dizzy. I shall be all right . . . in a minute."

Even as he spoke, he did not believe his own words, but it was true. The darkness passed. The strength returned to his legs. Straightening cautiously, he took a step away from his horse.

"Ye'll do, sir?"

"I'll do. Take good care of Saladin." He started to give minute instructions for the care of the charger.

Benson shook his head reproachfully. "Don't I know how to look after cattle, sir? I'll see to him meself, and he'll have everything o' the best, never fear. One of the men'll go with you indoors."

"No!" Damian snapped. Immediately regretting his curtness to the faithful old servant, he went on in a more conciliatory tone. "That is not necessary. Send my batman to me when the carriage arrives. It will be here soon. I rode at an easy pace."

"Aye, sir. We're all right glad ye're back, sir. We've been sorely missing Master Jack."

Damian acknowledged his awkward sympathy with a sober nod. Attempting a compromise between the firm stride required by his dignity and the delicate tread required by his back, he went into the house.

THREE

The butler, though apprised of the master's arrival and awaiting him in the great hall, had not considered it proper to assemble the household staff to be presented to him. Thankful to be spared that gauntlet, Damian patiently accepted Perkins's welcome and his properly expressed, but lengthy condolences on Mr. and Mrs. John's demise.

"Where is my mother?" he asked then.

"In the conservatory, I believe, sir. I shall bring refreshments at once."

Mrs. Perrincourt was reclining on a well-cushioned basketwork chaise longue among the orange trees and grape vines. Her eyes were shut, her mouth a trifle open.

Damian's first impulse was to rouse her from her nap with a kiss on her wrinkled cheek. However, he did not want her to wake to find him bent double and unable to straighten—or possibly flat on the flagstones beside her couch.

"Mama," he said softly.

Her hands went up to set her lacy cap in order even as she blinked drowsily.

"I was not asleep," she protested.

"Naturally not, Mama."

"Damian! Oh, my dear, I am so very happy to see you at last."

Eagerly, though not without difficulty, she levered herself to her feet and came to him. He managed to hug her and drop a kiss on her forehead without swooning.

"Sit down, darling," she said, subsiding onto the chaise. "You do not mind sitting out here for a while? I like to be where the children can reach me, however dirty they get, the scalawags," she explained indulgently.

Damian eyed the basket chairs with misgiving. "I had rather stand, Mama, though I apologize for towering over you. I am a trifle stiff from riding. Old age creeping up on me, I dare say."

"Oh, I know precisely what you mean! I am always horridly stiff after sitting for a while. But you are still young, Damian. Is it the wound you mentioned in your letter which troubles you?"

"A little," he admitted.

He did not wish to reveal the extent of his injury to her, or at least not just yet, so he quickly changed the subject. There were any number of topics in need of discussion, from the children's behaviour to the carriage accident that had robbed them of their parents. Yet what rose to his lips was an utterly irrelevant query.

"Do you know who has taken Merriman's Cottage?"

His mother accepted this unexpected byway with her usual placidity.

"A Miss Duckworth, I understand," she said. "It fell vacant soon after . . . after Jackie died. I left the letting to your lawyer. He said she had excellent references."

"No doubt. You have not called on her?"

"No, dear. I get about so little these days, I fear." She hesitated, with a puzzled frown.

"So, I presume, you know nothing of the uncouth female she employs to work in her garden," Damian said, ridiculously disappointed.

"No. Well, that is, I have heard she does her own gardening, even the heavy work, digging and so forth. Yet people say she is quite ladylike in other respects. It is really very odd, Damian."

"Excessively!"

"One does not know quite how to approach such a person, which is another reason I have not called. I feel it is very remiss of me not to welcome her to the village."

"Not at all, Mama. Either she is a . . . less than respectable woman who has learnt to ape her betters, but does not fully grasp the behaviour expected of a lady; or else she is a shockingly eccentric lady. I see no reason for you to approach such a person."

"Oh, no, dear. You know it is my duty as lady of the manor to make the acquaintance of all newcomers, whatever their degree. I simply must make the effort. I hope she will not be affronted by my tardiness."

Damian knew better than to argue. Despite her mildness, his mother was a determined woman when it came to her perceived duty.

Perkins brought in a tray just then. Damian was glad to see a decanter of Madeira as well as the pot of tea. A glass of wine would dull the persistent ache in his spine, he hoped.

As the butler left, he responded to his mother's last comment, his voice full of doubt as he recalled the woman's mud-smeared brow. "If Miss Duckworth is indeed a lady, she will properly ascribe the delay to your mourning for your son and his wife."

"Oh, Damian!" cried Mrs. Perrincourt. "It was perfectly dreadful. How I wished you were here!"

He was pacing as she told him about his brother's death, when he noticed two small, dirty faces and a tiny pink feline nose pressed to the glass wall of the conservatory. Thomas and Lucinda realized at once that they had been spotted. They snatched up the kitten and scurried away.

Again a twinge of guilt. He had not meant to make them afraid of him.

Nonetheless, he broke into his mother's enumeration of the guests at the funeral to say, "Mama, I am very sorry to see Jack's children so ungovernable."

She flared in their defense. "Not ungovernable, Damian. Tom and Lucy are exceptionally affectionate, sweet-tempered and willing to oblige. Indeed, it is quite charming to see how Tom takes care of his little sister. Boys are by no means always prepared to make accommodations for those younger and less able than themselves."

"I daresay they may be charming," Damian said skeptically, "but you cannot deny that they are undisciplined."

"Perhaps a little, just at present," said Mrs. Perrincourt with a guilty look. "If so, it is entirely my fault. They were both heartbroken when Jack and Melinda died, naturally. I could not bear to force them to follow their usual routine, when they were weeping their eyes out."

"But that was four months ago, ma'am! There were no tears in their eyes when I met them on my way up the avenue."

"No, though they still feel the loss *deeply*, I assure you. The trouble is, Miss Robinson was obliged to give notice, and I have not felt up to interviewing and selecting a new governess. I refuse to trust a lawyer's judgment in such an important matter, or even a friend or acquaintance! Besides, a little holiday, until after Christmas, I thought, will do the children no harm."

"Perhaps not," Damian conceded, "but then it will be past time for them to settle down. I shall find a governess for them."

"And you will be a father to them, I know, my dear. Yet I feel they are sadly in need of a mother. I am too old to carry on that role with any degree of success. Have you any thought of marrying?"

"It has crossed my mind now and then," said Damian hesitantly. "However, I saw no need of a wife. Being the elder by a dozen years, I have always been accustomed to considering Jack as my heir."

His mother heaved a sorrowful sigh. "Everything has changed. Do put your mind to it, darling."

"I will," he promised.

The next day, it rained all morning. When the sun peeked out in the early afternoon, Mariana found the ground was too soggy for digging. She decided to prune the brambles which were taking over one corner of her back garden.

Lyuba was eager to help. After a brief but painful encounter with the blackberry thorns, she came to the conclusion that they were as dangerous as the chickens. (A bold hen had pecked her enquiring nose on her second day at Merriman's Cottage, when she was not much more than chicken-size herself.) She went off to sniff in the hedges.

Even with gloves and long sleeves, Mariana had to agree that the brambles were dangerous. The low ones caught at her skirts and the high ones caught in her hair, and the ones in between pricked and scratched despite gloves and long sleeves.

Still, there was something eminently satisfying in the conquest of such a foe. Growing hot, she rolled up her unhelpful sleeves and battled on.

"Miss Duckworth!" Hetta called from the cottage. "Summun's come to call!"

"On me?" Mariana asked idiotically.

"Yes'm. There's a *footman* at the door, says Mrs. Prinket's out in the lane in her carriage and wants to know are you at home?"

"Oh, dear!"

A footman? Then Mrs. "Prinket" must surely be Mrs. Perrincourt, her landlord's mother. And here was Mariana with muddy boots, a rip in the hem of her gown, and her hair flying in all directions!

"What'm I to say, miss?"

She could not possibly receive the squire's mother in such a state. Yet to have Hetta deny her when she was obviously not away from home might very well set the seal on her exclusion from local society. Her disarray could accomplish that anyway, but it was perhaps a trifle more acceptable outdoors than in. Or so she hoped.

"I shall go out to the carriage, Hetta."

The torn skirt and the muddy boots could not be remedied. Mariana whipped off her gardening gloves and did her best to pin up her hair as she hurried around the side of the cottage. Bother it, she ought at least to be wearing a cap.

Too late. To keep Mrs. Perrincourt waiting while she changed her clothes was as unthinkable as to deny her or to receive her looking like the veriest slattern.

FOUR

An elderly lady awaited her, seated in an old-fashioned but well-kept landau. She wore a black, jet-trimmed bonnet and carriage robe. Mariana vaguely recalled the lawyer who handled her lease having mentioned that Mrs. Perrincourt's younger son had died that summer.

And the elder son was a soldier, she remembered now. So the high-and-mighty lieutenant colonel must be her landlord! No doubt he wished to disembarrass himself of his disreputable-looking tenant.

He would hardly send his mama to give her notice, however.

Mariana stepped up to the side of the landau, its hoods folded down on this fine afternoon.

"Mrs. Perrincourt?" she queried, with difficulty restraining herself from curtsying. Though the habit of decades was strong, she was an independent woman now, she reminded herself.

"Miss Duckworth." Mrs. Perrincourt gave her a slight, stiff bow, but her gaze seemed more curious than unfriendly. "My dear!" she went on unexpectedly, with a gasp. "What *have* you done to your arms?"

Looking down, Mariana saw several bloody scratches stitched across her arms, and one blob where blood had welled from a thorn's vicious stab. She had forgotten to roll down her sleeves.

"I do beg your pardon, ma'am," she said, hastily pulling the cuffs down to her wrists. "Not a pleasant sight, though no serious damage has been done, I promise you. I was hacking down blackberry bushes."

"A hazardous enterprise," said Mrs. Perrincourt, a twinkle in her eyes.

Emboldened, Mariana agreed. "Yes, but so very gratifying to see them fall, and thus to enlarge the garden by several square yards. I do enjoy gardening immensely, but it is a shockingly messy business, alas. As you see, I am in no fit state to entertain company, which is why I must apologize for not inviting you into the cottage."

"No, no, any apologies must come from me. I ought to have called many weeks since to welcome you to Wycherlea. My only excuse is that I have not been well since . . ." She bit her lip. "Perhaps you have heard about my son?"

"Yes, ma'am, I have. Please accept my sincere condolences."

Mrs. Perrincourt nodded. "Thank you. However, dear Damian—Jack's elder brother, you know—is at last returned just yesterday to Wych Court, and already I feel my health much improved. It was such a dreadful worry, his being in the army, in constant peril. He was quite badly wounded, in fact, but now he is at home, at least I am assured the French cannot kill him!"

"Indeed, I hope not." Mariana felt something brush her skirt and glanced down.

Lyuba deposited an egg at her feet and looked up with a short bark demanding thanks.

Mariana and Mrs. Perrincourt both burst out laughing, and the footman, standing by, guffawed.

"Good gracious," cried the squire's mother, "an egg-laying dog. It is the tenth wonder of the world, I declare."

Mariana picked up the egg. "Look, not a crack! One of my hens has been laying astray, but I never thought to send Lyuba to hunt for the eggs."

"She is a born retriever, Miss Duckworth. Damian

would buy her from you, I daresay, to train for when he is recovered enough to go shooting."

"She is not for sale, ma'am. Besides, I doubt Mr. Perrincourt would be happy with a dog who retrieves weeds from the compost heap."

"No, does she? Oh, see, what has she brought you now?"

"My glove! I dropped it when I was hurrying from the back garden."

"And here I am calling you from your work," said Mrs. Perrincourt remorsefully, "and keeping you standing when you had rather be butchering brambles. I am delighted to have made your acquaintance, Miss Duckworth. I hope you will come up to the Court to drink tea with me one afternoon soon."

"Thank you, I should like to."

And to be presented to Mr. Perrincourt—no, to have Mr. Perrincourt presented to her—Mariana thought as the landau bore Mrs. Perrincourt away down the lane. So he was wounded; he *had* been in pain when he scowled at her so.

The only remaining question was whether his scowl had been solely the result of his discomfort, or whether he had instantly taken her in contempt. It was too much to hope that he was sufficiently interested to be responsible for his mother's belated visit.

Hope? Fiddlesticks! Mariana rather liked Mrs. Perrincourt, but she cared not a whit for Mr. Damian Perrincourt's opinion!

Tired by the journey, Damian spent the day after his return to Wych Court in his chamber. He did not emerge until dinnertime, when he trod cautiously down the stately old carved oak staircase to join his mother.

"How do you feel, dear?" she asked anxiously.

"A great deal better than this time yesterday. And you, Mama?"

"A little tired, but that is because I was so full of energy this afternoon I drove out in the carriage to pay some long overdue calls."

Damian's thoughts at once flew to the outlandish Miss Duckworth, but all he said was, "I hope you have not overexerted yourself."

"Not at all. I have scarcely left the house these four months, but having you home at last has quite rejuvenated me. Our neighbours are all eager to welcome you home."

"Ah, I see," he said, laughing, "your mission was to confirm the rumours of my arrival."

"Well, naturally people wanted to know, and everyone was so kind when Jackie and Melinda . . . But there, we will not speak of that. I am afraid you will have a great many callers in the next few days. If you do not feel up to seeing them, we shall say you have a great deal of business to take care of after your long absence."

"As I shall have." Damian saw an opening. "I am sure many things have changed since last I was at home. Jack's new scheme for draining the west pasture, new tenants . . . Oh, by the way, you did not happen to call at Merriman's Cottage while you were out, did you?"

"I stopped at the gate and spoke to Miss Duckworth."

"Is she too vulgar for words?"

"Not at all. If her gentility is assumed, I could not detect the imposture. I thought her altogether a lady. Charming, in fact."

"You did not go into the cottage, though," he noted. "Did she invite you?"

Mrs. Perrincourt smiled and shook her head. "She said, quite rightly, that she was much too untidy to entertain a caller within."

"She does not sound at all like a desirable tenant."

Wrong word, Damian thought. His brief glimpse of her had shown her all too desirable, despite her greying hair and her dishabille. Odd, that. He was not accustomed to feeling such an instant attraction toward any female. "Not at all satisfactory," he hastily amended. "I wonder what sort of lease she has, and whether it can be broken."

"Pray do not try, Damian! She was untidy because she was clearing blackberries from the back garden. Old Foster neglected the place terribly. Surely you cannot ask for a better tenant than one who improves the property?"

"Yes, but . . ."

"Besides, I like her. And I confess that I am dying of curiosity to learn her history, and what brought her to live alone in Wycherlea."

Damian sighed. "Very well, Mama. Miss Duckworth shall stay, at least for the present."

"Thank you, darling." A trifle guiltily, Mrs. Perrincourt added, "By the way, I have invited her to drink tea."

"When?"

"Just 'soon.' I did not specify. I shall send a note, so tell me if one day or another suits you better."

Damian was not sure whether he wanted to avoid her or to meet her and judge her for himself. "Tuesday," he said at random. "You must promise to tell me if you discover that her past is less than respectable. Or her present, come to that!"

If he found her alluring, so might other men. The notion was oddly disturbing.

FIVE

Mariana's situation in life had not been such that she was accustomed to—or indeed comfortable—talking about herself. On the contrary, she had not infrequently found herself in the role of confidante, not always by choice. She was master of the sympathetic murmur, the encouraging exclamation, the general appearance of interest, sometimes feigned, sometimes altogether sincere.

Thus she was not at all surprised when Mrs. Perrincourt, after a few minutes of polite chitchat, started to talk about her recent sad loss.

Chilled after walking up to the house in a bitterly cold east wind, Mariana was by then warmed by a kindly welcome, a blazing fire and an excellent cup of tea in a snug sitting room. She listened with genuine sympathy and interest.

Allowing for a mother's pardonable partiality, Jack and Melinda Perrincourt sounded like a pleasant couple. Only a heart of stone, which Mariana did not possess, could fail to feel for their orphaned children. She had seen enough of the world, though, not to underestimate the benefits of a comfortable home with a doting grandmother.

She wondered how Master Thomas and Miss Lucinda got on with their unbending uncle . . . and whether he would put in an appearance at the tea table.

"Mr. John Perrincourt was your younger son, I think

you mentioned?" she said questioningly, hoping she did not sound too inquisitive, but eager to change the subject to his elder brother. "Yet he managed the estate?"

"Damian was always mad to go for a soldier," said Mrs. Perrincourt with a sigh, "since he was a little boy. His papa made him stay at home and learn to run the place, as he was to inherit it, but Damian still wanted to join the army. In the end, my husband gave in and purchased a commission for him."

"He has done well, has he not? If I am not mistaken, his insignia denotes a lieutenant colonel."

"Yes, though he has had to sell out now, what with—"

"Gran'mama?" A small, fair-haired boy peeked around the door. "We don't mean to disturb you," he said virtuously, "but we just came to see if we can come in. We went to Nurse first and got all washed and tidy," he added with still more conscious virtue.

"And Pirate," urged a loud whisper from behind him.

"And Pirate. Please, ma'am."

"Miss Duckworth, should you mind very much . . . ?" said Mrs. Perrincourt hopefully. "Pirate is a kitten."

"A *good* kitten," said the whisperer aloud.

Laughing, Mariana assured her, "I do not mind a bit. I happen to like kittens."

"And children?" enquired the little girl who entered behind her brother, kitten in arms.

"*Good* children," Mariana teased.

"Make your curtsy, Lucy!" hissed the boy, himself performing a creditable bow.

"Miss Duckworth, let me present my grandchildren, Thomas and Lucinda."

"How do you do, ma'am," said Thomas.

"*Mostly* good!" said Lucinda, wobbling a little as she curtsied. "It's difficult, holding Pirate."

"Lucy, darling, you are not lisping! Have your teeth grown back already?"

"No, Gran'mama, but Tommy's been teaching me to put my tongue in the right place so's I can say *ssss*. I've been practising and practising."

"Lithening to Luthy lithp was driving me mad," her brother said frankly.

Mrs. Perrincourt and Mariana laughed.

Damian heard laughter as he came down the passage. He hesitated. Though he was just outside his mother's sitting room, he still had not decided whether he wanted to meet Miss Duckworth.

It was his duty, he decided. Not only was he her landlord, and therefore bound to make her acquaintance sooner or later, but he ought to find out whether she was imposing upon his mother. Mama, always determined to think well of people, might be taken in by a clever assumption of ladylike manners. He, Damian vowed, would not.

He wished he could wait until his back allowed him to move more easily, but his mother had forced the pace. Ruefully he acknowledged that in any case the staff of Wych Court, most of his tenants, all the villagers, and half the neighbours knew of his disability.

Still, he would have preferred to keep it from Miss Duckworth—only because she might seek to take advantage of his weakness.

The pain and stiffness had already diminished considerably in the few days since his arrival. Here at home he was able to move, to sit, to lie down when and where the spirit moved him. If one position started to hurt, there was nothing to stop him changing to another. He was beginning to believe the doctors who prophesied almost full recovery.

He was fit enough to deal with Miss Duckworth. He pushed open the door and went in.

"Mama, can you spare me a cup of tea?"

"Of course, darling. Miss Duckworth, pray let me make known my son to you."

His bow was little more than a nod, and of necessity stiff.

Miss Duckworth rose and performed a slight—a very slight—curtsy. "How do you do, Mr. Perrincourt."

Her eyes were the deep, translucent green of Atlantic rollers passing beneath a ship's keel. Small lines radiated at the corners, the only sign of her age since most of her hair was decorously hidden by a frilly white cap with green ribbons. Damian guessed she was about his own age, somewhere between forty and forty-five.

Before he hastily averted his eyes from her full but shapely bosom, he noticed that her gown was green, clean, high at the neck and long-sleeved, all neatness and decorum.

"I trust you have no complaints about your cottage, ma'am?" he asked, taking a seat on a straight chair and accepting a cup of tea from his mother.

"None, thank you, sir." Was that amusement in her voice? "It is perfectly comfortable. The roof does not leak; the chimneys draw well; and the draughts are no worse than one must expect in an older building, of no significance, I do assure you."

"You have draughts?" Damian queried, concluding that her mealy-mouthed acquiescence was nothing but cover for a backhanded reproach.

Dammit, he would have the estate carpenter down at the cottage tomorrow. She must not have any justification for going about spreading tales of his inadequacy as a landlord.

At that moment, a gust of wind rattled the window-panes and made the fire flare up.

"No worse than you have here," said Miss Duckworth tranquilly.

Now Damian was sure she was teasing him. He shifted uneasily. Something small and white dashed from a corner and pounced upon the swinging tassel of his military boot.

"Pirate, come back!"

He batted the little creature away with a firm but gentle hand while he spoke sharply to the children, whose unobtrusive, silent presence he had not noticed before. "Did you ask permission of your grandmother and her guest to bring your pet in here?"

"Of course, sir!"

"He's good, really," Lucinda anxiously assured her uncle as she scooped up the kitten. "It's just that he's been quite quiet and still for simply *ages,* and now he wants to play."

Damian had seen little of his niece and nephew in the past few days. When he chanced to come across them, always in his mother's presence, they were distinctly subdued. When he had entered the sitting room, they must have made themselves small in the corner to avoid his censorious eye.

That was not the relationship he wanted with them, he realized. After all, they were still in the nursery. As their uncle, he would have a role in Thomas's upbringing when the boy was older. At present their nurse and the governess he was going to hire were responsible for teaching them to conduct themselves with propriety.

Besides, he was excessively conscious of Miss Duckworth's green, critical gaze upon him.

"Then, we must find something for him to play with," he said, "other than the tassels on my only decent pair of boots. I have had no opportunity to have shoes made since I came home, you see. Mama, perhaps you have some suitable scrap of ribbon?"

Mrs. Perrincourt dug into her work basket. Miss Duckworth regarded Damian with friendly approval, which he immediately resented. It was none of her affair how he treated his brother's children.

She rose gracefully, forcing him to the effort of standing up.

"It is time I was on my way, Mrs. Perrincourt," she said, and expressed her appreciation for the tea with unimpeachable gentility.

If her courtesy did not come naturally, she had indisputably learnt her lesson well. But who was she? What had brought a woman, a spinster, of her years to Wycherlea, to live with no relative or companion, and to do her own gardening?

Though she had departed, the answers would have to wait until the children also left. They were having such fun, with the kitten gamboling after a length of ribbon trailed across the floor, that he could not help but smile.

At once Lucy came to him and leaned against his knee. Looking up at him earnestly, she said, "You see, Pirate is good, isn't he?"

"Better than his name suggests," Damian said, laughing.

"That's because of the black patch over his eye," Tommy explained.

Eventually Pirate tired of the game. To everyone's surprise, he sprang up onto Damian's lap and settled there, kneading his thigh with tiny paws. His eyes closed, while a rumbling purr arose, astonishingly loud for such a little beast.

Tommy hurried over. "Sorry, sir, I'll take him."

"No, you can leave him." Damian stroked the soft white fur with one finger. "He is not using his claws on me, I am happy to say."

"I taught him to keep them sheathed, and he's pretty good about it; but I can't promise he won't scratch."

"He doesn't *mean* to hurt you," Lucy put in anxiously. "He's just a baby; he doesn't understand."

"I promise not to be angry with him if his angelic behaviour fails to hold. I shall bring him up to you in the nursery later."

Correctly interpreting this as dismissal, Thomas removed himself and his sister from the room.

"Well, Mama," said Damian, "what have you learnt of the mysterious Miss Duckworth?"

Mrs. Perrincourt reflected for a moment, then said with some slight perplexity, "Why, nothing, dearest, although we talked for quite a while before the children came in. That is, only that she is sympathetic and truly well-bred, and that when she is not gardening, she dresses well and modestly."

"She dresses well?" Damian enquired. "I know nothing of women's fashions."

"Oh, not in the height of fashion, or tricked out with frills and laces, but her gown was excellently cut and of good material."

"She did not speak of her past, or her family, or her situation?"

"Not a word. But you must not jump to the conclusion she was deliberately hiding something disgraceful, Damian. Now I come to think on it, I talked a great deal myself! I fear Miss Duckworth had little chance to put in her twopenny worth. If I had not chattered so, I daresay I should be able to satisfy your curiosity."

"I am not in the least curious about the wretched female," Damian hurried to deny. "I should just like to know a little more about the tenant of Merriman's Cottage. Without jumping to unwarranted conclusions, I do believe there is something havey-cavey about her. A respectable unmarried woman ought not to be living alone without any sort of chaperon."

"Come now, my dear, you are too exacting!" Mrs. Perrincourt exclaimed. "Miss Duckworth is certainly of an age not to need a chaperon."

"She is not so very old," Damian growled.

His mother looked at him with raised eyebrows, but did not comment. He quickly turned the subject.

SIX

"Squire said as you've got some nasty draughts about the house, miss."

Mariana regarded the hefty young man with puzzlement changing to amusement. The only reason she could imagine for Mr. Perrincourt to send a carpenter with such haste, when she had carefully *not* complained, was to ensure that she had nothing of which to complain.

He was determined not to put himself in the wrong where she was concerned. In other words, if anyone was at fault in any respect, it must be she.

"I told your master they are not bad," she said, "but since you have come, you might as well look."

Lyuba at his heels, the carpenter toured the cottage. The small but comfortable house, about a century old, had a sitting room, dining parlour, and kitchen below, and three chambers above. The puppy joined in peering—or in her case sniffing—at doors and windows as Mariana pointed out the minor cracks and gaps.

"I'll do me best, miss," the carpenter said doubtfully as they returned below stairs, "but these old places, they settle crooked, see. A bit o' putty here and there maybe'll help. Trouble is, you don't want to make it so's the doors and winders won't open and close."

"No, indeed! I shall be grateful for anything you can do, and I'll assure Mr. Perrincourt you did a splendid job. Is he a hard master?"

"Can't hardly tell yet, miss. His manservant, what was his batman in the army, I heard he says Squire's pertickler but fair."

"Fair enough," said Mariana.

She found herself still puzzled by Damian Perrincourt. Guessing the reason for his prompt attention to her insignificant draughts did not explain why he felt so strong a need not to be found lacking where she was concerned. Mariana was sure it was more complicated than a simple wish to do his duty as her landlord. She had sensed an inexplicably strong determination to prove himself morally superior to her, not merely her superior in station.

He had responded to his mother's introduction with a stiffness not wholly to be accounted for by his half-healed wound. All in all, it seemed he was resolved to dislike her, though he hardly knew her.

Did she like him?

One was naturally prejudiced against any person who regarded one with antipathy. She had not cared for his sharpness with the children, obviously not for the first time, to judge by their anxious apologies. Yet afterward he had begged Mrs. Perrincourt for a toy for them and the kitten.

She would keep an open mind, Mariana vowed. Time would show whether he was amiable or odious.

The former, she hoped—purely for the children's sake, and because she liked his mother. And, of course, as his tenant she was to some degree dependent upon his good will.

It was a great pity he had seen her first in such shocking disarray, she thought with a sigh.

News of Mariana's drinking tea with Mrs. Perrincourt—in her private sitting room, too, not the formal drawing room!—soon spread throughout the village and then the neighbourhood. Ladies began to call at Merriman's Cottage: the rector's wife and her sister, the apothecary's mother, the lawyer's spinster daughters, a genteel widow or two, someone's aunt and someone else's cousin.

By dint of letting it be known that she would be "at home" between certain hours, Mariana managed not to offend any of these good ladies by receiving them in her gardening dress. Besides, the December weather was rarely conducive to working out of doors.

Rain followed frosts and frosts followed rain. Lyuba, growing by leaps and bounds, insisted on a walk every day whatever the skies chose to do.

She was equally happy in the woods, where she chased squirrels and retrieved sticks, or in the meadows, where she chased rabbits and retrieved odds and ends—a crow's feather here, an abandoned field mouse nest there.

Mariana kept her strictly away from the Wych Court coverts and park. Though the pup was on the whole obedient, there was no guarantee she would come if called away from pheasants or deer. Best to keep her well out of the way of gamekeepers and their master.

In fact, she did not see Mr. Perrincourt at all in the fortnight after her first visit to the Court, though she called twice more. Mrs. Perrincourt received her kindly, and the children soon lost their reserve with her.

Which was delightful, but how was she to judge the squire if she never met him?

Then she received an invitation to a Christmas party at Wych Court. Everyone went, from cowherds to local gentry, she was informed by her new acquaintances.

The younger ones bemoaned the warning that this year there would be no dancing, because the family was still in mourning for Mr. Jack's death. Their elders told them they were lucky to have a party at all. The Perrincourts were generously entertaining as usual only so as not to disappoint their neighbours and dependents.

Mariana had only ever been to balls as a chaperon. She was not sure whether to be sorry to miss the experience, or glad that she would not have to worry about whether Mr. Perrin . . . whether any gentleman—or cowherd—would stand up with her.

Although Mr. Perrincourt probably would not have been able to dance anyway, with his injured back, she reminded herself.

At least she was bound to see him, to have a chance to form an opinion of his character.

There were lesser festivities in the village, and in the spirit of the season, Mariana was even invited by some of the nearby gentry to join the company at the tea table after dinner. The Perrincourts' recent loss excused their absence from these affairs.

One festive dinner party, however, they did attend. Lady Fortescue was Mrs. Perrincourt's dearest friend, though the property of Sir George Fortescue, Baronet, was some six miles from Wycherlea. (Because of the distance, Mariana was unacquainted with the Fortescues and had no expectation of an invitation.)

Damian had no wish to go, but his mother persuaded him. He was quite well enough for a mere hour's travel in the comfortable landau, "or you may ride if you prefer, my dear. Lady Fortescue will be happy to provide a chamber for you to change into your evening clothes. And who knows but you will find a bride among the company."

"Hardly likely, Mama!"

"You never can tell. Lady Fortescue's brother, Sir Everard Westin, is visiting with his family, including a daughter of marriageable age. He is a diplomat, you know, recently knighted for services to the Crown."

"And you think she would make me a suitable wife?"

"My dear, I have no idea. I have seen her only once, many years ago, when she was about Lucy's age. But the Fortescues have a number of other guests staying in the house, chosen to mingle well with the Westins, so there are bound to be other young ladies."

"To whom I have no notion of doing the pretty," Damian growled, but he agreed to accompany his mother.

At dinner, he was seated next to Miss Ariadne Westin. Much to his surprise, he found her charming. She was pretty without being vain, well-informed but not pedantic, conversable yet not a chatterbox.

She was twenty to his forty-four.

After dinner, the rugs in the drawing room were rolled back for a not quite impromptu hop. Watching the young people enjoying a vigorous country dance, Damian was glad of the excuse of his mourning, and his injury.

He had never much cared for dancing in his youth. Now he had no desire whatsoever to take part. The sight made him feel his age, though several of the older gentlemen joined in with verve and apparent pleasure.

He found himself seated on a sofa with Lady Westin, a grey-haired, distinguished-looking matron.

"What fun the young folks are having, are they not, Mr. Perrincourt?" she exclaimed with delight. "Ariadne adores dancing."

"Miss Ariadne is a thoroughly amiable young lady," said Damian sincerely. "I took the greatest pleasure in her company at dinner."

Lady Westin eyed him dubiously. "She is a good girl. We have been so much abroad that she has not had a proper come-out yet, but we intend to take her to Town in the spring. I think it best she should meet as many people as possible before she settles down."

"I am sure so charming a young lady will have not the least difficulty attracting a suitable *young* gentleman."

Damian ruefully noted Lady Westin's relief at his choice of adjectives. Though he had been reflecting not a moment since that he was too old for Miss Westin, or any of the other girls skipping about the floor, her ladyship's obvious concurrence made him wince.

"Thank you, Mr. Perrincourt," she said. "I hope it is not simply a mother's partiality which leads me to agree!"

"Not at all. You are to be congratulated on her upbringing, ma'am."

"Oh, not I! At least, I trust my influence has not been utterly negligible, but we owe more than I can say to her governess, a most excellent woman. Miss Duckworth came to us when—"

"Miss Duckworth!"

"My dear sir, do you know Mariana Duckworth? What a happy coincidence. Ariadne, love," she said as her daughter, becomingly flushed, breathless and laughing, came to her at the end of a set, "only think, Mr. Perrincourt is acquainted with your dear Miss Duckworth."

"Oh, splendid, Mama! I have been so very sad, sir, to have lost touch with Miss Duckworth. Will you give me her direction, pray?"

Damian obliged. Miss Ariadne vowed to call upon her former governess before leaving for London after Christmas.

A youth came to beg her hand for the next dance, and she went off.

Somewhat bemused, and feeling sheepish at having so misjudged his tenant, Damian asked, "How did you come to lose track of Miss Duckworth, Lady Westin?"

"I fear it is inevitable in Sir Everard's profession," she said with a sigh. "Diplomats move about so. My husband was attached to the Portuguese Court for many years, you know, first in Lisbon, and then in their exile in Brazil."

"And Miss Duckworth went with you?"

"To be sure. I cannot conceive how I should have managed without her. She was remarkably quick to pick up languages and foreign customs, the greatest help to me. Naturally, when Ariadne no longer needed a governess, we should have been happy to keep her on as a companion, or to pay her fare home if she so chose."

"She did not so choose, I take it?" Damian was more and more bemused.

"Far from it! She found a post with a Russian diplomat's family, and in no time, she was off to Russia."

"Good Lord!"

"She has not told you of her travels?" asked Lady Westin. "For all her attainments, she is the most modest thing in creation, and always excessively circumspect and proper. I daresay she does not wish to be considered boastful."

"I . . . I am only very slightly acquainted with the lady," said Damian evasively.

"Merriman's Cottage, you say, in Wycherlea? We shall certainly call. Is she living with a relative?"

"No, ma'am, on her own."

"She is not . . . Oh dear, I do hope she is not in need?" Lady Westin said anxiously.

"I believe not."

"That is a relief. I am so glad!"

Sir Everard came to speak to her then. Damian was in need of changing his position, so he went to talk to his host for a while. Afterward he chatted cordially with several others, but all the while his mind was revolving the extraordinary discovery of Miss Duckworth's prior existence.

He found it quite impossible to reconcile the "excessively circumspect and proper" governess with the mud-smeared woman in the garden.

Had her name been Jane Smith, or even Jennifer

Smithson, he would have been convinced the two were not the same. But how many Mariana Duckworths of the right sort of age could there be? He knew her name was Mariana, for he had seen it on the copy of the lease sent by his lawyer.

Miss Mariana Duckworth, governess extraordinaire, world traveler, digging weeds in a country garden?

SEVEN

"A governess? Did I not tell you Miss Duckworth is perfectly respectable, Damian?"

"You did, Mama," he admitted as the landau turned from the Fortescues's avenue into the lane. He nearly added, "But we do not know what she has been doing since she left the Westins, nor how she came by the money to rent Merriman's Cottage."

Biting back the words just in time, he recognized them as a feeble attempt to justify his unwarranted suspicions of the woman.

Thank heaven no one but his mother was aware of his mistrustfulness. He was going to find it difficult enough to face Miss Duckworth, knowing he had maligned her, without her knowing it, too!

"Is she coming to our Christmas fête?"

"Of course, darling."

Recalling the dreams he had had of her brought a blush to his cheek in the dark. If he had discovered her to be unchaste, and had she not lived on his own estate, he would gladly have set her up as his mistress.

The young girls he had met tonight, no matter how fresh and lovely, did not appeal to him in the slightest. He refused to make a fool of himself marrying a chit straight from the schoolroom just for the sake of an heir of his own body. Properly taught, Thomas would grow up to be a worthy squire of Wych Court.

No, no youthful bride for him. Yet he rather thought he should like to have a wife, not just a mature mistress. Someone to talk to at the breakfast table. Someone to come home to after a day riding about the estate. Someone to sponsor Lucinda when the time came for her to seek a husband.

A vision of little Lucy standing at the altar with a kitten draped over her shoulder made Damian smile.

She needed a mother as well as a governess. The trouble was, available women of the right age were either spinsters, with all the flaws which had deterred suitors in their youth, or widows, very likely with children of their own. Even if he found a suitable childless widow, he had no wish to have to compete against her memories of her first husband, good or bad.

Lucy might have to make do with a governess after all. She must have the very best.

Miss Duckworth?

He would never have the nerve, far less the gall, to ask her after having misjudged her so! Drat the woman, the best thing he could do was to stay out of her way.

Walking down the Wych Court avenue with the rector, his wife, and her sister after the party, Mariana pondered what she had learnt of Mr. Perrincourt in the past few hours. It was not a great deal.

She had noted three things. The first was in his favour: he appeared affable to all his guests, young and old, of high and low degree. The second she was glad of, whatever his faults: his back seemed much improved, to judge by his visible ease of movement.

The third was that he had avoided her like the plague.

Bother the man! she thought, wishing her companions good night and merry Christmas as she opened her garden gate. It was simply maddening not to be able to get

him out of her mind. She had too little occupation now
that the weather hindered both gardening and excursions
to the lending library in the nearest town.

Mariana was used to a busy life. She had enjoyed
teaching the ladylike accomplishments—music, drawing
and watercolours, fine needlework—as well as such aca-
demic subjects as her various employers considered suitable for their daughters. However, the only one she truly
appreciated for itself was music, and she was not yet
certain whether she could afford to purchase a pianoforte.

She had promised herself to incur no unnecessary expense for a full year after unexpectedly inheriting a competence from her long-forgotten godfather. Always
residing in other people's houses, not to mention abroad,
she had no real understanding of the cost of living. The
most recent bills for candles and coals had rather shocked
her.

Paying them would by no means land her in the briars,
but the purchase of a spinet was at present an unjustifi-
able extravagance.

No doubt the amiable Mrs. Perrincourt would be more
than willing to allow her to play upon the instrument up
at the Court. Yet Mariana could not bring herself to presume upon the old lady's good nature when her son was
so obviously—inexplicably—inimical.

And there she was thinking about him again already,
not five minutes after resolving to drive him from her
mind. Bother the man!

The day before the fête at Wych Court, Mariana had
received a note from Lady Westin. The Westins were
staying in the district, she said, and she and her daughter
would give themselves the pleasure of driving over to
call at Merriman's Cottage.

Her ladyship suggested the day before Christmas Eve, if it suited Mariana, and if the weather cooperated.

"After the snows of Russia and the rains of Brazil, you will think us grown shockingly soft," she wrote, and Mariana smiled to read it. "But what must be endured in case of necessity may be avoided when one's sole purpose is enjoyment. So, weather permitting, we shall call, for Ariadne is *aux anges* to have discovered your whereabouts."

Mariana was deeply touched. Ariadne had been her dearest pupil, and the Westins her most considerate employers. Nonetheless, for a governess to be remembered so kindly was unusual.

Hetta was set to baking and Mrs. Plunkett to scrubbing and polishing. Mariana took her best morning gown from the press, brushed it carefully and hung it to air. Though of the same modest cut as the rest, it had wide bands of lace at the neck and cuffs, and it was a rich burgundy colour which would have been most unsuitable when she was a governess.

She wanted to show the Westins that she was not only independent but lacked for nothing. Even Lyuba received a thorough brushing, much to her disgust.

A fine, frosty morning ensured that her preparations did not go for nothing. Shortly after eleven, a carriage was heard in the lane, and Lyuba barked a warning that it had pulled up at the gate.

Mariana suddenly wondered how she ought to address her callers. Not only had their relationship changed, but a new title must be taken into consideration.

My lady or *Lady Westin*? *Miss Westin* or *Miss Ariadne*? Would her former pupil be offended to be called *Ari*, her pet name when they were alone together, now that she was emancipated from the schoolroom?

As Mariana opened the door and started down the path

to welcome them, an elegant young lady jumped down from the carriage and ran to hug her.

"Darling Ducky!" she cried. "I have missed you so. Have you missed me?"

Lyuba came frisking out, and Ariadne stooped to hug her, too, allowing Mariana to greet her mother.

Smiling, Lady Westin held out her hand. "Miss Duckworth, what a charming cottage. We are all agog to hear how you have fared since we saw you last."

"Come in, do, Lady Westin, out of the cold. Ari, pray do not let Lyuba bounce up at you like that. I am trying to teach her manners, and she is not at all so apt a pupil as you were. Come in!"

Over tea, biscuits and cake before a crackling fire, they exchanged news. Mariana congratulated Lady Westin on her husband's knighthood.

"Papa is excessively happy," said Ariadne, "because it means he may hope for one of the best postings. Napoleon will soon be finished, and then we may go to Paris, or even Vienna. They say Vienna is the gayest capital in Europe."

"There is talk of a peace conference in Vienna," Lady Westin remarked. "If it comes about, the city will be aswarm with kings and princes and grand dukes."

"Should you like to marry a foreign prince, Ariadne?" Mariana asked.

"Not I," the girl said gaily. "An English diplomat would be best, but if I had to stop in one place, I should choose England, not some mouldy German *schloss*. I wish you would come with us to Vienna, Miss Duckworth, or to Paris."

"You will always be welcome to join us, Miss Duckworth, wherever we go," her mother confirmed.

Mariana found herself tempted. Vienna, Paris, Prague perhaps, or Italy. Turkey, India, China, how much of the world she had not seen!

She glanced around her cozy sitting room, at Lyuba, lying with her head on Ariadne's booted foot. She looked through the window at the apple tree in the front garden, bare now, but how much she looked forward to seeing it clad in pink and white blossoms come spring. And all the daffodil and crocus bulbs she had planted with her own two hands. . . .

Already she had put down roots here in Merriman's Cottage, in Wycherlea. She had acquaintances who—now that Mrs. Perrincourt had broken the ice—treated Mariana as an equal. Two or three of them she hoped were on the way to becoming friends, even intimates.

With the Westins, even as a guest and companion rather than an employee, she would never be quite on the same level. Living in someone else's house, however amiable, she would never be free to seek out friends of her own.

She was ready to settle down and find her place in a stable, pleasant, if humdrum community. The only fly in the ointment was Mr. Perrincourt's unaccountable hostility, but being without reason, it must surely lessen in time.

With familiarity, he would come to regard her simply as one of the village's eccentric spinsters.

Mariana sighed. "It is very kind of you to invite me, Lady Westin. However, unless for some reason I were forced to leave Wycherlea"—*unless,* she said to herself, *Mr. Perrincourt goes so far as to cancel the lease*—"I believe my traveling days are over. I do hope you will stay in touch, though. By the way, I have been wondering how you found me."

"Quite fortuitously, Mama happened to mention your name to a gentleman who came to dinner at my aunt's," said Ariadne. "A Mr. Perrincourt, who claimed some slight acquaintance with you. Was it not fortunate?"

"Mr. Perrincourt!" Mariana exclaimed in some confusion. "Yes, he is my landlord. Most fortunate indeed. His mother is a delightful person."

"I liked Mr. Perrincourt, too. He sat beside me at dinner and he seemed vastly amiable."

"Ah," said Mariana, "amiable, single, and reportedly quite well to do."

"And old. And not a diplomat." Ariadne laughed.

At the sound, Lyuba raised her head, then jumped to her feet and licked Ariadne's hand. She trotted to the writing bureau in the corner. Lying down, she reached out with one paw to scrabble under it. A moment later, she returned from the corner, triumphantly bearing a distinctly ratty old hairbrush with missing bristles.

This she dropped in Ariadne's lap.

"Her brush! She must have hidden it after last time I brushed her, the naughty creature. She hates being brushed, but it seems her retrieving instinct won."

"She brought it to *me*," said Ariadne. "I am honoured, Lyuba."

While she petted the proud puppy, Lady Westin said softly to Mariana, "Mr. Perrincourt seemed rather startled when he learnt you used to be a governess. I am so sorry to have given away your secret."

Embarrassed, Mariana shook her head. "Not a secret, exactly. I have no intention of trying to keep it secret. I suppose I have never mentioned it because no one has asked what I did before I came here. On the whole, people seem to prefer to talk about themselves."

"You are such a sympathetic listener, Miss Duckworth," said Lady Westin, and patted her hand.

After the Westins left, Ariadne promising to write often, Mariana thought about what she had said.

It was true she had not deliberately avoided mentioning her former profession, nor would she ever lie about it. Yet might she not, quite unconsciously, have led more than one conversation away from the subject of her prior life?

A governess occupied such an anomalous position in the world, neither servant nor lady. Not only could she never be quite sure where she stood, but the uncertainty often made others uncomfortably unsure how to treat her. As the people of Wycherlea came to know Mariana as herself, a pattern would be established which the discovery of her past need not alter.

After all, whatever she had been, Mariana was now a lady of independent means. If a certain stiff-rumped gentleman chose to regard her with contempt, that was his lookout.

EIGHT

"Must I go?" Damian groaned.

"Yes, dearest," his mother said firmly. "If you do not, you will offend the rector and set a shocking example to the village."

"The pews are so deuced uncomfortable!"

"That has been an adequate excuse since you came home, in consideration of your poor back, but there will be no long sermon to sit through on Christmas morning, especially as it is a Saturday."

"You will not make me go to church again tomorrow?"

Mrs. Perrincourt smiled. "You sound like a ten-year-old! Except that even at that awkward age you always enjoyed singing Christmas carols."

"I shall go with you today," Damian conceded with a sigh, then put down his foot, "but not tomorrow."

In truth, his chief objection to attending the Christmas service was not the discomfort of the pews, or the boredom of a sermon. He did not want to meet Miss Duckworth.

He had led his men through many a French bombardment, steadied them against the charges of Boney's cavalry, forded rivers with rifle bullets whistling about his head, even stormed the walls of Spanish citadels. Now here he was, panicking at the prospect of finding himself face-to-face with a middle-aged governess.

Not panicked, Damian reassured himself. Just wary.

He could not quite pin down the reason. After all, she did not know that he had suspected her of being a woman of easy virtue. She could not guess he had dreamt of her—often—in that guise.

The glimpses he caught of her at the Christmas fête had proved to him that his knowledge of her supremely respectable past did not make her less desirable. He had managed, not without difficulty, to avoid her then among the throngs of guests.

In the churchyard after the service, on such a fine day, it would be much more difficult to evade an encounter. Undoubtedly his mother would wish to speak to her. Best to get it over with, Damian decided.

Miss Duckworth was his tenant and his mother's friend. He was going to have to speak to her sometime.

In spite of anticipated embarrassment, he thoroughly enjoyed the service. Tom and Lucy had been taught the old, familiar carols by their nurse and grandmother, and they sang with splendid verve. Lucy proved to have an excellent ear for music and a sweet voice.

"Noel, noel," she warbled, turning to look up at her uncle with a joyful face as she sang. "Noel, noel!"

Damian wondered whether Miss Duckworth had a taste for music. He was glad to be sitting in the front pew, or he would have been searching the rows in front, trying to guess which was her bonnet.

Though the service was not long, and included as much standing as sitting, his back hurt by the time it ended. To his dismay, everyone else waited in their seats while the squire and his family walked down the aisle. He had not attended the village church in years, and had forgotten the custom.

Most of the congregation were chatting to their neighbours in the pews, but he felt as if everyone was watching him—Miss Duckworth included. Lucy's little hand in his, he attempted to walk naturally, not favouring his back.

As a result, when they emerged from the church after exchanging a word with the rector in the porch, the pain was worse. Damian was thoroughly irritated with himself and the world.

The carriage was waiting. They might easily have escaped had not Mrs. Perrincourt, as expected, wished to exchange Christmas greetings with any number of people—Miss Duckworth, of course, included.

She came out of the church chatting with the rector's wife and her sister, the most respectable of females. A burgundy red gown peeked out from her slate grey pelisse, and her grey bonnet had a festive sprig of holly pinned to the brim. She laughed at something one of her companions said, and Damian caught his breath.

For all her years, she was a lovely woman. And indubitably respectable, however eccentric. How could he ever have thought otherwise?

He felt an utter fool.

Naturally, feeling foolish made him angry, with Mariana Duckworth since she was the cause of his folly. It was her fault for misleading him with her bedraggled appearance the first time he saw her.

When she turned to him, after wishing his mother a very merry Christmas, it was all he could do to bid her a curt good day.

She gave him a forgiving smile, which made him angrier than ever, then stooped to give Lucy a Christmas kiss and ask after the kitten before moving on.

"Isn't Miss Duckworth nice, Uncle Damian?" said Lucy, adding fuel to the flames.

The New Year passed, and Twelfth Night. Damian's back improved, and with it his temper. He began to think he might now meet Miss Duckworth without scowling at her, but somehow he never seemed to encounter her.

However, he was still uncomfortable with the notion of asking her to be governess to his niece and nephew. Instead, he wrote to his lawyer in London, asking him to look about for candidates for the position. He would have been satisfied to trust the man's judgement. Since his mother was not, he requested that after a preliminary interview to weed out the obviously unsuitable, applicants should be sent at his expense to Wych Court.

The day after he dispatched the letter, the winter's first snow fell. When it stopped in midafternoon, a blanket three or four inches thick had transformed the gardens and park into a white wonderland.

Bundled in cloaks and coats and hoods and woolly hats and scarves and mittens, the children still somehow managed to race in circles like March hares, shrieking with glee. Damian watched from a window, tempted to go out and join them for a game of snowballs.

Next winter, he decided regretfully. Building a snowman would be equally bad for his back, but he could go out and encourage them.

He went, taking with him an old top hat and muffler, lumps of coal for eyes and buttons, and a carrot nose. Passing through the stables, he begged of Benson a pipe with a broken stem, and a broom.

The children were delighted, eager to set to making a ball for the body at once.

"Start at the top of that slope over there," Damian suggested. "When it is heavy enough, it will roll down and collect snow by itself."

They ran up the hill. Damian followed to direct the operation. Soon he judged the ball big enough to roll and told Tommy to give it a shove. It whizzed down the hill, Lucy and Tom sliding and tumbling after.

Out of nowhere, Pirate appeared, bounding after the

growing snowball and batting at it with paws as white as the snow.

"He thinks it's a giant white mouse!" Tommy cried.

Lucy laughed so hard she fell over and rolled the rest of the way down. She reached the bottom looking like a snowball herself.

Her brother righted her and brushed her down. The kitten, all in camouflage except for his black eye patch, pranced over to her, his paws barely dinting the snow. Scooping him up, she deposited him on his favourite perch on her shoulder, where he clung, looking pleased with himself.

"Do you think it is a good idea to bring Pirate out in the snow?" Damian queried.

"He's got a fur coat on," Lucy pointed out. "At first he didn't much like walking in it, but now he thinks it's great fun."

"The stable cats *live* outside, Uncle Damian," Tommy reminded him.

Pirate hung on to Lucy's shoulder as the construction of the snowman proceeded. Moving cautiously, Damian helped lift the head and balance it upon the rounded body. The children dressed up the sturdy figure with the bits and pieces he had brought. Damian leaned the broom against it, and they all stood back to admire their creation.

"He hasn't got a mouth," said Lucy, dissatisfied.

"I cannot recall what your papa and I used to use to make a mouth."

"You could use a curved twig," Tommy proposed. "He needs arms, too. Sticks would do for those."

"You had best go and find some," Damian said, beginning to feel chilled and rather tired.

"But we're not allowed in the woods alone," Tommy said virtuously.

"You may go this once. Stay at the edge, where you can see the house."

"We will, promise! Come along, Lucy."

They dashed off, still full of energy. Damian made his way back to the house.

In the library, Perkins—bless him!—had flip waiting for him, keeping hot over a spirit lamp. The sweet, spiced mixture of small beer and brandy quickly warmed him through.

Setting the half-emptied tankard on the desk, he sat down to work on his accounts. It was the one part of running his estate that he thoroughly disliked. Quickly bored, after a quarter of an hour he went to the window to see whether Tommy and Lucy had yet returned from the woods with arms and a mouth for the snowman.

Their creation still stood armless. No sign of the children. Damian frowned, wondering what sort of mischief they could have got up to in the woods.

He ought not to have let them go alone, when their grandmama or their nurse had forbidden it. They were such engaging youngsters, he had forgotten the lack of discipline which was bound to land them in a scrape, sooner or later.

Were they in trouble now? Should he go out into the chilly twilight to look for them?

Dusk was settling in even earlier than usual today. The thin grey overcast which had masked the sky since it stopped snowing had been replaced by heavy, ugly, yellowish clouds, threatening more snow. Assuredly the children must come in.

It would be unfair to send a servant out in the cold when it was his own fault Tom and Lucy were missing, Damian decided. With a sigh, he went to don boots, hat, and topcoat again.

He was scarcely a hundred yards from the house when he saw Lucy running toward him, not at her usual happy scamper, but stumbling tiredly through the snow. As she came closer, he saw tears streaking her face.

"Uncle Damian, come quick! Oh, please come!"

"What is it?" he asked sharply. "Is Thomas hurt?"

"Tommy? No." She took his hand and tugged him onward. "It's Pirate. He jumped down from my shoulder and went off into the woods and he won't come when we call and we can't see him anywhere."

Damian suppressed a groan. Finding a needle in a haystack was easy compared to a white kitten in a snowy wood. At least a needle could not run away.

NINE

Damian looked down at Lucinda. Her face was pale and weary, and she was sniffling and shivering.

"You go back to the house, Lucy," he said. "Tommy and I will find Pirate."

"But . . ."

"Do not argue. Go."

For a moment he watched her trudge sadly toward the house. She could only be a liability in what was already an impossible task. He turned and headed for the woods.

The trees were mostly oak and hornbeam, the latter regularly pollarded. Snow clung to every leafless limb and twig, and mounded the undergrowth, turning to featureless drifts the thickets of bracken, hazel and blackberry left as shelter for pheasants.

Perfect hiding places for a white kitten, Damian recognized with a groan.

"Thomas!" he called.

The little boy appeared from behind a large oak. "I can still see the chimneys," he said defensively.

"Good. Have you caught a glimpse of Pirate since your sister left you?"

"No. I can't see how we'll ever find him, Uncle Damian. He's *white*."

"Believe me, I know it."

"But I've got to go on looking. Lucy is in a dreadful pucker. Didn't she come back with you?"

"I sent her into the house, and you had best go, too. It is no use catching a chill."

"I'm not cold," Tommy said bravely, obviously suppressing a shiver. "Pirate's so little, though. He'll freeze to death. We can't just leave him without trying."

Damian decided another few minutes would not hurt the boy, as long as he kept moving. If they had not found the kitten by then, there was no point going on. Even the snow's reflective whiteness could not hold back the dark much longer.

A few flakes drifted down.

"We will just have to hope he sees or hears us and comes," Damian said unhopefully. "Here, take my hand, Tommy, and call him as we go. Pirate!"

"Kitty, kitty!"

"Here, puss."

"Come *on*, Pirate," Tommy cried despairingly.

They tramped straight ahead through the trees, one direction being as good as another. As the light faded, snow started to fall in earnest. Damian glanced at the child's wan face, scarcely visible in the gloom.

"We will have to give up for now," he said gently. "In the morning—"

"Look!"

Following Thomas's pointing finger, Damian saw a yellow dog galloping across their path, with something dangling from its mouth.

Something white and limp.

"It's got Pirate!"

Tommy set off after the dog at a run. He tripped over an invisible obstacle and measured his length in the snow, but in any case the dog was out of sight by now. Damian helped the boy up. He was crying.

"That dog killed Pirate!"

"I fear so," Damian said gravely, brushing him down

and turning him homeward with a comforting arm about his thin shoulders.

How the devil was he going to break the news to poor little Lucy?

He could not expect Thomas to do it. His mother might be the best person, but she would doubtless be almost as distressed as the child. Though her health had greatly improved since his homecoming, she was still a frail old lady. It was too much to ask of her.

Nurse? No, Nurse was undoubtedly an excellent person when it came to wiping away tears over scrapes and bruises, broken toys and the minor disappointments of childhood. The horrible death of a pet was altogether different. Nurse was much too bluff and hearty.

Lucy needed a mother.

Damian shied away from the inevitable conclusion. He refused to wed a chit half his age, and available older women had serious drawbacks. To marry solely for the sake of the children was a sure recipe for disaster.

"Uncle Damian, what are we going to tell Lucy? If we say Pirate's dead, she'll cry and cry and have nightmares, like she did after Mama and Papa got killed. 'Specially if we say a dog caught him."

Blenching, Damian said grimly, "I shall think of something, never fear."

They found Lucinda explaining to her grandmother about building the snowman, and the need to search for sticks, and how Pirate had run off into the woods. The little girl turned eagerly to her brother and uncle as they entered. Her face fell when she saw no kitten in their arms.

"You didn't find him?"

"I am sorry, Lucy," said Damian. "A white kitten is invisible in the snow."

"But he'll die of cold if he's out all night!"

"There are plenty of hollow trees where he could shelter overnight."

"And bushes covered with snow," Tommy said ingeniously, "where a little animal'd be warm as toast just like the Esquimaux igloos in my book."

"And rabbit holes," Mrs. Perrincourt backed them up. "Pirate is having a great adventure."

Lucy was slightly soothed, until a new difficulty sprang to mind. "But s'posing he comes home in the night and no one lets him in? He'll freeze sitting on the doorstep."

"One of the servants shall check outside every door regularly all through the night," her grandmother promised.

"I shall go out and search again as soon as it gets light tomorrow," Damian proposed, feeling guilty for misleading the child.

Later that evening, he told his mother what had really happened.

"A dog came out of nowhere with the kitten in its mouth," he said. "I did not honestly expect to find the creature, but nor did I expect so unpleasant an ending."

"Horrid!" Mrs. Perrincourt shuddered. "You were quite right not to shock Lucy with such a tale."

"I daresay, in the morning, she will accept that her pet is enjoying a life of freedom and mouse catching so much he does not choose to come home."

His mother shook her head. "She would be grieved to think Pirate has deserted her. Best to tell her he is dead, but not how. And bring home another kitten for her, if you can find one."

"There are none in the stables at present, but undoubtedly someone in the village or on the farms will have a litter. I shall see what I can do."

* * *

No more than another inch or two of snow fell during the night. Early next morning, when Damian rode down the avenue, the earth's white coverlet sparkled dazzlingly in the rays of the rising sun, and crunched like starched linen beneath his horse's hooves.

With luck the beautiful day would put Lucy in a cheerful frame of mind. Damian was not at all sure telling her Pirate was dead was a good idea, or that another kitten would compensate for her loss. Nonetheless, he had decided to follow his mother's advice, for want of a better notion.

What on earth would his army companions think if they knew his errand? he wondered ruefully. Lieutenant Colonel Perrincourt riding out at daybreak in search of a kitten to comfort a little girl!

The second cottage he came to on the way to the village was Miss Duckworth's. Glancing over the hedge, he saw her standing on the doorstep.

He tipped his hat.

"A glorious day!" she called, smiling.

Her head was bare, her pinned-up braids glossy in the slanting sunbeams. The nip of the frosty air had brought a becoming colour to her cheeks. She must have just stepped out to admire the scene, for she wore neither pelisse nor gloves. Her blue gown, in spite of its demure neckline and long sleeves, displayed her maturely elegant figure to advantage.

Damian was seized by a burning desire to make up for his previous gruffness, to mend relations between them. Miss Duckworth, now moving down the path toward him—she had on boots, he was glad to note—seemed quite prepared to let bygones be bygones. He could do no less.

He wanted to present himself in a favourable light. An ex-governess would approve of his efforts on Lucy's behalf, he thought, and perhaps she knew of a litter of kittens in the village. He might even ask her advice as to whether he was doing the right thing for the child.

He drew rein.

Around the corner of the cottage pranced a yellow dog. Damian instantly recognized the colour, the size and shape, the long, blunt muzzle, floppy ears, and feathered tail.

"Your misbegotten hound killed my niece's kitten!" he burst out furiously.

Miss Duckworth gave him an icy look and turned back toward the cottage.

"Come, Lyuba!" she said. The dog followed her.

Damian was not going to let her get away with ignoring his complaint. He swung down from the saddle, scarcely conscious of wrenching his back in his haste. Flinging his mount's reins over the gate post, he stormed after her up the snowy path.

"Did you hear me, madam? Your wretched whelp caught and killed Lucinda's kitten in the woods! The child is heartbroken. If you cannot discipline the vicious brute and teach it to behave itself, I shall—"

The door closed in his face.

Raising his hand to bang the knocker, Damian hesitated. It would be more dignified, and very likely more productive, to write to her, warning that he would have the beast shot if she failed to train it not to kill. A vivid but calm description of Lucy's sorrow was more likely to rack Miss Duckworth with guilt than shouting at her.

He had frightened her . . . or had he? She had not fled, but retreated in good order before his boorish attack. Why did he find it so impossible to treat her with ordinary, gentlemanly courtesy, as he did every other female of his admittedly limited acquaintance?

The door opened.

Miss Duckworth stepped out, closing the door behind her. In her arms she bore a fluffy white kitten with a black patch over one eye, a purring kitten which she deposited in his hastily extended hands.

"Might I suggest," she said coldly, "that in future you attempt to ascertain the facts before going off at half cock? Good day, Mr. Perrincourt."

She went back into the house and shut the door.

TEN

Just before her front door thudded shut, Mariana heard a yelp of pain. Seething, she attempted to ignore it. The latch clicked into its slot, and she turned away.

Lyuba gazed up, her bright brown eyes innocent, loving—and just a trifle reproachful?

With a sigh, Mariana addressed her: "So you wish me to heap coals of fire upon his head, do you? I daresay he merely raised his hand to push on the door, and bashed his knuckles against it."

The tip of the puppy's tail swished gently, but she continued to regard her mistress with unwavering reproach.

"Or is it that you want your new little friend back?" Mariana sighed again. "No, you are right, I must at least see if the chucklehead has damaged himself."

Once more she opened the door. Mr. Perrincourt stood there, half bent over in an awkward posture, one hand pressed to the small of his back, the other arm cradling the kitten. His face was shockingly pale, and below the brim of his top hat, Mariana saw beads of sweat bespangling his brow.

"My dear sir, what is it?" she cried, alarmed. "You are in pain. Come in and sit down!"

"I cannot move without support," Mr. Perrincourt choked out. "Have you a walking stick? Or an umbrella . . ."

She flew to his side. "Here, give me the kitten." She

could not resist a sly dig: "If you trust me with him. Now, can you put your arm across my shoulders? I am strong, sir, you need not fear to put your weight on me. That is it. Be careful of the step."

"The step is where I came to grief," he said ruefully, leaning on her heavily as they crossed the threshold. "I moved backward without care and twisted to keep my balance. My back . . ."

"Mrs. Perrincourt has mentioned your injury. What will suit you best?" Mariana asked, supporting him into her sitting room. "A straight chair, or to lie upon the sofa?"

"I am best off lying flat upon the floor," Mr. Perrincourt confessed with embarrassment, "but quite apart from the discourtesy, I fear I cannot get down there without aid, far less rise again when your patience is exhausted."

"I shall call my maid and, if need be, send for your servants to help you up when my patience is exhausted," she said dryly. "Hetta!"

Grumbling under her breath, the maid lent her assistance. Soon the squire was flat on his back on Mariana's rug, with a cushion beneath his head and another under his knees. Though the procedure obviously hurt him a good deal, not a murmur escaped his lips until he was settled there, when he produced a groan of relief.

The dog, an interested spectator, trotted over to lick his face.

"Lyuba, come away!"

"No, let her be," said Mr. Perrincourt. "I deserve that she should bite off my nose. I do *not* deserve that you should be so kind."

"I cannot but agree," Mariana said cordially, sitting down upon the sofa.

Pirate was sitting there, where she had dropped him, diligently washing himself. Now he jumped down and went to curl up on Mr. Perrincourt's stomach, purring. Lyuba lay down with her chin on the squire's ribs, her nose touching the kitten's paw.

"As you see," Mariana continued, "they are the best of friends."

"So I see," he said, looking still more abashed.

"Lyuba ran off when I let her out into the garden yesterday evening, and came dashing back a few minutes later, bearing the kitten. I was not sure he would survive—he was soaking wet and chilled through. I dried him as best I could, and he managed to drink some warm milk. Then Lyuba took charge again. She carried him to the hearth rug and lay down beside him. I believe her mothering saved him."

"Her rescue surely did. I most humbly beg your pardon, and hers. You will observe, I abase myself."

Mariana smiled. "The proper position for self-abasement is facedown, I believe. Tell me, sir, do you customarily jump to conclusions on no evidence and with such a vengeance?"

"Not no evidence," he protested. "Thomas and I saw the pup—Looba is her name?"

"Lyuba. It is the Russian pet-name for a girl called Lyubov, which means love."

Mr. Perrincourt twisted his tongue around the unfamiliar sound. "Lyuba. How do you do, Lyuba," he added as she raised her head to look at him.

She stretched out her neck to lick his chin, then subsided again. Mr. Perrincourt raised his hand and gently pulled her ear.

"We saw her, with Pirate limp in her mouth," he said, continuing to stroke her neck. "You must admit it appeared pretty damning."

"I suppose so, if you do not know her. She has the softest mouth imaginable." As Mariana spoke, she watched his hand caressing Lyuba, and then she became aware that he was watching *her* mouth. Suddenly, unaccountably, her cheeks grew hot, and illogically, she rose and went to poke up the fire. "Are you warm enough, sir?"

"Perfectly, thank you." His voice was a trifle unsteady. For a moment she wondered if an incautious movement while her back was turned had exacerbated his injury, but he went on. "And the pain has subsided considerably. I shall not try your patience much longer."

"Believe me, Mr. Perrincourt, if there is any one quality a governess is obliged to cultivate, it is patience!"

"I daresay it is a quality in which you consider me sadly lacking. All I can plead in my own defense is that Lucinda was heartbroken at Pirate's disappearance, and I dreaded having to break it to her that he was dead."

"I wish I had sent a message up to Wych Court last night, but it was snowing. I did not care to go out, or to send Hetta in such weather. When you saw me on the doorstep just now, I had just decided to walk up myself with the kitten, though I ought to have been doing my accounts. I was quite sorry when you appeared, since you deprived me of an excuse for a walk on this beautiful morning."

"And I soon made you still sorrier for my arrival, did I not?" he said wryly. "As well as depriving you of your walk. Pray do not feel you must stay in to entertain me just because I am prostrate on your floor."

Mariana laughed, and Mr. Perrincourt smiled in response. His smile transformed his rather severe features. Somewhat to her surprise, Mariana decided she quite liked him, at least when he was not being pompous or outright rude.

"I have the best of excuses not to do my accounts now," she said. "I shall go and fetch someone to assist you."

"I dislike accounts quite as much as you possibly can,

so I am happy to have provided an excuse for you to postpone working on them."

"I do not mind when they add up correctly the first time, but they so rarely do!" She stood up. "Excuse me, pray, while I go and put on my outdoor things."

"Dress warmly, Miss Duckworth," Mr. Perrincourt urged. "The sun is pleasant, but in the shade the air is icy. I should not wish you to take a chill on your errand of mercy."

Lyuba dashed ahead up the stairs to her chamber. Mariana donned hat, gloves, and her warm pelisse, adding a shawl. When she returned to the sitting room, the sight of the squire, flat on the floor with the kitten asleep on his middle, struck her afresh, and she could not repress a chuckle.

"I suppose I must look utterly ridiculous," he said disconsolately.

"I beg your pardon, sir, I did not mean to laugh at you. That was disgracefully rude of me, especially since you are in pain."

"Very little now, I assure you. In fact, I daresay I can lift myself to my feet now, and walk home, if not ride." He raised his head and put out his hand to move Pirate, who stepped down, stretched, and began to wash. "I shall save you the errand."

"No, no!" Mariana stooped to press his shoulder to the floor. "Pray do not be foolish! Would you deprive Lyuba and me of our walk?"

"By no means, ma'am. You may go where you please—or walk with me." As he spoke he cautiously rolled over and pushed himself up onto hands and knees, with no more than a grunt of effort. "My mother would be pleased to see you, and the children, also. You must know that Lucinda bestowed upon you the accolade of that all-purpose adjective, *nice.*"

"I am honoured." Looking down at him, crouched on

all fours, Mariana smiled at his valiant determination. "What are you going to do now, Mr. Perrincourt? You will not be comfortable for long in that position, I fear."

"What a wretched tease you are, ma'am! With just a little assistance from your maidservant, I shall be up on my feet directly."

"Why trouble Hetta? I am sure I am quite as strong as she is, after all the work I have done in my garden. Come, let me help you up."

With her support, he stood. Whereas she had helped him in from the front step with no thought but for his pain, now his closeness, the warmth and weight of his touch, made her feel most peculiar. Her breath caught in her throat. She was not accustomed to the proximity of the masculine half of creation, and Mr. Perrincourt seemed to her a particularly masculine example.

As soon as she was sure he was steady, she hastily moved away, unnecessarily straightening her bonnet. He picked up his hat from the table where she had set it.

"Thank you, Miss Duckworth," he said in a constrained voice. "I shall do very well now."

Not sure if his sudden reserve betokened embarrassment to match hers, or physical discomfort, Mariana asked, "Do you honestly believe you will be able to walk all the way up to Wych Court?"

"Yes, if I take it slowly. However, if it will not discommode you, I shall leave my horse tied to your gatepost and send a groom down for him. Were I to lead him, I could not answer for keeping my feet should he toss his head or pull on the bridle."

"I am not at all certain you are fit to walk so far," Mariana said with a frown, picking up the kitten. "Will you not sit here and let me send your carriage?"

"No," he said obstinately, and went slowly but steadily to hold the door for her.

With Pirate, much to his noisy fury, confined in a lidded basket, and Lyuba racing around in the snow, they set off up the lane.

"What a stubborn man you are," said Mariana conversationally. "Why would you not remain at the cottage until your servants came to fetch you? I hope it was not because you dislike being beholden to me?"

"Not at all, Miss Duckworth. I am already under more obligation than I can well express. No, I did not want to alarm my mother, without good reason."

She raised her eyebrows at him. "Indeed? I wonder why I should have imagined you were simply reluctant to have any more witnesses to your prostration on my rug?"

"I wonder what could have led you to that conclusion?" Mr. Perrincourt said with a sheepish grin. "But it is quite true—as you see—that my back is improved quite enough to get me home. Incidentally, I prefer to consider myself determined and self-disciplined, not stubborn."

"I daresay," said Mariana tartly. "Fortunately, the English language has more than sufficient synonyms to allow all of us to give our faults the names of virtues."

"There speaks the governess!" he crowed. "Didactic is the word."

His turn to tease, Mariana acknowledged, pleased to see his eyes sparkling like the snow in the sun. He was walking more easily as they proceeded, still slow and careful, but no longer stiffly tense.

"I prefer instructive," she said with a smile, "thereby proving my point."

"So you do." He sobered. "Miss Duckworth, I have a favour to ask of you. I trust you will think me considerate, not cowardly, if I beg you not to mention my mistake over the kitten to Lucy, or my unforgivable rudeness to my mother."

"Of course I shall not," Mariana said warmly. "It could only distress them. Besides, you are forgiven."

"You are too good, ma'am. Dare I hope we may cry friends?"

"If Lyuba and Pirate are friends, Mr. Perrincourt, then I see no reasonable alternative for us!"

ELEVEN

When they reached the house, Miss Duckworth said hesitantly, "I had better not come in. I should have left Lyuba at home. Pray convey my respects to Mrs. Perrincourt."

"Balderdash!" said Damian, opening the front door. "My brother always had dogs about the house, and I shall again when I am fit to train them to behave themselves. The pup is the heroine of the hour. Bring her in. The children will want to make much of her."

"To heel, Lyuba!"

To Damian's surprise the dog obeyed at once. Though she had not killed but rescued the kitten, he still thought of her as an undisciplined creature.

Perkins came across the hall toward them. Lyuba promptly dashed to greet him, tail wagging madly, and leapt up at him.

"Down!" commanded the butler firmly, in chorus with Miss Duckworth.

Lyuba grovelled, rolling over onto her back. With an apologetic glance at his employer, Perkins bent to scratch her tummy. She squirmed in ecstasy.

"I am so sorry," said Miss Duckworth. "She is still learning. She is very young. Lyuba, come here, you naughty girl."

"Better too friendly than nervy, miss," Perkins observed as Lyuba pranced back to her mistress, not at all ashamed of herself. "The nervy ones generally end up nipping. Beg pardon, sir!"

"Perkins, tell Benson to send a groom for Saladin," Damian ordered. "He is at Merriman's Cottage. Is my mother come down yet?"

"The mistress is in her sitting room,"

"Good. Will you go to her, Miss Duckworth, while I take Pirate up to the nursery?"

Hearing his name, the kitten set up an angry yowl and started clawing the inside of the basket.

Under cover of the noise, Miss Duckworth murmured, "Are you really ready to tackle the stairs?"

Damian eyed the staircase dubiously, reluctant to admit to finding the prospect of climbing three flights a trifle daunting.

Perkins saved him. "Master Tom and Miss Lucy are outside, sir," the butler reported. "Miss Lucy insisted on going to look for her puss, though Master Tom said you would find him if he was to be found. As you did, did you not, sir?"

"Yes. Have someone fetch them in, if you please. Miss Duckworth?" He escorted her to his mother's sitting room, Lyuba docile at their heels.

They had scarcely time to explain the situation to Mrs. Perrincourt before the children burst into the room, pink-cheeked and tousled, with snow on their boots. Their excited exuberance at Pirate's reappearance, none the worse for his adventure, scared the kitten into scrabbling up the curtains and perching on the rod, out of reach.

Naturally Lyuba joined in the general commotion. Damian could not blame her, as Lucy and Tom kept hugging her. They rolled around on the floor together. The puppy licked the children's faces whenever she managed to reach them, leading to shrieks of glee and more hugs.

Mrs. Perrincourt and Miss Duckworth were helpless with laughter. Damian was glad to see his mother in high spirits, but it was Miss Duckworth's mirthful face that brought the grin to his.

He ought to chastise the children, but weakly he let them romp on.

Lyuba escaped from the heap on the floor and frisked around the room, barking. Grabbing a cushion from one of the chairs, she went to drop it in Miss Duckworth's lap.

Miss Duckworth caught her collar. "All right, that is enough," she said. "Mrs. Perrincourt, this is no time for a quiet chat. May I call again later?"

"Of course, Miss Duckworth, I am always happy to see you, with or without the dear puppy."

Damian called the children to order, and they said polite goodbyes and thank-yous. But as he left the room with Miss Duckworth, he heard them start to squabble about how to get the kitten to come down.

"I fear they are shockingly in need of discipline," he said. "They ought to know better than to come rushing in like that, with snow on their boots and their hair uncombed. And then to create such riot and rumpus, especially when there is a visitor present."

"The return of Pirate from the dead was reason enough for a little ebullience," Miss Duckworth argued. "Discipline has its place, but one must make allowances."

"Discipline is the glue which holds the world together," Damian said vehemently.

She looked at him in surprise. "You feel very strongly upon the subject."

"I learnt in the army that without discipline, everything falls apart. Undisciplined troops are no better than a mob; undisciplined civilians are mere rabble." Aware that his tone was grim, he tried to lighten it with a smile. "Yes, you might say I feel strongly."

"You have been a soldier since you were a boy?" Miss Duckworth asked.

"I was always mad for the army, ever since I was in short coats. It has been my life."

"And you always found it perfectly satisfying?"

He grimaced. "Until the Peninsula. Things were pretty bad there at times—from the retreat from Corunna to . . . But I shall not bore you with details." To his astonishment, he found himself confessing, "I might have sold out when my father died, but that Jack had everything well in hand, and I did not care to dispossess him."

"You must have been very fond of your brother," she said softly.

"Jack was the best of good fellows." In the weeks since he heard of Jack's death, the agony of grief had faded to a dull, ever-present ache, like his back. Like his back, it was liable to flare up unexpectedly. "I miss him!"

She laid her hand on his arm, in silent sympathy for a few moments.

Then she said, "Everyone tells me Mr. Jack was an excellent farmer and landlord, and husband and father, an admirable gentleman. Your military rank speaks for the fact that you were an excellent officer. Yet pray do not attempt to convince me that you and your brother never created riot and rumpus!"

"I should catch cold at that, for you have only to consult Mama! So you think I am too concerned over the children's misbehaviour?"

"It is not for me to say."

"But I wish you would, Miss Duckworth. I value your professional opinion."

"Very well." She gave him a slightly mischievous smile. "Let us return to near synonyms. I believe what your niece and nephew need is not so much discipline as guidance."

"Quibbler!" he laughed. "At any rate, you will surely agree that they need a governess. I have written to ask my lawyer in London to find a suitable person for them. However, I see no need to go so far afield. Miss Duckworth, may I beg you to consider taking on the position?"

"I cannot stop you begging, Mr. Perrincourt," she said dryly, "but in return I must beg you not waste your breath. I have retired. I am in no need of the salary, and besides, I was never a nursery governess. No, I regret disappointing you, but I am done with governessing."

As she set out homeward down the avenue, Mariana was filled with chagrin. So Mr. Perrincourt's sudden desire for friendship was merely a result of his realization that she might be useful to him, she thought sadly.

A moment's reflection sufficed to disabuse her of the notion. He had known for some weeks of her former profession. Today he had talked to her like a friend, revealing his feelings, not at all as if he simply wished to mend fences in order to offer her a position.

Moreover, the way he had approached her today was hardly conducive to good relations—first berating her, then forced to recognize his error, and then mortified by his collapse.

Poor man, he had suffered a difficult morning!

Many a gentleman would have hated her forever for witnessing his weakness. Mr. Perrincourt had risen above such pettiness. All in all, she had to believe his latter cordiality grew from his better acquaintance with her. Previously, they had had no occasion to get to know each other. Apart from a brief parley on the subject of the draughts in her cottage, they had scarcely exchanged how-d'you-dos.

He had taken her refusal of his request like a gentleman. Mariana hoped he would continue not just coolly gentlemanly but friendly.

She was encouraged in her hopes by the delivery, that afternoon, of a basket of apples, pears, oranges, and a large marrowbone. The accompanying note, explaining the gift as a mark of gratitude from the children for Pirate's safety, was written by Mrs. Perrincourt.

However, she added a postscript: *The above was dictated by my son, and the basket was entirely his notion. You have quite won him over, my dear. I am so glad.*

By next afternoon, the snow was gone from all but the most deeply shaded spots. Mariana was in the front garden, examining with a thrill the crocus, snowdrop, and winter aconite shoots already springing where she had planted them, when Mr. Perrincourt rode up.

"Come and see!" she cried, straightening, then hurried toward the gate. "No, pray do not get down if it will risk injury to your back."

"As long as I am careful . . ."

Anxiously she watched him dismount. That manoeuvre successfully accomplished, she bethought herself of the cause of her excitement.

"I fear you will think me sadly foolish, Mr. Perrincourt. I have made you descend only to see a few green sprouts poking through the earth."

He laughed. "I meant to come in anyway, to . . . er . . . to make sure you received the children's basket. Ah, I see Lyuba received her bone, at least!"

Lyuba looked up from chewing on her treasure and gave a rather perfunctory wag of her tail.

"She is not allowed to take it indoors," Mariana said. "It was very kind of you . . . of your mama to send it. And the fruit. I arrived too late to plant a vegetable garden last year, and I had no time to make preparations to put up preserves; so it is particularly welcome."

"Good! Now show me your precious green shoots, and explain why they are so precious to you."

"Oh, partly because I have not seen an English spring these many years, but mostly because I planted the bulbs myself. Look, here, and here."

"They have indeed come up." He took her hand and solemnly shook it. "Congratulations, Miss Duckworth."

"You are laughing at me," Mariana said resignedly, "but indeed, when one is new to gardening, as I am, it is a cause for elation."

"And that makes up for the labour of planting them?"

"Absolutely. Besides, you may find it difficult to believe, but I enjoy dabbling in the soil. For so many years, you see, I was obliged to observe the most minute details of propriety. Both Portuguese society and Russian are far more rigid than the English in their limits on the behaviour of young ladies. As I wished—with their parents' concurrence—to allow my pupils certain freedoms, I had to be particularly circumspect in my own conduct to compensate."

"So now you are free," Mr. Perrincourt said warily, "you choose to defy convention."

"Only in the most minor matters! And not simply for the sake of oversetting people's expectations. I truly enjoy gardening. At least," she added honestly, "I cannot say I enjoyed clearing brambles, though it was satisfying in a way, and digging is quite tiring. I have not accomplished all I hoped to be ready for planting come spring."

"I have been unable to give all the attention I would wish to the farms," said the squire. "Jack left everything in excellent heart, but now I am fit enough I must start relearning the business."

"Your mishap yesterday has not set back your recovery, sir?"

"Not at all, thanks to your prompt assistance. I cannot say . . ."

"Pray do not try, Mr. Perrincourt."

"And after I so maligned you!" he said in heartfelt tones.

"Not me, but Lyuba," Mariana said lightly. "I do not wish to hear another word on the subject."

He obeyed her, and shortly took his leave to go and visit one of his tenant farmers.

Early next morning one of the Wych Court gardeners arrived, with instructions to do any heavy work Miss Duckworth commanded. He brought a basket of winter vegetables.

For the next few weeks, Mariana was never without broccoli, brussels sprouts, cabbage, leeks, cauliflower, or celeriac, and turnips, onions, and potatoes. There were jars of preserves, too, and even pheasants and rabbits. The rich, brown, weedless soil of flower beds in the front garden and a vegetable plot in the back awaited the spring planting season. The apple tree was pruned and the hedges trimmed. Next time snow fell, it was shovelled from her path within the hour.

Mr. Perrincourt would take no thanks. She had forbidden him to utter the word, he said, and what was sauce for the goose was sauce for the gander.

She met him often, and he always stopped for a chat, after church, in the village, out walking in woods and fields, when she called upon his mother. Soon she found it hard to believe she had ever considered him odiously inflexible.

One February day, when Mariana was drinking tea with Mrs. Perrincourt, the old lady looked up from the fringe she was knotting and said quietly, "My dear, I dare say you must be aware that Damian's affections are engaged."

Mariana's heart plummeted. Whom did he love? She was not even aware that he had the remotest interest in any young lady. Still, it was none of her business, and she was about to say so when her hostess spoke again.

"You will forgive my speaking, I know, but I should hate to see him hurt. I believe him to be most sincerely attached to you. I hope if you cannot return his affection, you will take care to—"

"My dear ma'am!" Mariana's laugh was shaky. "I am persuaded you mistake the matter. Mr. Perrincourt's kindness to me arises from a generous heart, and perhaps from a hope that gratitude will lead me to accept the post of governess to his niece and nephew!"

"It is true that he has not been satisfied with any of the candidates sent down from London," said Mrs. Perrincourt doubtfully. "Still, I am far from convinced . . . There is only one way to find out. My dear Miss Duckworth, do you accept the position, and we shall watch how he conducts himself toward you then!"

"I see you are in league against me!" Mariana exclaimed. "Very well, ma'am, I accept, and I vow you will soon observe how fast Mr. Perrincourt's interest in me wanes."

TWELVE

Mariana laid down firm rules for her employment. She declined to live in, but would go up to Wych Court for a few hours every day except Sunday. Lyuba was to go with her, for she did not care to leave the puppy with Hetta. And lastly, she must have a free hand with the children, not hampered by Mr. Perrincourt's notions of discipline, or by Mrs. Perrincourt's overindulgence.

The Perrincourts demurred at nothing, so the following Monday she took up her new duties.

She found Tom and Lucy delightful, with eager, enquiring minds and very willing to learn. The playful kitten proved an unmanageable distraction, but once Pirate was banished from the schoolroom, everyone settled down, including Lyuba.

Mr. Perrincourt also had to be banished from the schoolroom. At first Mariana assumed the reason for his frequent appearance was to impose his strict ideas, in contravention of her rules. However, having enquired after the children's lessons, and admired their writing and their pictures, he always fell into general conversation with their preceptress.

In fact, he was more of a distraction to Mariana than to her pupils. Reluctantly, for she enjoyed their talks, she asked him to limit his visits to five minutes.

He complied, but he continued to turn up daily. He

also, unless out on business, joined the schoolroom party's daily walks on fine days.

The baskets of provisions continued to arrive regularly at Merriman's Cottage, and the gardener called weekly to ask if there was work for him. Mr. Perrincourt instituted thrice-weekly afternoon tea drinkings in his mother's sitting room, which he invariably attended. When the weather was the slightest bit inclement, Mariana found the landau at the door waiting to take her home. She was invited to stay for dinner far more often than she felt it proper to accept.

In short, Mr. Perrincourt continued to dance attendance on Mariana. The attraction she had felt for him from their first meeting, in spite of his then gruffness, grew as she came to know him better.

She might very easily fancy herself in love, she realized, if she were not well past the age for such nonsense.

Sometimes she suspected his mama might be right about his feelings for her. More often, she convinced herself that he, too, was past the age of romantic attachments. And if not, then a younger woman was far more likely to catch his eye.

But if, by chance, he had come to care for Mariana, why did he not speak? He had every opportunity, and nothing she could see to make him hold back.

No, Mrs. Perrincourt must be mistaken, she decided mournfully.

Damian groaned.

Lyuba looked up from her place on the hearth rug. She had taken to following him down from the schoolroom sometimes, after his daily visits. Now she came over to the desk where he sat and laid her head on his thigh, gazing up at him with sympathy in her big brown eyes.

Pirate, curled up on one corner of the desk, slept on, oblivious of Damian's travails.

He fondled Lyuba's silky head. "It is hard for an inarticulate soldier," he told her. "I have been trying for days, and somehow I simply cannot get beyond 'My dear Miss Duckworth.' Or do you think it ought to be 'My dearest Miss Duckworth'? No, that sounds ridiculous. 'My dearest Mariana . . .'?"

The pup shook her head. Actually she shook all over, really more a wriggle of pleasure in his caress, but Damian chose to interpret it as a negative.

"You are quite right," he went on. "I have no right to speak her Christian name. But that brings up another question: Shall I speak, or shall I address your mistress by letter, the coward's way? Either way, I must plan my approach."

He turned back to the desk and picked up his quill. Lyuba sighed and settled at his feet.

"My dear Miss Duckworth," he read on the sheet of notepaper lying in front of him. He dipped the pen in the inkwell, and stopped with it poised over the paper.

Too formal. He crumpled the sheet into a ball, set it aside, and began again.

"My very dear Miss Duckworth." Ah, that was better. She was very dear to him.

He had felt a physical attraction right from his first sight of her in her muddy gardening dress, mud streaked on her forehead. It had grown until it kept him awake at night, aching with desire, and haunted his dreams. Since he had come down off his high horse—or toppled off, rather—and learnt to know her, he had come to love her gentleness and humour, to admire her competence and her independent spirit.

Her independence, there was the trouble. How could he expect her, after years of living at the beck and call of others, to give up her independence and become his wife?

It went without saying that she would never marry him for his wealth or position. All he had to persuade her with was his love.

The best he could do was to stop dithering and pour out his heart, whether he decided in the end to send the letter or to con it well and utter the carefully prepared phrases aloud. He dipped the pen again, and wrote.

This time the words flowed easily.

"Your . . . most . . . devoted . . . loving . . . ," he said aloud as he wrote the final line. "Damian," he signed it.

Damian? Damian Perrincourt? D. Perrincourt? In any case, that would be left off if he made a speech of it. Was the last line above his signature too effusive? It might embarrass her, he thought, frowning.

He read what he had written. The whole thing was too emotional. All very well if she accepted his offer, but shockingly embarrassing to her, and mortifying to him, if she refused him.

"Damn!" he swore.

Lyuba raised her head. Pirate stood up and stretched.

"Damn," Damian repeated more softly. He picked up the sheet of paper, crumpled it into a ball, and tossed it onto the desk top.

Pirate sprang upon the splendid new toy. He patted it back and forth. The ball slid across the polished wood as if it was alive. He pounced. The paper made a fascinating crackling noise. He hit it again, and chased it as it slithered to the edge of the desk and fell off.

Lyuba seized it. She pranced around the library, tail swishing, eyes turned to Damian as if to say, *Look at me, aren't I clever?*

"Lyuba, come! Bring it here!" Damian jumped up and reached for her as she passed nearby.

She eluded him with ease. A few feet away, she stopped to look at him teasingly. As he strode toward her, she dashed to the half-open door and disappeared into the hall.

Mariana was halfway down the stairs when Lyuba galloped into the hall. The puppy scampered up to meet her and proudly dropped a ball of paper at her feet.

Holding one of the carved oak banister posts for balance, Mariana stooped to pick up the crumpled paper. It was damp, but only one corner was irretrievably soggy. In an attempt to salvage whatever her naughty pup had stolen, she smoothed the creases.

The first few words caught her eye: *My very dear Miss Duckworth.*

"Oh!" she said faintly, and sat down upon the stair.

The sudden weakness in her lower limbs did not affect her eyes. She read on.

Footsteps sounded in the hall below, unmistakably a man's hurried stride.

"Oh, the devil!" groaned Mr. Perrincourt.

Feeling her mouth quiver in a tremulous smile, Mariana kept her face averted.

"Miss Duckworth, I did not mean you to read that!"

She held up her hand to stop him. "One moment, sir, I have all but finished." *Your most devoted, loving . . .*

"Please . . ."

At last she looked at him, puzzled and a trifle apprehensive despite the warmth that flooded through her. He stood at the foot of the stairs, his hand on the carved water lily topping the bottom post, his eyes cast down as if the toes of his boots had suddenly become objects of the greatest interest.

"I would not have read it had I not seen my name. It is addressed to me, yet you say you did not wish me to read it? Why not?"

"Sentimental claptrap," he muttered, scarlet-faced.

"Oh," Mariana exclaimed joyfully, "I was afraid perhaps you might have changed your mind since writing it. There is nothing wrong with sentiment, if these are your true sentiments. And it is not claptrap, I hope, if you take claptrap as a synonym for mendacity. Or *have* you changed your mind?" she asked anxiously, in a small voice.

"No, my beloved governess, I have not changed my mind!" He took the stairs two at a time. "I used claptrap as a synonym for verbosity, and those are indeed my true sentiments." Stopping on the step below her, he said seriously, "I was afraid of embarrassing and disgusting you with unwelcome ardour. Is it unwelcome?"

"No," Mariana admitted, smiling up at him without a trace of the maidenly modesty she had so often recommended to her former pupils.

Damian sat down beside her and took her in his arms.

Sometime later, this idyllic interlude was interrupted by a butlerian cough from below.

"Ahem! Mrs. Perrincourt desires to know, miss, whether you will be joining her for tea?"

As Lyuba, who had been lying on the stairs, skittered down to greet her friend Perkins, Mariana emerged with a dreamy smile from Damian's embrace.

"Yes, Perkins, I am on my way."

"We are on our way," Damian corrected, his arm still about her waist as she stood up.

"Are you going to be married?" asked a youthful voice hopefully.

Mariana realized Thomas and Lucinda had been sitting at the top of the stairs for some time, quiet as mice. She blushed as she thought of what they had been watching. So oblivious had she been that Pirate had somehow gone past her up to the children without her noticing. He was draped in his usual pose on Lucy's shoulder.

"Yes, we are going to be married," Damian told his

niece and nephew, "as soon as possible. At my age I cannot afford to wait."

"The first of May," said Mariana, "after the daffodils bloom, the ones I planted myself."

He laughed down at her, the corners of his eyes crinkling. How she loved him!

"Very well," he said. "That will give us time to look about for a new governess. I fear, however, it will prove utterly impossible to find another the equal of the incomparable Miss Mariana Duckworth!"

A FELINE AFFAIR

by

Mona Gedney

As Graham Livingstone turned from the main road to make his way toward Ivy Hall, he sighed deeply. This was scarcely the way he wished to be spending his time. The weather had grown cold and bleak with the onset of winter, and if he were in Town as he should be, he would be enjoying himself in the most comfortable of circumstances instead of bouncing his bones down a narrow country lane.

"Insanity, Winchell, sheer insanity!" he remarked cryptically to his valet, who was clinging valiantly to the luggage.

"Yes, sir," remarked the valet sympathetically, clearly needing no explanation.

"And that, Winchell, must be the ancestral home of the dreaded Miss Alyce Brightman. Robert described it to me in distressing detail, down to the ostentatious *B* in the wrought-iron gate—quite as showy as the *y* in Alyce. I believe he hoped it would keep me away from here— and it very nearly did." He waved his whip vaguely in the direction of a very Gothic-looking manor perched atop a low hill, then slowed and stared at it more intently.

"Good Lord, Winchell! Look at that! She has all the instincts of a bloodhound!" he exclaimed under his breath, his eyes widening in horror. "I thought she was still in London, but I believe that is Alyce riding toward the gate! What a nightmare it will be if she intercepts us. Hang on for your life, Winchell! We will pass that gate before she arrives there or die trying!"

And, true to his word, he raced the team past the gate, and they kept their frantic pace until they had left the far wall of the park safely behind them. Graham Livingstone was devoted to his bachelorhood and had clung to it tenaciously for the ten years that he had been an ornament to the *ton*. Miss Brightman, however, appeared unable to grasp that concept and had spent the last three seasons pursuing him with a single-minded determination that horrified him.

"My apologies, Winchell," he said penitently, having noted the servant's wild-eyed expression as he attempted to keep their belongings—and himself—from bouncing into the road, "but I can imagine nothing worse than encountering her again—especially here on her home turf."

"I quite understand, sir," responded Winchell, loosening his hold for a moment so that he could wipe the beads of perspiration from his forehead. "Have we much farther to go to Ivy Hall?"

"Courage, Winchell, courage!" he cried hearteningly, feeling quite robust now that his nemesis was safely behind him. "We are almost there. I told my brother when he purchased this estate that he had done me a disservice by placing himself so close to Miss Brightman and that he needn't expect to see me here—and yet here I am!"

"So you are, sir," agreed Winchell, fully willing to indulge his master if he had need of stating the obvious.

"Well, what I mean to say, Winchell, is that if I can do this—come here against all my inclinations—then so can you. We are both in this together." He eyed the valet for a moment. "Does that improve your spirits, Winchell?"

"Indeed it does, sir," responded Winchell, his voice carefully devoid of expression.

Livingstone burst into laughter. "You are a liar, Winchell—but you are always refreshing."

The valet allowed himself a wisp of a smile. He had served Graham Livingstone faithfully for ten years and would have followed him to far worse places than the far reaches of Yorkshire—if there were worse places, which Winchell privately took leave to doubt. He shuddered briefly as he looked about him and then closed his eyes. Never had he gone so far from London and civilization.

Nor was he cheered when he heard Livingstone sing out, "Take heart, Winchell! We're almost there!"

A brief glance confirmed the valet's worst fears. Ivy Hall did not live up to its inviting name. In fact, he could see no ivy at all, although he privately felt that humble plant could have gone far toward softening the square grey outline of the building they were rapidly approaching. It looked fully as bleak and wind-scoured as the countryside through which they had been riding. Master Robert had wanted to take up the life of a hermit when he left London two years ago, and he had clearly found the perfect hermitage. Winchell could not imagine anyone other than a devoted family member deliberately seeking out such a place.

It was clear that his master shared his opinion. As they entered the hall, they were set upon by a pack of spaniels that seemed determined to fling them to the flagstoned floor so that they could become more closely acquainted. Livingstone stared down in horror at the muddy paw prints on his immaculate doeskin breeches and the blotches that desecrated the shining surface of his riding boots. The butler tried to fend them off, but could do nothing with them. Not until their own master entered the room and called them sharply to order did they obey, tumbling cheerfully from the hall at his command.

Livingstone shook out the capes of his greatcoat before handing it to the butler and turned to his brother crossly. "Good Lord, Robert! Why don't you keep those beasts out of doors where they belong? They have quite destroyed me. Why, it will take Winchell hours of work to restore my boots alone."

"And I am delighted to see you, too, Graham," responded Robert, a small smile playing over his lips. "It is reassuring to see that you haven't changed."

"Well, you might have seen that I haven't changed if you lived closer to civilization so that you could get into Town occasionally."

"Yes, but I didn't want to get into Town at all," returned Robert simply. "That was precisely what I wished to avoid." This time his smile was genuine. "And, as you see, I have avoided it."

Graham stared about him disapprovingly. "Indeed you have! But you know, Robert, you needn't have moved to the ends of the earth simply because your little romance hit a bump in the road. You might at least have thought of the inconvenience making such a trip as this would cause me!"

"You must forgive me, Graham," replied Robert Livingstone ruefully, regarding his brother with amusement. "I had no idea, you see, that you would make such an effort merely to see me. Naturally I should have considered that first when choosing my home."

"Well, of course you should have thought of that!" returned Graham, his irritation mounting. "After all, you are all the family I have, and I do feel some responsibility for your well-being!"

"Very kind of you, I'm sure," observed Robert, guiding him into the library and away from the interested gaze of his butler, who was deliberately lingering in the hall. "I had no idea that my well-being was threatened in any way, however."

Much to the butler's disappointment, he shut the door of the library firmly behind him before turning back to his brother to resume the conversation. "Just why have I become the subject of your concern, Graham?"

"Oh, I don't know just why it should trouble me," was the caustic response. "However, when I am in White's enjoying a comfortable game of whist or a dinner with friends and am continually asked when you are coming back to Town and why you have stayed away two years and whether or not you have stuck your spoon in the wall, I begin to feel that I should look into the matter."

"I should think that anyone with a grain of intelligence would know why I am here," responded Robert coolly, pouring them both a glass of sherry. "After all, everyone in the *ton* knew that Marian broke off our engagement just two weeks before the wedding. It was certainly not a secret."

"Well, that's scarcely reason for running off to some far corner of the earth and walling yourself up!" snapped Graham. "It isn't as though such things never happen, nor that there was any shortage of pretty young women waiting to console you. Damme, Robert, engagements are broken every day."

"Such things hadn't happened to me." Robert stared for a moment at the display of Roman coins on his wall.

Graham studied him for a moment. Certainly his brother had never had to face rejection. He was the perfect picture of a young girl's hero, broad of shoulder and brow, his dark good looks striking. Graham himself was a handsome, well-made man, but he had never placed himself in the same category as his younger brother.

"I suppose I should really be grateful to Marian, however," Robert continued, still staring at the coins and fingering a handsome gold brooch. "If she hadn't left me, I never would have pursued my interest in the Romans, and the study of antiquities has been most gratifying—far more than following her about from drawing room to drawing room would have been."

Graham looked at him blankly and then glanced at the coins. "The Romans?" he asked. "Do you mean to tell me, Robert, that you go about looking for those antiquated bits that farmers sometimes turn up in their fields? Is that the way you spend your time nowadays?" His younger brother, popular with the *ton* for his good looks and his abilities as a sporting man, had evidenced no scholarly interests since childhood.

Robert nodded. "And it is far more satisfying than lying about at the club or boxing at Cribb's Parlour, spending my time with people I don't really care a fig for and who care nothing for me."

Graham sank back in his chair and nursed his glass of sherry uneasily. "You can't mean that, Robert! It sounds to me as though you're still blue-deviled and using all of this as an escape. Are you not still grieving over losing Marian? We all thought that was why you hadn't come home again."

Robert laughed. "She probably did me the greatest favor in my life by not marrying me," he returned. "I far prefer this quiet life."

"I don't know how I'll be able to explain this to Hornsby and some of the others at the club who have been demanding that I restore you to Society," his brother moaned. "They won't believe me if I tell them the truth."

Robert shrugged. "I can't see why they would really care one way or the other. It isn't as though I had any particular friends there." He turned to the fire and kicked at it idly with the toe of his boot. "Is that really why you've come all this way—to tell me that I am missed and that I must go back? I won't, you know."

Graham stared at him uncomfortably. "Well, now that you mention it, there is a little bit more to my trip than that."

Robert nodded. "I thought there must be, but, to be frank, I couldn't imagine what it might be."

Graham, usually quite self-possessed, began to grow more restive. "It all began at a ball a few weeks ago," he began slowly. "Now, I daresay that you might not be taken by the idea immediately, Robert, but I think that if you give it a little time, you may—"

"Give what a little time?" interrupted his brother curiously. "What have you been up to, Graham?"

"It seemed quite a knacky notion at the time, you see. I bumped into Marian at Lady Fotherington's ball—"

"Is she in Town at the moment?" inquired Robert, still poking at the fire. "I should probably send off a thank-you note for my freedom."

"No need," said Graham unhappily, deciding that forthrightness was the only way to broach the subject. "She will be here tomorrow and you may tell her yourself."

There was a brief silence as Robert turned to stare at him in disbelief. "Marian will be here? At Ivy Hall? Are you quite mad, Graham?"

"Well, how was I to know that you weren't still wearing your heart upon your sleeve?" demanded his brother. "The last letter you wrote to me was chock-full of your misery at losing her."

"That was written well over a year ago!" Robert protested.

Graham shrugged. "How was I to know that you had changed your mind?"

"You might have asked me! Have you actually invited her here?"

Graham nodded. "She and her mother will arrive tomorrow afternoon."

Robert rubbed his forehead in disbelief. "Mrs. Blakeley, too! My cup runneth over." A sudden thought struck him, and he turned to eye the culprit sternly. "Have you invited anyone else, Graham?"

"Well, of course I have not! This is your home, after all!"

"Precisely my point! Whatever possessed you, Graham—you who pride yourself on being so awake on every suit? You must have been three parts disguised to have done such a hen-witted thing."

"I was no such thing!" exclaimed Graham indignantly. "We fell into conversation quite by accident, and it seemed to me that she showed the deepest regret for breaking off your engagement."

"Did she indeed?" responded Robert, his disbelief written clearly on his rugged features, sharply in contrast with his brother's finely chiseled profile. "How well she has hidden it from me for two years!"

"Well, what would you expect her to do? What could she do? Come crawling back and beg your forgiveness?"

"I don't know that I would have required the crawling," responded Robert, appearing to consider the matter carefully, "but I would have greater belief in her sincerity had she at least returned her engagement ring to me instead of clinging to it like the scheming little fortune hunter she is."

"Her engagement ring?" said Graham blankly. "Do you mean she didn't return Mother's ring?"

Robert shook his head. "She knew very well what that ring meant to me, yet she could not trouble herself to return it. She was welcome to keep the other bits of jewelry I had given her, of course; but the ring was different, and she knew that perfectly well."

Graham was silent, studying the fire. Their mother's ring was an antique piece that had been in their family for generations. It was irreplaceable, not only because of its value, but also because their beloved mother had worn it every day of her life from the time she first received it from their father until her death. Marian was well aware of that, for Robert had told her so when he presented it to her. Since Graham had no intention of ever marrying himself, he had approved his brother's use of the ring so that the family tradition would continue.

"That doesn't seem in character," he finally said slowly. "Although I have spent little enough time with her, it simply doesn't seem like something Marian would do. Her mother, possibly," he added as an afterthought, "but not Marian."

"Apparently neither of us knew her quite as well as we thought," returned Robert. "I should have heeded the gossip about her desire to marry anyone with money."

Graham dismissed his remark with a wave of his hand. "You know that the Town Tabbies say that about anyone they take a dislike to—and Marian had every eligible young man hanging after her, so of course she was an object of gossip."

He paused and looked unhappily at Robert. "In view of what you have told me, though, both about the ring and about the current state of your feelings for her—or I suppose I should say your lack of feelings for her—I can only apologize for inviting her here."

He sighed and sank back into his chair. "It really is too bad, you know," he said regretfully. "I rather fancied myself in the role of Cupid."

Robert shrugged. "You meant it for the best, I'm sure. At any rate, it is far too late to undo it—we shall have to muddle through it as best we can. I can scarcely pack them off to an inn when they arrive. The only place in the neighborhood is that godforsaken Royal Rooster down the road—and I wouldn't allow my stable boy to put up there."

He closed his eyes for a moment, picturing the disappearance of his bachelor ease under the onslaught of feminine company. "I suppose I had better ring for Jarvis so that he can prepare for guests." He smiled grimly. "At least this will give the servants something to talk about.

Aside from you, they will be our first guests at Ivy Hall since I arrived."

He had just reached for the cord when a sudden thought struck him, and he looked at his brother with deep misgivings. "Just how long a visit did you invite them for, Graham? Tell me it was only for two or three days."

There was a slight pause, and then Graham smiled weakly. "Only for a fortnight, Robert," he murmured. "After all, this is quite a trip to make for a visit of only a day or two."

Robert groaned. It was quite as bad as he had suspected. His comfortable life, to which he had grown happily accustomed, was falling to pieces about him.

"I hope that you are feeling very entertaining, my dear brother," Robert remarked dryly, "for rest assured that you are the one that shall be with them. I have my work, you see."

Graham was still mulling over his brother's words as he prepared for bed that evening. What Robert meant, of course, was that he had every intention of closeting himself in that rat's nest of books and boxes he called a library and emerging only at mealtimes—if then. Or, worse still, he would think of some brief trip he had to make in order to look at some antiquity and abandon Graham completely to the Blakeley ladies.

He paused a moment, suddenly envisioning the lovely Marian. He had been quite taken aback when she had approached him at Lady Fotherington's ball. She had appeared so distressed as she spoke regretfully of the broken engagement.

"It wasn't a wise decision," she had confessed, her hand lingering warmly on his arm. "I was just a foolish girl then, however, so I must excuse myself on that account."

"Of course," he had responded with equal warmth, suddenly realizing that Robert's days as a hermit might be drawing to a close if he could only bring the two of them together. "I understand completely."

He had looked earnestly into Marian's dewy blue eyes and found himself thinking—if only for a moment—that he could understand why Robert had become a recluse after losing such a beauty.

Remembering the moment, he smiled to himself. A mild flirtation would pass the time away quickly enough if Robert chose to continue in his present stubborn course. He could not, after all, allow Marian to be disappointed after so long a journey since he himself had been responsible for it. He could at least see to it that she enjoyed herself. For the moment, he put aside all thought of Mrs. Blakeley.

He was just congratulating himself upon his selfless decision when a piercing shriek tore the air. He stared at the curtained window wildly, for it had seemed to come from just outside it.

"Winchell!" he shouted, quite forgetting that he had sent his valet to bed some time ago as an apology for their troublesome journey—and for the mud-spattered boots and breeches that he had to clean.

After realizing that Winchell was out of earshot, Graham stood perfectly still and listened. Rain was peppering the windowpanes, and the branches of a tree were scraping against the house in the wind, creating together a most unmelodious duet that made him grateful to be inside by a warm fire. For a few moments he heard nothing more than that, and he was about to attribute the earlier noise to the storm when the same shriek suddenly shattered the night again.

Ripping the curtains aside, he flung the window up,

fully prepared to see someone being murdered on the lawn below. Huge drops of icy rain immediately soaked the sleeves and front of his nightshirt, chilling him to the bone, but what momentarily unnerved him was the tremendous thump on the chest he received from what appeared to be a flying object.

Still certain that there was a murder in progress and that he had been attacked as a possible witness, he hung out the window, peering into the inky darkness below. The shriek was not repeated, however, and he could hear nothing save the storm. Puzzled, he slowly lowered the window and pulled the curtains snugly closed again and turned back to the room, curious to see what had been flung at him. To his surprise, there was nothing on the floor except a puddle of water.

Even more puzzled now, and freezing as well, he stripped off his dripping nightshirt and dried himself in front of the fire, eager to go to bed and quietly to sleep. Trust Richard to choose such a place, he muttered to himself! He had referred to the neighborhood inn as a godforsaken place, but Graham was of the opinion that the entire county could be described in precisely the same manner.

"I daresay there's not a pennyworth to choose between the Royal Rooster and Ivy Hall," he said bitterly, carefully avoiding the puddle as he made his way across the room.

Pulling aside the heavy velvet curtain that sheltered the bed cozily from drafts, Graham prepared to make himself comfortable and warm once more. To his indignation, however, he saw that his bed was already occupied.

A sodden, bony-looking cat of an unfortunate shade of orange lay precisely in the center of the bed, carefully making her toilette. This, then, had been the object that had attacked him and that had been responsible for the nerve-shattering shrieks.

"Here now!" he exclaimed, attempting to shoo the beast from her nest. "Off of there immediately!"

The cat paused, one paw in the air, and studied him for a moment. She appeared to have no intention of moving.

Taking advantage of her momentary attention, Graham tried once more to displace her. "I am planning on sleeping in that bed myself, small beast—or at least I am after Winchell puts on fresh linens—so you might as well remove yourself at once."

The cat returned to the beautification of the paw in question, apparently unimpressed by Graham's plans for the evening.

"Well, I've no intention of soaking yet another nightshirt by picking you up and removing you myself," Graham announced. "Winchell shall have to attend to it." And, disregarding his earlier plan of allowing his valet an early evening, he pulled the bell cord with a vengeance.

Winchell soon appeared, a trifle heavy-eyed to be sure, and with wisps of hair standing on end, but looking highly competent as he always did. "You rang, sir?" he inquired.

Graham pointed toward the bed. "You will see that I have an uninvited visitor, Winchell, and I wish for you to think of something to do with her."

Curious now, Winchell peered around the curtains, prepared for almost anything. At the sight of the interloper, he chuckled. "The cat appears quite comfortable, sir. Just what did you wish for me to do with her?"

"To take her away, of course!" responded Graham indignantly. "How am I to sleep in a bed that has been soaked by that unhealthy-looking beast? We shall probably have to burn the mattress. I hope that Robert has an extra one."

"How did she get in?" asked Winchell curiously.

"Through that far window," responded his master, pointing at it crossly. "She was making enough noise to wake the dead, and I thought someone was being murdered. She proceeded to shoot into the room like a cannonball and make herself at home."

"I can see that she did," responded Winchell, amused. "Did you wish for me to put her back out the same way that she came?"

Graham paused for a moment, listening to the wind and the blowing rain. "Perhaps we shouldn't put her outside until morning," he said reluctantly. "After all, it really isn't a fit night for man nor beast. Why not leave her downstairs?"

"And what of the dogs, sir? Master Richard lets them run free, you know, particularly at night. They might make short work of a cat set amongst them. Particularly one that appears to have had a hard time of it."

Graham groaned. "Wouldn't you know that Richard would think of another way to complicate my life?" He regarded the cat unhappily. "She does look like she's been chewed up a bit, doesn't she?"

Winchell, who was fond of cats, nodded. "Possibly she's already met the spaniels."

"Well, I suppose there's nothing for it," sighed Graham. "Get me fresh linens for the bed, Winchell, and we'll put these on the floor by the fire. She might as well be comfortable."

Winchell allowed himself a small smile. He had known just how it would be. For all his meticulous, demanding ways, his master had an unexpectedly tender heart. That, coupled with the fact that Graham Livingstone was always a credit to his valet, kept Winchell faithful to his master, despite those who tried to lure him away with the promise of a higher salary. "Just as you say, sir," he responded politely.

"And bring me a glass of brandy," added Graham as Winchell opened the door.

"Yes, sir."

"And, Winchell," he added reluctantly.

The valet paused to look back at him. "Yes, Mr. Livingstone? Is there something else you would like?"

"A dish of milk," sighed Graham. "And perhaps a small plate of chopped chicken if there is such a thing to be had in my brother's pantry."

Candle in hand, Winchell departed to face the spaniels and the uncharted depths of the kitchen below.

The next morning, despite the cold, Graham left the window invitingly open, calling the cat's attention to it before leaving the chamber to go down for breakfast.

"Do you think she will actually leave, sir?" inquired Winchell, eying the cat, who was snugly encased in her covers by the fire, both dishes empty beside her.

"Of course she will," returned Graham confidently. Striding once more to the window, he called to the interloper. "See here, cat! Why not rush out there and find a mouse? I would check down by the stable if I were you."

At the sound of his voice, the cat raised one eyelid sleepily and appeared to regard him benevolently for a moment before curling herself into an even tighter ball of fur and lapsing once more into sleep.

"I place no confidence in her," observed Winchell. "What an odd color she is—very much the color of ginger. And she has such an odd, lumpy shape for a scrawny cat."

"Unfortunate beast," agreed Graham. "It is certain that she will win no prizes for her looks."

Ignoring these slurs upon her appearance, the cat slept on.

That afternoon the crunching of gravel under the wheels of a carriage and a flurry of activity on the part of the butler and a footman forewarned Graham that the Blakeley ladies had arrived. Abandoning his book in the drawing room, he hurried to the library door.

"They're here, Robert!" he announced in a whisper.

"Are they indeed?" inquired his brother coolly, not troubling to look up from his desk.

"Well, come along, man! You can't be so rag-mannered as not to welcome them to your home."

"Why could I not? You invited them—you may go and make them welcome as their host. Jarvis will show them to their chambers, and you have my blessing to make them fully at home—except in the library."

Abandoning all hope of persuading his brother to act in a reasonably civilized manner, Graham returned to the hall to try to atone for his absence.

"Marian, Mrs. Blakeley, welcome to Ivy Hall." He beamed upon them as the footman carried in their baggage.

"How well you are looking, Mrs. Blakeley," he declared, taking her hand.

"I have survived the trip, Mr. Livingstone, if that is what you're referring to," she returned brusquely. She was a small, thin woman, whose sharp eyes missed nothing. "And where, pray tell, is your brother?"

Marian intervened smoothly, extending her hand to Graham. "How charming to see you again, Graham. I have looked forward to having more time to talk with you. Our chat at the ball was sadly brief."

"So it was," said Graham, grateful to her for rescuing

him. "Rest assured that here at Ivy Hall there will be an abundance of time to talk."

"So I should imagine," said Mrs. Blakeley, looking about her. "It didn't appear to me that there is much to do in this country aside from talk."

"And as for Robert," Graham continued, trying to overlook her extremely accurate observation, "he appointed me his deputy to welcome you, and he will be with us at dinner."

"Indeed?" returned Mrs. Blakeley, glancing at him sharply. "It seems a strange business that the host should not be present to welcome his guests."

"Not at all, Mama," said Marian. "I am sure that Robert has business to look after now that he has an estate to oversee."

"Just so," responded Graham quickly, casting her another grateful glance. "And now if you will allow Jarvis to show you to your rooms, I will see to it that refreshments are prepared for you."

"How very kind," returned Marian, smiling at him gently.

Graham watched her glide up the steps behind the butler and her mother. He thought with satisfaction that Robert must be strong, indeed, if he could resist her charm for the next two weeks. A sudden thought followed hard on the heels of that one. Perhaps it was possible that was why Robert was remaining within the fastness of his library—to protect himself. Perhaps he was afraid that being too much with Marian would once again make him vulnerable to her all too evident charm.

Mulling over this interesting thought, Graham bustled away to see to the refreshments that he had promised the ladies. It would be just his lot in life, he reflected darkly, to find himself left with Mrs. Blakeley to entertain for two weeks while Robert and Marian wandered about the house smelling of April and May.

When Robert appeared at dinner, however, he showed no sign of any such vulnerability to Marian's charm. Indeed, the majority of his conversation—if it could be termed conversation, thought Graham bitterly as he considered the matter afterward—was directed most pointedly to Mrs. Blakeley.

"You might as well have hung out a sign saying, 'I don't even know you are here, Marian,' " he hissed at his brother after dinner. The ladies had retired to the drawing room and the two gentlemen were going through the motions of drinking their port before joining them.

"I could do that if you would prefer," remarked Robert idly.

"How can you be so callous to someone who has come so far to see you?" demanded Graham. "I can't believe that you look at that lovely young woman and then deliberately ignore her."

Robert grinned at his brother. "If you find her so lovely, Graham, you have my permission to pay your addresses."

Graham choked on his port. "Pay my addresses? Have you lost what little wit you had, Robert? You know my feelings on that subject."

Robert nodded and raised his glass to his brother. "Just as you, dear brother, know my feelings on this particular subject."

Defeated, Graham retired to the drawing room to entertain the ladies alone, grateful that Marian could—and would—play the pianoforte and sing. It helped to fill the evening, although he could feel Mrs. Blakeley's icy gaze and periodically was compelled to make brief attempts at conversation with her.

Unfortunately—or perhaps fortunately—she put a quick end to all of his attempts, observing with a sharp sniff that she wondered about the manners of a host who would abandon his guests immediately after dinner. Since

Graham was in perfect agreement with her, that appeared to put an end to the subject. Never had he been so grateful to see coffee served, and at the first moment decently possible, he, seconded deftly by Marian, suggested that an early evening might be agreeable for the ladies after their journey.

"It was hell, Winchell, absolute hell!" he exclaimed the next morning as he attempted to tie his cravat in the newest fashion, wrecking its pristine freshness before his valet's agonized eyes.

"I'm sure it was, sir," murmured Winchell, who was going through his own private hell as he watched his master make a snowy tangle of the cravat. "If I may, sir," he said finally, deftly managing to separate Graham from the piece of linen. Laying it aside, he picked up a fresh one and began work himself.

"I've got to think of something to entertain them today, Winchell, but what is there to do here? If I don't provide some sort of amusement, I shall be compelled to have that old harpy peck at me until I produce my brother."

Winchell made soothing sounds as he tied Graham's cravat and smoothed the final immaculate fold. "I have complete confidence that you will think of something, sir," he said calmly, "or perhaps just your company will do. After all, every hostess in the *ton* considers you a prime catch for any dinner party or rout. The ladies have always been very fond of you."

"Yes, that is true," returned Graham, brightening suddenly. "I shall surely do better with Mrs. Blakeley today—and Marian of course is a pleasure to be with."

"Just so, sir," replied Winchell, surveying his handiwork with satisfaction. "And it appears that the storm is behind us, too," he observed, pulling wide the curtains. "There may even be a bit of sun today."

As the shaft of sunlight cut across the floor, Graham noted a sudden glint of light on his pillow. Curious, he walked closer to see what had caught the sun.

"Winchell!" he gasped. "Look at this!" And he held up a graceful diamond bracelet. "Where could it have come from?"

Winchell's eyes widened slightly. "Unless you have had lady callers other than the unfortunate Ginger, I'm sure I couldn't say, sir."

"Well, of course I haven't!" Graham exclaimed. "But the blasted thing wasn't there when I awoke this morning, and I don't believe the maid served it with my tea."

"That doesn't appear likely," agreed his valet dryly. "Perhaps you should ask Mr. Robert about it—or the two ladies."

"Yes, I can just feature that!" said Graham bitterly. "I could certainly say, 'Excuse me, Marian. I found this bracelet on my pillow this morning. Could you have left it there?' "

"I see your point," said Winchell, nodding. "Your brother, then, is your most likely prospect."

"If he will allow me into his sacred library," observed the aggrieved Graham. "He is fully capable of forcing me to stand in the hall and shout my problem through the keyhole."

As it happened, however, Robert was in need of a diversion, and Graham was allowed to present the interesting development to him, dangling the glittering thread of diamonds in front of him as he did so.

"Well, I certainly have never seen it before," he assured his brother. "What are you going to do with it?"

"That's why I'm talking to you," responded Graham in irritation. "I haven't the slightest notion."

"You do realize that Winchell is right—you will have to ask the ladies if they are missing a bracelet."

Graham sighed. "I suppose so." He brightened for a moment. "At least it will give us something to talk about for a little while—not that that would be a matter of concern for you," he added bitterly.

Robert retired into the volume he had been studying when his brother entered the library. "Quite right," he observed, not looking up even when Graham opened the door to leave. "Quite right. Not my concern at all."

Neither Marian nor her mother had seen the bracelet before, however, although they both exclaimed over its loveliness.

"What will you do if you don't discover the owner?" asked Marian curiously, still holding it to the light and admiring its sparkle.

"I shouldn't think he is likely to find the owner," observed Mrs. Blakeley. "After all, it isn't likely to be the housekeeper or the scullery maid, and we are the only female guests."

"Well, someone must be missing it," Marian sighed, placing it reverently on the tabletop, her fingers lingering on it.

"You're very fond of jewelry, aren't you?" enquired Graham absently, his mind straying suddenly to the engagement ring. "That's quite a lovely ring you're wearing now," he observed, glancing at the ruby that shone against her pale skin like a drop of glistening port.

"Thank you," she returned, smiling and twisting the ring absently. "My grandmother left this to me because—as you say—I am fond of jewels."

"Of course you are," inserted her mother tartly. "What woman of taste and good sense is not? Not only are they beautiful themselves, but they also lend their beauty to the wearer—to say nothing of the fact that they are often the only things of value that a woman may own in her own right."

"Mother is imminently practical," said Marian, coloring slightly.

"If Mr. Livingstone is a sensible man," returned Mrs. Blakeley—and Graham noticed that she placed undue emphasis on the *if*—"he will know that I am correct."

Graham inclined his head in gracious agreement. He would have had no intention of taking issue with Marian's mother even if he had felt her to be quite wrong. As it was, he felt her statement to be accurate, although it was not a matter he had given much thought to. It was very possible, he reflected, that she spoke from personal experience. Perhaps the old tabbies in London had been right on the mark when they said that Marian—because of her mother, of course—was a fortune hunter.

When he looked at that young lady, however, his heart misgave him. She was regarding him with a worried expression, a small crease between her lovely eyebrows.

"Things have not always been easy since my father died, you see," she said softly. "I hope you will not think the less of us because of Mother's frankness."

Mrs. Blakeley sniffed loudly before he had a chance to reply. "It would matter little enough it he did. And I doubt that Mr. Livingstone has ever had to spare a thought for the cost of anything he desired."

Marian colored more deeply still and turned away. Ladies, naturally, did not discuss matters like money and the cost of making one's way through life. A woman of a lower class might be expected to do so, but not a lady.

"Mother, please," she protested in a muffled voice.

"Your mother is quite right, Marian. I have never had to think about the cost of anything—nor has Richard. I must agree with your mother, for I know that the position of a lady is often more subject to the whims of fate than that of a gentleman—so it is very farsighted of her to think to protect herself and you in such a manner."

Marian smiled at him gratefully, and Mrs. Blakeley looked at him with raised eyebrows. "Well, young man, that's the most sensible thing—perhaps the only sensible thing—I've heard you say."

Graham decided that a gracious nod would suffice as a reply to this very questionable accolade, and he soon managed to make his escape to his own chamber under the pretext of putting the bracelet away.

"What a perfect terror that woman is!" he murmured as he entered the safety of his room. "And to think that poor Marian must live with her day in and day out."

He paused a moment to inspect his breeches carefully. He had successfully evaded all of the spaniels except one that seemed particularly determined to become his boon companion. With relief he saw that the damage this time had been negligible.

A slight movement on the bed caught his eye, and he glanced up apprehensively. The worst of his fears were realized. On the counterpane stretched the scruffy, ginger-colored cat. He snatched up a stray boot and heaved it at her, for the moment careless of his wardrobe. At the last moment, however, she rolled out of the way, and it came to rest beside her on the bed. She raised one eyelid casually to regard the boot and its owner with a blissful expression, then collapsed in a boneless heap, chin resting comfortably upon the boot.

"Winchell!" he called sharply, hoping that his valet was somewhere within earshot.

"Yes, sir?" he responded, appearing in the doorway. Nor did he appear alone. Robert was close behind him.

"What is all the noise about, Graham?" he demanded.

The outraged tenant of the room pointed at the recumbent cat, who was peacefully oblivious to the commotion she was creating.

"Is that yours, Graham?" asked his brother, astounded. "I had no idea that you went in for pets." He looked at Graham reproachfully. "You might at least have asked before bringing the cat with you."

"You know that beast is not mine," responded Graham indignantly. "I have no doubt that it is another member of the menagerie you keep in your household. Why, you should charge admission to this place! You would make a fortune!"

"Yes, but I don't need one," Robert pointed out. "Nor do you. And I don't believe that little Ginger here is a member of the brigade of cats that inhabit the stable. I believe that I would recall that singular color."

"Well, where *does* she belong? She can't take up residence in my room, as she keeps trying to do."

Robert shrugged. Graham noted with irritation that he seemed to shrug a great deal these days when he had no wish to answer a question. "It doesn't seem to be my problem, dear boy. I'm not the one whose company she's seeking."

Having managed to outrage his brother beyond the capability for speech, Robert strolled from the room, pausing only to glance back once and chuckle.

"Good luck, Ginger," he said, and closed the door softly behind him. The cat, seeming to recognize her name, opened one eye briefly in acknowledgement, stretched lazily, and returned to slumber.

Glancing at his master's face, Winchell said quickly, "I will take care of the matter, sir."

Reassured, Graham managed to grow calm and strolled downstairs, secure in the knowledge that he would find no cat upon his counterpane when he returned—unless, he thought uneasily, Ginger made it her business to return. Surely, however, they would be able to outwit a cat.

To his delight, Marian was alone in the drawing room.

Her formidable mother had retired to her chamber with a headache, announcing that she wished to be left alone.

"I hope that my mother didn't shock you when she spoke so frankly about financial matters," said Marian.

Seeing that she was really quite distressed, Graham hastened to her side. "Not at all," he said reassuringly, drawing her to a sofa near the fire. "Her view is an extremely practical one."

"Yes, but she need not be sharing such comments with someone who scarcely knows her. I am sure that you were shocked."

Graham patted her arm comfortingly. "Far from it. And, after all," he added, attempting to achieve a lighter note, "we were almost family, so that puts us on a more intimate footing."

To his dismay, Marian colored deeply and turned away. "I'm afraid that I have been most indiscreet," she murmured, sounding on the verge of tears. "I should never have accepted your kind invitation here. Robert is angry that we're here, isn't he? That's why he spends all of his time in his library."

Inwardly cursing his brother, Graham turned her gently toward him and lifted her chin. Two or three tears slid down her cheeks, and he reached for his handkerchief to blot them tenderly. Few women could cry without becoming red about about the eyes and nose, and he noted with satisfaction that Marian was one of those few. She was lovelier than ever, her blue eyes made a deeper blue by the gathering tears.

"I have a terrible confession to make," he said gravely, his eyes twinkling in direct contradiction of his serious tone. "I hope that you will not be shocked."

Diverted—and ready to be pleased—she shook her head. "What is it? What is your confession?"

"Robert has become a scholar," he replied, in quite

the same tone that he would have confessed that his brother had become a murderer.

"A scholar?" Marian asked, her eyes widening.

Graham nodded. "He has taken up with the Romans and spends his time rooting about in dusty books and examining old coins and bits of pottery. It's really quite distressing."

"Are you serious, Graham? Is that really why he is spending all of his time in the library?"

Seeing that she looked more cheerful, Graham sacrificed truth without a qualm. "Yes—I don't believe that he is really aware that the rest of us are here."

"You cannot know what a relief that is," Marian replied, a smile lighting her face. She took his hand without seeming to realize that she had done so. "I was so afraid that he might be angry—that he might still—" Here she broke off in pretty confusion, suddenly looking down so that her bright curls hung about her face and concealed it.

"That he might still be in love with you?" finished Graham gently, once again putting his hand under her chin so that she would look at him.

She nodded silently.

"But isn't that what you hoped when you came here?" he asked. "I thought that when you said your decision wasn't a wise one, that you meant that you regretted breaking off the engagement."

"No, Graham—I meant that I regretted accepting his offer and then having to break it off when I knew that I couldn't go through with it."

"Did you never love him, Marian?" he asked, again remembering the comments about her being a fortune hunter.

She shook her head. "Never. I was very young and impressionable, and Robert is a very handsome, impressive man. I thought that that would be enough, but the closer we came to the wedding, the more I thought about my own parents' marriage and how unhappy they had been together, how little they had in common. And by then I knew that Robert and I were just the same. Why, we could never think of anything to say to one another when we were alone together."

"A pity you didn't know about the Romans," observed Graham, determined to keep the tone light.

Her chin quivered, but she smiled. "Not even that would have helped," she returned, "for the mere thought of the subject bores me to distraction."

"Thank heavens," murmured Graham in relief. "One scholar in the house is enough."

"But it was very thoughtless of me to wait so long to break the engagement," she said, apparently set upon making a full confession. "I hurt Robert and my mother both."

He had a sudden vision of what Mrs. Blakeley's reaction must have been and shuddered, patting her hand. "It must have taken a great deal of courage to break it off, my dear. I admire your honesty."

She gripped his hand more firmly and looked into his eyes. "Since we are being honest with one another, Graham—and since my mother was so brutally frank about our finances this morning—you must know that she has had it in mind that I must marry well."

He nodded. "It would appear the only practical thing to do," he agreed. "I can see that she would have been grieved to see Robert go on that account."

"She has been grieved about several others who have offered." Marian stood up suddenly and pressed her hands to her cheeks. "What must you think of me, Graham! I sound conceited beyond belief!"

"Nonsense," he returned firmly, drawing her back down beside him on the sofa. "Anyone with half an eye knows that a young woman as lovely and charming as yourself must have had many offers for her hand."

For a moment Marian sat silently, staring at the fire.

"Why didn't you accept any of them?" he inquired curiously. "Was it because you felt the same way about them as you did about Robert?"

She nodded, not looking at him.

It seemed quite natural to him to reach out and once again take her soft hand in his and to pat it reassuringly. "Then, you were quite right to refuse them."

Marian looked at him then, her eyes bright. "Do you really think so, Graham?" she asked eagerly, leaning toward him.

"Of course." And, he told himself afterward, it would have seemed quite cold to have drawn back from one so obviously in need of reassurance. Drawing her into the circle of his arms and kissing her comfortingly seemed the only gentlemanly thing to do.

The kiss was a tender one, deeper than he had intended and with considerably more warmth than he had anticipated. As they drew slightly apart and looked into one another's eyes, a sudden thought struck him.

"Marian, if you didn't come here to see Robert, why did you come?"

"Because of you," she replied simply, moving close to him once more and kissing him.

It spoke volumes for her charm that Graham did not flee the room immediately. Instead, denying all his natural instincts of self-preservation, Graham heard himself murmuring, "Poor Robert!"

Indeed, the end of their tender interlude was not brought about by Graham, but by the sound of loud voices from the hall. Startled, Graham and Marian drew apart and hurried to the door.

Astonished, they saw that the hall was occupied not only by Robert, the butler, and two footmen—all of whom one expected to see there—but also by the cook and several maids, all in full cry.

"Trying to make it up the back stairs, he was!" exclaimed the cook, waving a wooden spoon to emphasize her point. "I screamed for Bevis"—and here she indicated one of the footmen, a sturdy fellow who nodded in modest affirmation—"and Bevis made a run for the bounder, but he got clean away!"

"I'm certain that Bevis did all that could be expected," said Robert soothingly, thinking of his dinner and wishing to redirect the cook's thoughts into a more productive channel. "And I daresay that we will have no more trouble with the fellow. Jarvis and I will personally inspect all of the locks tonight so we may all rest easily." This came after a muttered observation that they would all be murdered in their beds.

"And I'm certain that you would all enjoy a little wine with your own dinners tonight," he added. "It will help to calm your nerves. Jarvis will see to that as well."

This happy thought allowed Jarvis to shepherd his flock back to their proper precincts, leaving Robert looking after them ruefully.

"There's no telling how much that will cost me," he observed. "I believe that Jarvis will serve with a generous hand—and probably the best that I have."

"Well, never mind your wine cellar, Robert! What on earth happened!" demanded Graham. "Did I hear them properly? Was someone trying to get into the house?"

Robert nodded. "Just a little shell game set up by some passing peddlers. A man came to the door and was showing them ribbons and trinkets while his partner tried to get upstairs to help himself to whatever was available."

Marian's hand flew to her throat apprehensively. "Do you think they will be back, Robert? Are you certain that we're quite safe?"

"Yes, of course we are," he said reassuringly. "Jarvis

will lock everything up as tight as a drum, and I'll go round and check everything afterward. We will have no problem."

Graham looked at him with raised eyebrows. "This is quite a lovely neighborhood you have chosen. Is this something that happens with regularity?"

Robert snorted. "No, dear brother, it is not. This is the only bit of excitement that we've had in two years, I assure you."

"Well, Marian, we must count ourselves fortunate. This must all be happening in our honor," Graham responded.

"Perhaps you're quite right about that," said Robert unexpectedly. "Perhaps he is the one that dropped off the diamond bracelet and he had just come back by to pick up his goods."

"You know that's absolutely impossible," spluttered Graham. "There's been no stranger planting jewels in my room."

"Indeed?" enquired Robert, one eyebrow still raised. "You think it was a friend or family member, then?"

Before Graham could respond to this provocative remark, Winchell appeared at his side.

"I just thought, sir, that you would wish to see this," he announced, and produced from his pocket an ornate, old-fashioned amethyst brooch. "I found it on your pillow."

They all stared at it, transfixed. Finally Graham looked at Marian. "Does it belong to you or your mother?" he asked hopefully.

Marian shook her head. "I've never seen it before." She put out her hand and took it from Winchell, holding it up for inspection. "It is very old-fashioned, of course, but the amethysts are lovely."

Graham looked at Robert, but he shook his head firmly. "It's not in my line of things at all, Graham. Now, if it were a Roman brooch, that would be quite a different matter."

"Where on earth are these things coming from?" demanded Graham. "And why are they appearing on my pillow?"

Winchell coughed self-deprecatingly. "If you will permit me, sir, a thought had occurred to me."

Graham looked at his valet expectantly. "Yes, Winchell, what is it?"

"The brooch was not the only thing on your pillow," Winchell observed, and then paused to see what effect this announcement had had on his audience.

Graham clapped a hand to his forehead. "Don't tell me there was more jewelry!" he exclaimed.

Winchell shook his head. "No, I disposed of the other item. It was a dead mouse."

They all stared at him intently; then Graham began to laugh. "Don't tell me, Winchell, that you think the cat is responsible!"

"Do you mean Ginger?" demanded Robert, his eyebrows high.

"What cat are you talking about?" asked Marian, looking at them in astonishment. "Are you saying that a cat brought the jewelry to Graham?"

Winchell nodded. "I believe that well may be, ma'am," he replied in a deferential voice. "The cat has been coming and going quite freely, and"—here he paused and glanced at his master—"she does seem very fond of Mr. Livingstone."

Robert broke into laughter at his brother's pained expression. "Beware of a cat bearing gifts, Graham! Have you no scruples? Do you accept gifts of jewelry from just anyone?"

Graham looked at his brother crossly. "It seems to me that if we grant the fact that the cat might be bringing them—and given the evidence of the mouse, I suppose there's not much choice about that—then it seems to me that the question we should be asking is where she is obtaining those jewels."

Robert stopped laughing, and they all looked at Graham blankly.

"Well, it stands to reason that a cat might catch a mouse almost anywhere, but where in blazes is she going to go for jewels?"

For the moment, Graham's questions seemed unanswerable, and they all were extremely careful about checking the locks upon every door and window that evening, protecting themselves against the unknown evil.

They did not really have long to wait for their answer to Graham's question, however. The next morning a peremptory knocking at the door sent Jarvis hurrying to answer it. To Graham's horror, he ushered in Alyce Brightman.

Glancing around the dining room hurriedly, he saw no means of escape, so he prepared himself for the inevitable. Amazingly enough, however, she didn't seem even to notice him. Instead, she marched straight toward Robert, her head held high.

"I need to speak to you, Mr. Livingstone," she said firmly, ignoring Jarvis's attempts to announce her.

"Of course, Miss Brightman," responded Robert affably, glancing at his brother's stricken expression with satisfaction. He remembered distinctly Graham's horror of this young woman who had stalked him so relentlessly. "Perhaps you have met Miss Blakeley in Town."

The two ladies nodded briefly to one another, and Robert smiled at his brother. "And I'm certain that you remember my brother."

Miss Brightman, focusing for the first time on Graham, momentarily lost her stern expression and fairly glowed.

"Graham," she said warmly, hurrying forward to take

We'd Like to Invite You to Subscribe to Zebra's Regency Romance Book Club and Give You a Gift of 4 Free Books as Your Introduction! (Worth $19.96!)

If you're a Regency lover, imagine the joy of getting **4 FREE Zebra Regency Romances** and then the chance to have these lovely stories delivered to your home each month at the lowest prices available! Well, that's our offer to you and here's how you benefit by becoming a Zebra Home Subscription Service subscriber:

- **4 FREE** Introductory Regency Romances are delivered to your doorstep

- **4 BRAND NEW** Regencies are then delivered each month (usually before they're available in bookstores)

- Subscribers save almost $4.00 every month

- Home delivery is always **FREE**

- You also receive a **FREE** monthly newsletter, *Zebra/ Pinnacle Romance News* which features author profiles, contests, subscriber benefits, book previews and more

- No risks or obligations...in other words you can cancel whenever you wish with no questions asked

Join the thousands of readers who enjoy the savings and convenience offered to Regency Romance subscribers. After your initial introductory shipment, you receive 4 brand-new Zebra Regency Romances each month to examine for 10 days. Then, if you decide to keep the books, you'll pay the preferred subscriber's price of just $4.00 per title. That's only $16.00 for all 4 books and there's never an extra charge for shipping and handling.

It's a no-lose proposition, so return the FREE BOOK CERTIFICATE today!

Say Yes to 4 Free Books!
Complete and return the order card to receive this $19.96 value, ABSOLUTELY FREE!

(If the certificate is missing below, write to:)
Zebra Home Subscription Service, Inc.,
120 Brighton Road, P.O. Box 5214, Clifton, New Jersey 07015-5214
or call TOLL-FREE 1-888-345-BOOK

Check out our website at www.kensingtonbooks.com.

FREE BOOK CERTIFICATE

YES! Please rush me 4 Zebra Regency Romances without cost or obligation. I understand that each month thereafter I will be able to preview 4 brand-new Regency Romances FREE for 10 days. Then, if I should decide to keep them, I will pay the money-saving preferred subscriber's price of just $16.00 for all 4...that's a savings of almost $4 off the publisher's price with no additional charge for shipping and handling. I may return any shipment within 10 days and owe nothing, and I may cancel this subscription at any time. My 4 FREE books will be mine to keep in any case.

Name _____

Address_____ Apt._____

City_____ State _____ Zip _____

Telephone ( ) _____

Signature _____ RN129A
(If under 18, parent or guardian must sign.)

AFFIX STAMP HERE

ZEBRA HOME SUBSCRIPTION SERVICE, INC.

120 BRIGHTON ROAD

P.O. BOX 5214

CLIFTON, NEW JERSEY 07015-5214

his unwilling hand, "how lovely to see you again. I had no idea you were in the neighborhood." She glanced briefly—and disapprovingly—at Robert. "Of course, none of us ever see your brother, who lives here as a perfect recluse."

"Yes, Robert appears to have renounced the world," agreed Graham, trying to disengage his hand. "You're looking very well, Miss Brightman," he added weakly, as she directed the full force of her gaze upon him.

"Oh, not Miss Brightman," she protested. "Surely we have put that formality behind us long ago, Graham."

Graham stared at her for a moment, trying to see her impartially. She was, he supposed, quite a beautiful woman—not to his taste, of course, but still a beautiful woman—tall and slender and fashionably dark.

"As you wish—Alyce," he murmured, finally managing to regain possession of his hand.

"That's much better," she responded softly, her voice almost a caress.

Robert appeared to be enjoying himself hugely. "We had just finished breakfast. Do join us in the drawing room, Miss Brightman," he said warmly, guiding her in that direction, "or perhaps I, too, might call you Alyce since we are neighbors."

"Of course," she agreed, allowing herself to be escorted into the room and seated. Graham seated himself at a secure distance from her and devoted himself to trying unsuccessfully to catch Marian's eye.

"I am delighted to see you, of course," said Robert encouragingly, "but you appeared to have something of consequence on your mind when you arrived."

"Yes, yes indeed," Alyce agreed, suddenly remembering the purpose of her errand. "It is about your cat."

"My cat?" returned Robert, startled. "Which cat are you referring to?"

"I haven't seen it myself, but one of my servants described it as quite a scrawny beast of a peculiar shade of orange."

The other three looked at each other in astonishment.

"You know it, then?" said Alyce, noting the exchange.

Robert nodded. "We met Ginger very recently," he returned. "She appears to have adopted my brother."

Graham glared at him. "Well, this is your house after all, Robert. You must answer for the beast."

"What is it that interests you about this unfortunate-looking cat, Alyce?" inquired Robert. "Do you wish to adopt it?"

"Certainly not!" she returned brusquely, looking a little taken aback by his question. "I merely wish to reclaim what is mine."

"Reclaim what is yours?" asked Graham apprehensively. "You wouldn't be referring to jewelry, would you, Alyce?"

She nodded. "Yes, indeed. The cat has apparently stolen both a bracelet and a brooch from my dressing table."

She paused a moment and, taking their silence for disbelief, added, "Yes, I know what you must be thinking; but my maid saw her crawling out my window this morning, and one of the stable hands saw her go streaking across the meadow in this direction. Upon inquiring, one of my servants reported that he had seen a cat of that description when he was at Ivy Hall yesterday."

"Well, at least that takes care of our little mystery," said Graham in relief. "I have your jewelry, Alyce. The cat had brought both pieces to my room."

"Indeed?" she asked, looking somewhat startled. "Why would a cat do such a peculiar thing?"

"As I said earlier, Alyce," intervened Robert, "Ginger appears to have a real fondness for Graham. The pieces of jewelry appear to be presents for him."

The others stared at Graham for a moment; then Alyce

exclaimed suddenly, "How very gallant of you, dear Graham!"

Feeling that they had missed a line in a play, the rest looked at her curiously.

"What do you mean, Alyce?" asked Graham apprehensively, recognizing her expression all too well. She was a past master—or mistress—of misreading his actions to suit her own purposes. "What in thunder does losing your jewelry to a pilfering cat have to do with my being gallant?"

Alyce cast him a warm, lingering glance, her thick, dark lashes fluttering flirtatiously. "However did you manage to get your cat to do such a thing, Graham? How unusual a way to capture my attention."

"I did no such thing!" exploded Graham, leaping to his feet and pacing up and down the room. "Most certainly I did not train that cat to steal, and I had no notion that those pieces belonged to you until you arrived here!"

Alyce shrugged, clearly disappointed. "Very well, Graham. What *is* the explanation, then? Why did your cat do such a thing?"

"She is not my cat!" he returned vehemently. "And I have no idea why she would do such a thing! It's not as though she were a magpie that is attracted by bright objects."

"Yes, that is the question, isn't it?" said Marian suddenly. She had sat quietly through the conversation, mulling over the curious situation. "Why did the cat suddenly appear here and who *did* teach her to steal? I find both those questions quite unsettling."

The others looked at her, and for a moment there was no response.

"You are quite right, Marian," Robert agreed slowly. "Perhaps we should think this through more carefully. Ginger may not be working alone."

"Now there's a happy thought," replied Graham caustically. "I suppose you think she is the head of an entire gang of thieving cats."

Marian spoke before Robert could respond, shaking her head. "I think it is possible that the cat has been trained by a gang of human thieves. Just think of the man who tried to enter the house only yesterday."

"What man was this?" demanded Alyce. "What is going on here, Graham?"

"I wish I knew," he said, putting his hand to his forehead and sinking into a chair. He was beginning to have a headache.

Robert explained briefly what had taken place, and Alyce's dark eyes widened in horror. "Then, we may, indeed, have a gang of thieves in the neighborhood! What a terrible time for my parents to be away! I shan't be able to sleep a wink tonight!"

"Certainly you must not stay alone," said Robert decisively, a sudden mischievous and thoroughly satisfying idea coming to him. Graham might have inflicted the Blakeleys upon him, but he was about to have his revenge. "Go home and pack your things, Alyce. By all means you must stay with us until your parents return or until we have this matter properly disposed of."

Graham gasped in horror and tried frantically to catch his brother's eye.

"You see," Robert said, firmly avoiding Graham's gaze, "Graham quite agrees with me. We must have you protected."

"How very kind of you both!" exclaimed Alyce, her eyelashes fluttering once more. Graham reflected that they fluttered so ferociously that he should have felt the coolness of the breeze. "I shall go and pack at once."

"We will expect you in time for dinner this evening," replied Robert smoothly. "It will be a delightful evening, I'm certain—perhaps the beginning of many delightful evenings. Who knows how long it will take us to solve this little problem?"

Graham shuddered convulsively. He was suddenly far less certain that this evening—and the succeeding ones—would be at all delightful. He spared his brother a baleful glance as Robert left to escort Alyce to her carriage.

"Miss Brightman seems to be on very close terms with you, Graham," remarked Marian, playing idly with a tassel of braid on her gown so that she could avoid his eye.

"Don't be misled, Marian," he replied earnestly, mentally comparing her appearance with that of Alyce. There could not have been a sharper contrast than that between her gentle fairness and Alyce's sharp, dark features. For all the world, lovely though he knew she was, Alyce reminded him of a hunting dog, for she had all the sharpness of a pointer. Marian, on the other hand, made him feel protective, and her gentle demeanor drew him irresistibly.

"I assure you, Alyce thinks that we are on much closer terms than we are," he continued. "I know that it will seem ungentlemanly of me to say this, but—"

"If it would be ungentlemanly, perhaps you should not say it," she interrupted, smiling gently as she rose.

"No, please don't go, Marian," he pleaded, wondering for a moment if this could be his own voice that he was hearing. "Stay for a moment."

She paused and looked back at him, and he took advantage of the moment to draw her down next to him on the sofa. "You mustn't believe what isn't true," he continued. "There is nothing between Alyce and myself except the most casual of friendships."

"She did not appear to think that," pointed out Marian. "And I'm afraid that because I allowed you more liberties than I should, you think that you should pacify me so that I allow you to continue."

"You mustn't think that, Marian!" he exclaimed, horrified. "I am not taking advantage of you—not that I don't enjoy an elegant flirtation," he added hurriedly, being a stickler for the truth.

Marian tried to rise once more. "I would prefer not to be one of your flirts, Graham, no matter how elegant the flirtation might be."

His arm encircled her waist firmly to keep her from rising. "You must believe me, my dear," he whispered into her ear, for her face was turned away from him. "I am not trifling with you."

"Naturally you would say that," returned Marian, still refusing to look at him. "What accomplished flirt would not?"

"Please look at me, Marian, so that you'll know I am telling the truth," he begged. "If you will just—What the devil!" he exclaimed, his loverlike tone changing abruptly.

Ginger had made a sudden, uninvited appearance in the drawing room, sandwiching herself between the two of them and depositing herself in his lap. There she began with satisfaction to tidy her muddy paws, paying no heed either to the damage of Graham's breeches or to his promises of immediate retribution.

"So this is Ginger," laughed Marian, thoroughly enjoying the scene before her. "Do you suppose she has brought you another offering, Graham?"

He blanched at the mere thought, and shook his head vehemently. "Certainly not! Surely she hasn't had time for another outing to Alyce's."

"Perhaps you should go up and check," advised Marian, seeing a way of extricating herself from the present awkward situation.

"Yes, you're quite right," he agreed readily, reaching for her hand as he spoke. "But, Marian, before I go, will you promise to walk with me in the garden in an hour?"

"Walk in the garden?" she asked in surprise. "Isn't it rather cold for that?"

"A trifle chilly," he admitted, "and I grant that Robert doesn't have much of a garden, but it's the only opportunity I see for having a private moment with you."

Marian considered the matter for a moment and then nodded. Her mother was safely in bed, still nursing her headache and a French novel. Surely there could be no immediate danger in taking a brisk walk in a rain-soaked garden—a walk very likely chaperoned by a watchful cat and a handful of interested servants.

Graham pressed her hand and glanced down at the offending cat. "Perhaps I should introduce you," he said, a twinkle in his eye.

To his surprise, Marian patted Ginger on the head with her free hand, disregarding the fact that aside from being decidedly unattractive, the cat was also decidedly stiff with mud. Ginger stretched her scrawny neck toward Marian, eyes half-closed, and purred unmistakably.

"I would say that you have met with her approval," he observed. "I see that you must, indeed, like cats if you would spare the time for one so disreputable-looking."

"Oh, she will not be so bad when she is cleaned up and her hurts are mended," said Marian, studying the animal judiciously. "I can take care of that a little later if Robert can supply me with one or two things that I will need. And she will not always be so oddly lumpish in shape, you know."

"What do you mean?" inquired Graham curiously. "She is rather oddly shaped—but I had thought that just part and parcel of her very unattractive appearance."

Marian gave Ginger a final pat as she withdrew her hand from Graham's and prepared to leave. "Not at all," she said, dimpling. "I would say that once she has borne her litter, she will be uniformly skinny, a condition which you can easily repair with a good diet."

And so saying, she left the startled Graham staring down at the blissful beast in his lap.

"Kittens?" he demanded incredulously. "And I suppose they will look just like their mother!" Ginger continued to purr, ignoring his tirade.

Another hideous thought struck him. "And if Robert thinks he is going to foist you and your offspring upon me to take back to London, he is quite mistaken," he assured Ginger sternly. "I shall do no such thing, you may be assured. You, small beast, will take up residence in the barn with your kind."

Ginger reached out lazily with one paw and patted it gently against his waistcoat, leaving a pattern of unmistakable prints across its pristine whiteness. In despair, Graham tucked her under one arm, until, remembering her condition, he thought better of it and cradled her in both arms, whereupon both of them set forth in search of Winchell.

They discovered the valet in Graham's room, putting the final touches upon the jacket he would wear to dinner. He greeted their arrival with a pained expression, his eyes going immediately to the wreckage of his master's clothes.

"I had no choice, Winchell, I assure you," said Graham. "I was set upon and had no opportunity to defend myself."

Here he set the cat down carefully. Noting his extreme delicacy, Winchell looked at him curiously.

"Miss Blakeley told me that she is in the family way," he explained, looking a little ashamed of his weakness.

"Indeed?" returned Winchell. "I hadn't given it any thought; but now that you have pointed it out, I am quite certain that she is correct."

"And we are not taking them back to London with

us," Graham announced firmly, looking with distaste at Ginger, who had arranged herself in front of the fire to continue her toilette.

"I am relieved to hear it, sir," said Winchell gravely. "The trip here in the curricle was quite crowded as it was. With a cat and a litter of kittens, the journey would be quite unthinkable."

Graham shuddered, just thinking of it, and allowed Winchell to help him out of his muddy attire and into his dressing gown.

"You know, Winchell, I think I shall rest for just ten minutes. No longer than that, though, for I must be ready to meet Miss Blakeley in less than an hour."

Winchell regarded his master with interest. He had not displayed this much interest in a young lady—barring his fearful flight from Miss Brightman—during the ten years Winchell had known him.

"I shall have you ready in time, sir," he said reassuringly.

Graham eased himself onto the edge of the bed, feeling that today had already been a very long one. "I haven't told you the worst, Winchell," he said in a defeated voice. "My brother has evinced a streak of wanton cruelty that I had not realized he possessed."

"Mr. Robert?" inquired Winchell, his eyes wide. Whatever peculiarities the brothers had, cruelty was not among them.

Graham nodded sadly. "Even though he knows my relationship with Miss Brightman, he has invited her to be a guest in this house. She will join us this very afternoon."

"No!" exclaimed the valet, properly horrified. "Why ever did he do such a thing? And doesn't the young lady live just down the road?"

Graham nodded again and leaned back against his pillow. Winchell's distress on his behalf was extremely satisfying. "He did it quite deliberately, Winchell, to repay me for what he considers my perfidy in inviting Miss Blakeley and her mother here."

Winchell shook his head in disbelief. "I don't understand how he could have done such a thing, sir. After all, you invited Miss Blakeley here in perfect good faith."

"Exactly!" agreed Graham vehemently. "And he knows very well—" He broke off suddenly and put his hand behind his head. "What the devil is this lump in my pillow?" he demanded.

Winchell glanced up in concern.

"What's wrong, sir?" he asked. "Have you gotten the headache again?"

Graham shook his head and held up his hand. In it glittered a ring, a rare blue diamond in a simple gold setting. "It was my mother's," he said simply.

He stared at the cat a moment. "I devoutly hope that you didn't get this from Marian's room," he said bleakly, all of Richard's unpleasant accusations coming back to him with a rush. He had pushed them out of his mind when he had first seen Marian again. Now that he knew her better, he could believe them even less.

Ginger paused in her ablutions a moment to stare up at him, her odd golden eyes glinting in the firelight. Quite as though she understood, she rose and trotted toward the bed. Before Graham realized what she was about, she had leapt first to a chair and then onto the counterpane beside him.

"What the devil is that cat about now?" he exclaimed, leaping from the bed. He had no desire to have Ginger cuddling next to him.

That, however, did not appear to be what the cat had in mind. A moment of burrowing among the covers brought something else to light—a simple gold brooch.

Both he and Winchell stared at it for a moment. Finally

Winchell ventured, "It looks rather like some of the bits that Mr. Robert takes such an interest in."

"So it does," agreed his master, a sudden thought striking him. "So it does." And, placing the brooch and the ring in the pocket of his dressing gown, he announced, "I will be back shortly, Winchell. I have some investigating to do."

As he opened the door, Winchell observed mildly, "Might it not be best if you did your investigating fully dressed, sir? You might encounter one of the ladies along the way. I daresay Miss Blakeley's mother might take exception to your attire."

Graham glanced down at the burgundy splendor of his dressing gown and grinned. "You are quite right, Winchell. Mrs. Blakeley would be outraged, and she would give it full voice."

Turning to his valet, he spoke briskly, "Well, let's do it with all possible speed, Winchell. If I am right in what I am thinking, I would like to know immediately."

Only ten minutes later—a record time for master and servant to outfit him—he was knocking at the door of his brother's library. When Robert did not answer immediately, he opened the door and marched in, intent upon his errand.

The room was just as much a disaster area as it had been the first day he had seen it. Books and boxes were stacked upon every available piece of furniture and across the carpet as well. He had to thread his way among them with the utmost care to keep from tumbling something over.

"How can Robert think in the midst of all this clutter?" he remarked in disbelief. He himself required a meticulous order to all of his belongings or he could not function. In such a place as this he would have gone mad in minutes.

"Just how am I to find what I'm looking for in all of

this clutter?" he asked himself, prodding an empty box aside with one boot. "It would have to have been something opened fairly recently, though."

And, so saying, he withdrew to a corner of the room and studied the area before him methodically, beginning at one side and working his way across in a narrow strip, careful to omit nothing from his scrutiny. Dividing the room into ribbons, he worked his way back and forth across it, carefully moving boxes and books from the surface of things and peering inside anything that had been opened.

At last he found a box that was approximately the right size, and he rummaged about, looking for its wrappings. It had been, naturally enough, addressed to Robert Livingstone, and an inspection of the papers within the box revealed a calling card that belonged to Marian.

Armed with his evidence, Graham prepared to track his brother to earth. His quarry, however, entered the room just then.

"Graham!" he exclaimed, startled to see his brother standing there. "Were you looking for something?" he asked, gazing at the box in Graham's hands.

"I've found it," Graham responded. Digging into his pocket, he produced the gold brooch. "Is this yours?" he asked.

Robert stared at it for a moment, then reached out for it. "Yes, it certainly is. I managed to get this for my collection just a month ago. Where did you find it?"

There was a brief silence, and then Robert's eyes widened in disbelief. "Not the cat!" he exclaimed. "Has the animal been pawing about in my library?"

"I would say so," returned Graham grimly. "Look at what else Ginger discovered when she was investigating your lair." And he held up their mother's ring.

"That can't be! Marian had the ring—Ginger must have found it in her chamber!"

"I might be inclined to agree with you—if I held the same opinion of her that you do—except for this." Graham waved the small box in the air.

"What about it?" demanded his brother. "There are dozens of boxes in the room. What is so special about that one?"

"Indeed, there are dozens," agreed Graham, looking about him with distaste. "I can't imagine how you can have a coherent thought in this mess."

"Well, I can," retorted Robert. "Never mind about the mess! Tell me about that box, Graham."

"Addressed to you, is it not?" Graham inquired, holding up the wrapping so that he could see it.

Robert nodded. "So it would appear."

Graham drew Marian's card from the box. "And if you will direct your attention to this," he said smoothly, "I think you will understand the importance of the box."

"Marian's card?" said Robert blankly.

"Marian's card in an empty box," returned Graham pointedly. "And the brooch from the library appeared in my room at the same time the ring did."

Graham looked about them, shaking his head. "And if you put that information with the chaotic character of this room where books and boxes could disappear for months on end, I think that we have enough evidence to exonerate Marian."

Robert sat down abruptly, still clutching the card. "So we do," he murmured.

"Did you ever ask Marian about the ring?" Graham demanded.

Shamefaced, Robert shook his head. "Only when she first broke the engagement. After that, I assumed that she had simply decided to keep it. I didn't want any contact with her, so I never asked her about it again."

"And so if that miserable cat had not decided that this particular box made a good toy and had not boxed it about until it tore open, you would still be saying that Marian is a thoughtless, self-serving woman!" Graham responded in disgust.

"You are right, of course," said Robert, rubbing his forehead with the back of his hand. "I'm grateful that I've not expressed that opinion of her to anyone but you."

"I should hope so," replied Graham slowly.

He was beginning to grow a little uneasy as he watched Robert, who was showing every sign of being properly distressed by his mistake. That was gratifying, of course, but he did not wish for Robert to be *too* distressed. After all, that might signify a lingering interest in Marian. Perhaps now his brother would change his mind about Marian completely and wish to renew their engagement.

It wouldn't matter a whit if he did, Graham told himself abruptly, straightening his shoulders. After all, wasn't that why he had invited Marian to Ivy Hall? He had wanted to help Robert mend his broken heart and take his place in Society once more. And perhaps, thanks to Ginger, he was about to do it.

After all, he had no personal interest in Marian otherwise. She was a very charming young woman and a delightful companion, but there the matter ended. He conveniently put from his mind all memory of assuring Marian that his attentions were no mere flirtation. Undoubtedly the return of the ring would go far toward restoring her relationship with Robert.

Handing the ring to Robert, he said, "Here. You should put it in a safe place until you need to use it again."

"Use it again!" exclaimed Robert. "I scarcely think so! I can't imagine myself marrying until I am quite an old man."

"Do you think Marian will wait that long?" asked Graham indignantly. "You needn't be completely selfish!"

Robert looked at him in amazement. "Marian!" he exclaimed. "I thought I had made myself quite clear on that point!"

"But that was before you knew the truth about the ring," his brother pointed out.

"That doesn't matter," Robert responded. "Having the ring returned doesn't make me any more eager to marry her—or anyone else."

"Indeed?" responded Graham, straightening his shoulders as he turned to leave the room.

"Who knows?" remarked Robert casually as Graham opened the door to leave. "Perhaps you will be the one to use Mother's ring."

Graham closed the door with rather more emphasis than was needed and started toward the stairs.

"Graham!" called Marian from the door of the drawing room. "Are we not going for our walk?"

Suddenly remembering their engagement, Graham hurried toward her.

"I beg your pardon, Marian," he began, "but I found another deposit of jewels on my bed, and so I've just been returning them to Robert."

"To Robert!" she exclaimed in surprise.

Graham nodded. "Just some of his Roman trumpery," he said, dismissing it with a flick of his hand, "but doubtless the cat felt that I might be interested in it."

Marian began to laugh. "You know, Graham, Ginger is unmistakably fond of you. You will be compelled to take her back to London with you."

"Never!" he said manfully. "Winchell and I have made a pact that we will do no such thing—no cat and family are going home with us. It would be far too inconvenient."

Marian looked at him, and he saw with sudden emotion that her eyes were tender. Graham was acknowledged as one of the most polished flirts of the *ton,* but—precisely because of that—he was not prepared to deal with emotions. He was accustomed to playing at lovemaking. No other woman that he could remember— except his mother, of course—had looked at him with such genuine warmth in her eyes. He felt as though someone had suddenly robbed him of his breath.

"I might have believed that earlier," she replied, the corners of her lips dimpling in what he privately considered the most delightful manner, "but now I've seen you with Ginger, you know, and I noticed that you did not fling her to the floor as I expected when she muddied your clothes. You were rubbing her behind the ears instead and getting mud all over your hands. Besides, I got Winchell to tell me about the first night that she adopted you."

"Betrayed by my own valet," he murmured, sitting down on the sofa and drawing her down beside him.

She looked at him for a moment as she sank down next to him; then her hand gently traced his eyebrow and the plane of his cheek. Graham had been having some difficulty breathing as it was, and for a moment he thought that he had stopped altogether.

"I told you that I came here because of you—and it's true, you know, even if it is unladylike to say so," she murmured. "I have always liked you better than any of the others because you are so amusing—and now I have learned that you are kindhearted as well."

She lowered her hand, and Graham was able to breathe again—although not as regularly as he would have liked. Smiling with what he hoped was careless aplomb, he said smoothly, his lips close enough to move the soft tendrils of hair next to her ear, "I am overcome by the accolade, Marian. I had no idea that being amusing could have such an impact."

She laughed and drew away, patting his cheek. "But it does, Graham. Of course it does. I have told you that I couldn't bear being bored. Imagine marrying someone who bored you to distraction—someone whose very presence turned every day into a murky greyness, making you tired before you even arose in the morning."

Graham shuddered. "A most unattractive prospect," he agreed. "You were wise to avoid it."

He looked down at her, noticing that her head was resting on the back of the sofa, distressingly close to his shoulder. "What makes you think that life with me would be any different?" he asked, suddenly overcome with curiosity.

She smiled gently and patted his cheek again. "Graham, in the two days since we have been here, you have brought to light a series of robberies committed by a cat, been the cause of an attempted break-in and—"

Here she broke off and glanced down for a moment.

"Well?" he inquired curiously. "And what?"

"And made love to me most charmingly," she added, coloring prettily.

"And you call *me* an accomplished flirt?" he demanded in mock astonishment. "You shock me, Miss Blakeley!"

"This should shock you, I know," she replied seriously, not catching his eye for a moment. "After all, a young woman pursuing the brother of her former fiancé? And you have heard Mother, so our need for money—which you have—is no secret. Why should you not be shocked?"

He acknowledged to himself that everything she said was true, but he could not feel himself shocked in the least—and the reason for it occurred to him suddenly.

"Perhaps it is because of your candor, Marian," he said gently, forcing her to look at him once more. "You need not have told me the truth about anything, you know—but I somehow feel quite certain that you have been honest in everything."

He was about to kiss her when an unexpected interruption stopped him.

"How very touching this is, to be sure," observed Robert lazily, standing in the doorway. "Please don't allow me to interfere with your pretty love scene." And he left, closing the door gently behind him.

Marian looked at Graham with wide eyes. "Is he angry, do you think?" she whispered.

Graham shook his head. "Robert cannot act. If he were angry, we would know it."

He suffered a momentary misgiving, wondering if perhaps he were dismissing Robert's feelings too lightly. It was perfectly possible that if he still had a *tendre* for Marian, he had been hurt by what he had just witnessed. He did not allow the thought to linger, however. Robert had never made a secret of his feelings, and he could not imagine that he would begin now.

Readily accepting a brother's assessment of the situation, Marian laid her head on Graham's shoulder. "Well? Are you going to allow his interruption to interfere?" she asked softly.

"Never," he responded, returning his full attention to the matter at hand.

Several pleasurable minutes had passed before they became aware that they had a guest. Ginger had joined them, managing to entangle herself in their embrace so that she was partially caught between them.

Laughing, they extracted her, but Marian stopped the laughter when she glanced toward the door.

"Graham, Robert closed that door when he left, and it's still closed. How did Ginger get in?"

Graham glanced up, startled, and then smiled. He pointed to an open window at the end of the drawing room. "Apparently all she requires is a window," he observed. "That seems to be her favored mode of entering a room."

"I am pleased to see that you have a chaperon, even if it is only a cat," observed an acid voice.

Turning abruptly, they saw Mrs. Blakeley standing stiffly in the light of the now open door.

"Mother! Are you feeling better?" Marian asked guiltily.

"I am able to walk and speak today," observed her mother, "which is quite a bit more than I was able to manage yesterday."

"I'm very glad to hear it," said Graham mendaciously, trying to sound cheerful. He would have been happier had she been unable to speak. "May I have Jarvis bring you something to eat?"

"No," she sniffed. "I don't believe that I could swallow anything."

She paused a moment in thought. "Perhaps I could manage tea and dry toast, however," she said. "And, if it isn't too much to expect, perhaps you could sit with me while I have it, Marian," she added.

"Of course I will, Mother," replied Marian meekly, rising to follow Mrs. Blakeley from the room. "Perhaps we will be able to take our walk a little later, Graham," she added in a low voice as she passed him.

Graham watched them leave. It remained a mystery to him how a dry stick of a woman like Mrs. Blakeley could have a daughter as gentle and winsome as Marian.

And he tried not to think what it might be like to have a nearer connection with Mrs. Blakeley than that of host and guest. The thought was simply not a tenable one.

Irritated by the loss of Marian, he wandered toward his brother's library for company.

"Oh, do go away, Graham," snapped Robert ungraciously when his brother tried to slip unobtrusively into the room. "Have you lost your playmate and come looking for a substitute?"

"Well, you needn't sound so cross, Robert," he responded sharply. "After all, it's not as though you have any interest in her now. You made that perfectly clear to me."

"Did I, indeed? When Miss Brightman comes to call, you may find yourself with one too many lady friends."

"You needn't throw Alyce Brightman up to me!" he responded indignantly. "She wouldn't be coming here at all if it weren't for your spiteful nature!"

"Spiteful?" gasped Robert. "How can you say that to someone who has lost his fiancée to his own brother? Why, I'd be the laughingstock of White's if anyone knew about it!"

"Marian isn't your fiancée, and you had no wish to have her here at Ivy Hall," Graham reminded him. "I am surprised at you, Robert, for behaving in such a small and spiteful manner."

Before Robert could respond in kind, Graham walked briskly to the door. "If you will give me just a moment, Robert, I will give you the opportunity to prove me entirely wrong."

"And I will!" Robert called after him. "Make no mistake about it! I will!"

It took only five minutes for Graham to return, this time escorting a beaming Mrs. Blakeley on his arm.

"I told Mrs. Blakeley how eager you were to have the opportunity to spend some time with her," he informed Robert smoothly, smiling at him.

"Dear Robert," she cooed, fluttering toward him, "I am so very glad to see you doing well. I had been wondering when we would have the opportunity for a tête-à-tête."

Graham watched her in amazement. He had had no idea that she was capable of such a deceptively sweet manner. Robert watched her with the fascination of the transfixed victim of a cobra.

"You can't imagine how delighted I was when dear

Graham told me that you had asked me to have my tea and toast sent in here so that I could chat with you."

Graham, astounded by the ease with which he had gone from "Mr. Livingstone" to "dear Graham," watched his hapless brother with amusement. Robert had drawn a chair close to the fire—supplying the screen necessary to protect a lady's complexion from the heat, of course—and placed a low table next to it for her tray. Recognizing that he had no option, he seated himself next to Mrs. Blakeley to while away the afternoon.

Immensely cheered by the scene he had left behind him, Graham went in search of Marian. Mrs. Blakeley had made it abundantly clear that she still considered Robert an eligible prospect as a son-in-law, and his company would undoubtedly occupy the lady for the duration of their walk. It would do Robert a great deal of good, too, he thought with satisfaction. He would have the opportunity to reconsider the matter of being engaged.

Together the two of them braved the chill of the garden, and Graham was relieved to see that they were not escorted by Ginger. He had feared that she would not be able to resist such an outing.

"I left your mother with Robert," he informed Marian cheerfully. "I believe that they will have a pleasant chat while we are out."

Marian looked dismayed. "Oh, poor Robert!" she groaned. "I shouldn't say that, of course, but Mother has been quite determined that we will renew our engagement on this trip. She will hound him relentlessly, I'm afraid."

"I'm glad to hear it," returned Graham, pleased. "Or at least I am pleased that Robert will have a bit of a problem."

He took Marian's arm and turned her to look at him. "And you are certain, Marian, that you don't feel as your mother does—that the engagement should be renewed?"

"I have told you how I feel about Robert," she reminded him. "He is not at all the man to interest me. Perhaps he and Mother might suit."

Graham smiled at this sally. "And do tell me more about the man who does interest you," he said encouragingly, and stepping behind a high hedge, he pulled her close to him and kissed her. Suddenly he was oblivious to the autumn chill and to all else save Marian.

"You are quite shameless," she laughed as she emerged breathlessly from his embrace. "You know very well that you are that man, and it isn't the part of a gentleman to force a lady to confess her passion."

He was about to pursue that interesting statement when Alyce walked briskly around the end of the hedge.

"Oh, there you are, Graham!" she said brightly. "I had been wondering where you got to. Robert told me he thought that you had gone for a walk in the garden."

She nodded stiffly to Marian, who smiled in return.

"Good day, Miss Brightman," she said politely. "It is refreshing to get a little fresh air after being indoors all morning. Personally, I have found the walk invigorating." She glanced up at Graham and smiled wickedly.

Alyce, who had not missed the intimate glance, remarked coolly, "If you are tired, Miss Blakeley, allow me to encourage you to return to the house. It wouldn't do to exhaust yourself. Perhaps you should take a nap."

"Well, I don't know that I will take a nap, but I believe that I will go in now," remarked Marian, glancing at her escort.

"And I will accompany you," responded Graham with alacrity. "I have had enough fresh air for the moment."

Alyce pouted prettily, gazing up at him through a fringe of dark lashes. "Why, Graham, I thought that you would escort me through the maze so that I don't lose my way."

Graham was unmoved. "Never fear, Alyce. If you do

not come in for dinner, I shall have Robert come and find you."

Ignoring the edge to his remark, Alyce laughed merrily, just as though he had made a particularly clever joke, and she quickly took his other arm as he turned back toward the house.

When they arrived in the hall, Graham saw in disappointment that Mrs. Blakeley had not managed to trap Robert for long. Mrs. Blakeley had just started upstairs, but when she saw them, she came back down.

"Well, Graham, you may count yourself fortunate that you have a brother who looks after your best interests."

"Indeed?" inquired Graham, his eyebrows lifted. "And just what has Robert done to assist me?"

"He managed to rid you of that ridiculous-looking cat that has haunted the house," she announced, waiting for his pleased reaction.

To her surprise as well as his own, however, there was no such reaction.

"He got rid of Ginger?" he exclaimed angrily. "Why would Robert do such a thing? Ginger is my cat!"

"Since when did you take such a liking to that cat?" asked Robert curiously, emerging from the library at the sound of voices. "You have done nothing save remind me that she is my cat and not yours. I thought that I was doing you—and the rest of us—a favor by sending her on her way."

"I would certainly agree that you were," agreed Alyce. "Any animal that steals my belongings is not welcome where I am."

Ignoring his longing to tell her that she need not stay, Graham turned back to his brother. "What did you do with her, Robert?"

"I didn't have to do anything," he responded. "It was all done for me."

"And just what does that mean?"

"Some uncouth-looking individual came to the door asking for 'the gentleman of the house.' Jarvis didn't want to let him in; but he appeared ready to make a scene, so he came in to fetch me."

"You have never seen the like of this man in a gentleman's house," inserted Mrs. Blakeley. "It was shocking that poor Robert was forced to have any dealings with him at all."

"I could have put him out immediately had I wished to," responded Robert crossly. "I wasn't 'forced' to do anything at all."

"And so the fellow just announced to you that he wanted Ginger and you went and fetched her for him?" demanded Graham, determined to have a full explanation of the matter.

"Of course not. He described the cat—which is quite unmistakable, you know—and I sent Jarvis with a bag up to your chamber in case the cat was there. She was sleeping soundly, so Jarvis bagged her easily enough and brought her back down to the man."

"Bagged her!" cried Marian, horrified. "You must be careful of her, Robert. She is about to give birth to her litter."

"Well, really, Marian!" exclaimed Mrs. Blakeley, equally horrified, although for another reason. "Be careful of your subject when you speak in front of gentlemen! And I must say that I would think you would be grateful that the muddy beast is gone!"

"*I* certainly am!" announced Alyce. "Robert, you did the proper thing. The cat was nothing but an eyesore and a problem for those who encountered her."

"It appears that everyone except Marian forgets one important fact—Ginger was my cat, and I should have been consulted before you packed her off in such an unthinking manner," announced Graham, more irate than anyone in the room, including Robert, had seen him before. His anger surprised even himself. "If you will excuse me, I am going upstairs."

Robert kept country hours, so the five of them gathered for dinner only a little later, which allowed Graham a reasonable amount of time to discuss the outrage with Winchell.

"It is simply not to be borne!" he informed his valet bitterly as Winchell deftly arranged his cravat once more. "Robert has always accused me of being high-handed, but it appears to me that he has outdone me by half."

"Just so," Winchell murmured comfortingly. "I know that you were growing very fond of the cat."

"That is not the point at all," responded his master crossly, unwilling to admit any such weakness. "It is the principle of the matter! He knew very well that Ginger was *my* cat, and yet he assumed a very cavalier attitude toward her disposal."

He began to pace the room, disregarding the fact that Winchell was having to hurry along beside him, still working with the cravat.

"Indeed, he did, sir," said Winchell, valiantly keeping up with him. "What do you plan to do about it?"

Graham stopped stock-still. "Do about it? What do you mean, Winchell?" he demanded. "What can I do about it? The cat is gone."

Winchell looked thoughtful. "Well, you could make inquiries about where such a man might be staying. Clearly he doesn't live at one of the homes in the neighborhood."

"Not according to the description of him that Robert gave," Graham agreed. "But there isn't anyplace else that I know of."

"I beg your pardon, sir, but wasn't there mention of an inn?"

Graham brightened immediately. "Of course there was!" he agreed. "The Royal Rooster! Robert said that it was a disreputable sort of place—just the spot where such a fellow might put up!"

"Just so, sir. You could ride there in the morning to check on the matter."

"So I could—and I will. It's a pity that it's grown so late now—and that dinner is waiting. I suppose I must go down."

"I'm certain that Miss Blakeley would be disappointed if you did not, sir," ventured Winchell. "I should imagine that she favors your conversation."

"She would have to, considering her other choices," agreed Graham. "You're right, of course. I can't abandon Marian to their tender mercies."

Cheered by the fact he now had a plan, Graham went down to dinner in a more pleasant frame of mind, greatly to his brother's relief. Robert was not a conversationalist at the best of times, and he was relying heavily upon Graham's social skills to see them through the evening.

The drapes were drawn snugly against the dark and the gathering storm, and a fire crackled cheerfully in the dining room. By the time they had reached the second course, they could hear the wind flinging icy shards at the windows.

Despite Robert's hopes, Graham had become unusually silent during dinner, concentrating on his food and his thoughts. Having made another futile attempt to draw his brother into conversation, Robert had just begun to chat about the weather when Graham suddenly erupted into speech.

"He is undoubtedly a thief!" he announced suddenly, laying down his fork.

"Who is?" demanded Mrs. Blakeley, startled.

The others stared at him in consternation, but Marian understood him immediately and nodded. "Undoubtedly!" she agreed. "The rogue has trained her to steal for him! She was probably sent to rob this house the night you saved her from the storm, Graham."

The others were still staring at them both.

"Are you talking about Ginger?" asked Robert. "Do you mean that she was supposed to rob us that night?"

Graham nodded. "If you recall, Jarvis told us that someone had tried to pry open one of the downstairs windows that night. He discovered it when you did your check of all the windows and doors. That was probably done by the same fellow that came to the door today."

Pushing his chair back from the table, he stood up abruptly. "I am going to the Royal Rooster now!" he announced.

"Why now?" asked his brother. "You know what the weather is like out there. Why can't you wait until morning if you must go?"

"There's no telling what they will have done with Ginger by then," he returned. "They might even try to make the poor cat go out tonight. I should have gone this afternoon as soon as Winchell remembered the existence of that inn."

"Well, what's the harm in having the cat out tonight?" asked Alyce idly. "It seems a great fuss over something relatively unimportant."

"How would *you* like to be out tonight?" asked Graham, turning to her. "And you're not underfed, nor wounded, nor in the family way."

"Well, I should say that I am not!" she exclaimed indignantly. "How could you be so rag-mannered as to say such a thing, Graham?"

Robert shook his head in sympathy. "You do seem to be losing your grip on things, old boy," he agreed. "Why not just have another glass of claret and be glad that you're warm and out of the storm?"

Graham paused a moment. What his brother said was perfectly sensible, but he knew he could not do it. No one seemed to care a whit about the cat—except Marian, of course—and Winchell. Considering the matter more carefully, he suddenly realized that those three were also the only ones that he felt sure truly cared for him. A rather odd group, he thought—but they were *his* group, and he had an obligation to take care of them.

"I'll see you later this evening," he said directly to Marian, who nodded, and then he left without a word to the others.

"Well, of all the—Robert, is your brother all about in his mind? He seems not to be himself at all!" exclaimed Alyce angrily.

Robert shook his head, mystified. "I've never seen him like this before."

"Well, everyone cannot be as level-headed as you are, Robert," sniffed Mrs. Blakeley. "I must say that I have always considered Graham a little unstable."

"He is no such thing, Mother!" said Marian defensively. "You don't know him at all, so you really should not be making such pronouncements. He is a very intelligent, very loving man."

"Well, you should certainly know about that," remarked Robert, acid in his tone.

Both Mrs. Blakeley and Alyce looked up sharply at this remark, but Marian appeared unmoved.

She smiled slowly at Robert. "You are quite right, Robert. I am, indeed, in a position to know."

Mrs. Blakeley groaned, and Alyce rose to leave the room. "This is all becoming too much for me," she announced. "I will be in my chamber if anyone needs me."

As it didn't appear that anyone had any immediate need of her, she hurried from the dining room, telling herself that this was the oddest house party she had ever attended. Perhaps it was fortunate, she thought, that she had not managed to bring Graham to heel. It could have been a dreadful mistake. With this comforting thought, she was able to face the rest of the evening with equanimity.

The three left at the table looked at one another. The only one who seemed quite comfortable was Marian.

"I apologize for my ill-natured remark, Marian," said Robert stiffly. "I shouldn't have said that at all. I had no right to do so."

Marian nodded. "That's true, of course, Robert, but I don't hold it against you. I'm sure that it's a thought that is difficult to grow accustomed to."

"What is difficult to grow accustomed to?" demanded Mrs. Blakeley. "I am your mother, after all, Marian. Explain to me what you are talking about."

"Merely that it is difficult for Robert to see his former fiancée in love with his own brother," Marian said simply.

Mrs. Blakeley shook her head. "I don't know how you could have become so slow-witted," she said. "You are, after all, my daughter. Everyone in the *ton* knows that Graham Livingstone will never marry. You are merely another of his flirts."

Marian rose. "I will take a leaf from Miss Brightman's book," she announced. "I shall be in my room if anyone needs me."

Mrs. Blakeley and Robert were left staring at one another.

"I'm not at all certain, Mrs. Blakeley, that Marian is another of Graham's flirts," said Robert slowly. "I've never seen him behave just like this before."

"Addle-witted, do you mean?" inquired Mrs. Blakeley acidly. "Miss Brightman is right. He seems to be all

about in his head, saddling up in a winter storm to go
in search of a cat."

As Graham made his way slowly against the icy wind,
he felt that addle-witted might very well describe the
condition of a man who would undertake such a ride.
By the time the lights of the Royal Rooster came into
view, he was virtually frozen to his horse, and it required
two stable boys to help him down.

He paid them handsomely to look after his horse, hoping that the amount would be enough to keep them from
stealing the animal. Then he turned his attention to the
inn.

It was as disreputable-looking a place as one could
imagine, thought Graham grimly. Several of the wooden
shutters that covered the windows were missing, and others were banging loudly in the wind, threatening to pull
loose at any moment.

The taproom he entered was dark and uninviting, its
few inhabitants looking as though they had recently escaped from Newgate. Graham became suddenly aware
of the elegance of his own dress and hoped that they
would not decide to rob him of all he possessed.

He forced himself to look nonchalant as he stood before the smoldering fire to dry his jacket, tossing down
his beaver on the table and calling for a tankard of ale.

"A cold night," observed the innkeeper curiously.
"Did you lose your way in the storm, sir?"

Graham shook his head. "I was coming here," he announced.

All conversation in the room stopped, and he felt several pairs of eyes boring into the back of his head.

"I'm looking for someone," he explained.

"Are you, indeed?" asked the innkeeper dryly. His customers were not of a class that expected—or wel-

comed—callers. "Who would someone like you be look-ing for here at the Rooster?"

"I'm looking for a man who came to my brother's house today," responded Graham.

Before he could go on, the innkeeper interrupted him. "If he caused any trouble, I don't want to hear about it," he observed. "I'm not responsible for what my customers do."

"Well, who said you were?" responded Graham, puz-zled.

Convinced that Graham was not going to try to call him to account for some runagate relative or customer, the innkeeper relaxed a little.

"What's the cove's name?" he asked, ready to be help-ful if possible.

"I don't know his name, but I can describe him," re-plied Graham, and he proceeded to do so.

"Jack Ware, that would be," responded the innkeeper. "Too fond of the heavy wet is old Jack. It'll be the death of him."

"Is that so?" asked Graham. "I hope he hasn't been partaking too freely just now, for I would like to talk with him."

The innkeeper shrugged. "Jack's gone," he said. "Left this afternoon without paying his shot."

"Gone?" exclaimed Graham in disappointment. "Did he take his cat?" he asked.

"Must have. That bag of bones isn't here," was the response.

"Do you know where Ware might have gone?" Gra-ham asked, unwilling to give up.

"If I did, I'd be after him to collect the five guineas he owes me, wouldn't I?"

Wearily Graham returned to the stable, where he found the two boys asleep next to his horse, each hoping for another tip. Grateful that he still had a horse, Graham paid them again, thereby making two lifelong friends for himself. However, not even his new friends could shed any light on Ginger's whereabouts.

Discouraged, he rode slowly home despite the storm. Somehow they had all become tied together in his mind—Marian, Ginger, Winchell, himself. Together they were a unit—strange though the thought seemed to him—but with any one of them missing, nothing seemed complete.

"You've got rats in your upper works, old man," he told himself. "It's probably time that you got back to London and knocked the cobwebs out." The thought of London did nothing whatsoever to improve his mood, however. He realized that with a sudden, painful start. For years London had been his primary enjoyment in life, and now he couldn't even bear to think about going back there.

By the time he reached Ivy Hall, he was once again fairly frozen into his saddle. This time, at least, there would be hot food and a glass of brandy. He would put all of this behind him. After all, Ginger was only a cat—a spectacularly unattractive cat. A cat that was very likely dead or having her kittens out in the cold so that the whole lot of them were as good as dead, he told himself dismally.

As he approached the door, Marian flung it open and ran out to help him in. Everyone appeared to be bustling about him, and he decided that he must have been colder than he had thought. Even Robert and Mrs. Blakeley were doing what they could to make him more comfortable.

He was pushed close to the fire after his coat had been stripped from him, and Robert plied him with brandy. The fiery liquor began to have its effect almost immediately, and he could look about him with interest.

"I shouldn't have let you ride out alone," Robert observed contritely, his brows drawn closely together. "If I hadn't been so self-absorbed, I would have realized that you shouldn't wander off into the storm alone."

Graham grinned at him. "I thought that you would want to come for the pleasure of my company, Robert."

"Well, at least you are beginning to sound more like yourself," said Robert in relief. "When you were gone so long and then you came in looking like a snowman, I was afraid that I had made a much more serious mistake than I had thought by letting you go."

"Afraid I'd stick my spoon in the wall and you'd be blamed for it?" inquired Graham, cocking an eyebrow in his brother's direction.

Marian, who had been gone for a few minutes, suddenly reappeared.

"Graham, do you feel like walking with me for just a little?" she inquired.

"Do let him rest, Marian!" responded her mother tartly. "The poor man is half frozen—let him thaw by the fire."

"I am touched by your concern, Mrs. Blakeley," Graham replied, "but I really do feel that walking a little might help my circulation."

And he rose and offered Marian his arm, which she accepted with a smile.

"How delightful you look, my dear," he said, smiling down at her as they walked slowly up the stairs. It was surprising to him just how happy he felt as he looked at her. "Just where are you taking me?"

"To your chamber," she replied demurely, her dimples showing.

"You shock me, Miss Blakeley!" he exclaimed in mock horror. "Surely you don't plan to take advantage of me in my weakened condition."

"I would not be above doing so," she confessed, stepping into that room as Winchell opened the door for her.

"I'm glad to see you back, sir. I thought perhaps we'd best put some dry clothes on you before you take your death," he observed.

"A very good thought, Winchell," he agreed. "Won't it be a little inconvenient with Marian here, however?"

"Never mind being clever," returned Marian, guiding him toward the bed. "Come along with me."

"Only too gladly, madam," he said blithely, "but I'm afraid that we may shock Winchell."

He turned and looked back at his valet, who was looking at them benevolently. "You'd best shut your eyes, Winchell—or better still, I shall ring for you when I need you."

"Yes, sir," responded Winchell, not moving an inch.

When he turned back to Marian, she pulled aside the heavy curtain that sheltered the bed, and he gasped. There lay Ginger—not on the counterpane, but on his pillow. It appeared to Graham that she had been recently dried, for her fur seemed to be as fluffy as he had ever seen it—and she was no longer lumpish in appearance. Tucked close to her were the four reasons that Ginger had regained her figure. One of them, he noted, looked precisely like Ginger.

Graham put out his hand and patted her very carefully on the top of her head. "Nice work, old girl," he said approvingly, and Ginger began to purr deeply.

"Are they all alive?" he asked.

"Indeed, they are," Marian assured him, "and they are doing very well."

"How did she come to be here again?" asked Graham.

"She must have escaped from the bag and come back through the storm," Marian responded. "She was soaked through and half-frozen when she arrived."

"But how did she get in?" he persisted. "I know she didn't knock at the front door."

"That was Miss Blakeley's idea, sir," said Winchell,

who had started for the door. "She came upstairs and left the window here open—storm or no storm. Then she kept checking here regularly, thinking that the cat would come back if she could, and as you see, she was quite right."

Graham looked at her gratefully. "Thank you, my dear," he murmured, drawing her into his embrace and pressing her tightly against him.

"Did you deliver the kittens yourself?" he asked, the thought suddenly occurring to him.

Marian shook her head, her face still pressed against his shoulder. "Ginger took care of that herself. Winchell and I just cleaned them up."

Graham grinned over his shoulder at Winchell. "My thanks, Winchell."

The valet nodded. "Ring for me should you need me, sir," he said crisply, closing the door behind him.

Graham looked at the group on the bed and smiled down at Marian. "It appears that I now have a family, Marian." Drawing her closer still, he inquired, "Dare I hope that you will preside over it with me?"

Marian put her arms around his neck and pulled his lips firmly down to her own. "I have planned to do precisely that for some time, sir. Wild horses could not prevent me."

"I believe, madam, that this belongs to you," he murmured into her curls, slipping his mother's ring from his pocket and onto her finger.

"Yes, I believe it does," she replied. "And this time it fits perfectly."

He pulled back suddenly to look down at her. "You are not planning on spending all of my fortune on jewelry, are you?" he demanded, his eyes twinkling. "You have made your love of it all too clear to me."

"Oh, here will be no need for that, Graham," she replied calmly. "You must remember that we have Ginger—she will supply all that I need."

He laughed, clapping his hand to his forehead. "How right you are, my dear. I had forgotten that we have a cat that must be reformed so that she may take her proper place in Society."

And he gathered Marian close to him again, ignoring her protests that Ginger was in need of no reform while she, Marian, was very badly in need of jewels. He quieted her at last by the most practical and pleasant of means—a kiss.

The silence that fell on the room was complete, except for the steady rumble of satisfied purring and Graham's sigh of satisfaction as he realized that everything that he wanted in life was within his reach.

MUCH ADO
ABOUT KITTENS
by
Valerie King

ONE

Lord Cheriton sat in his well-appointed barouche, coachman-driven, stealing glances at his betrothed now and again, his thoughts drawn toward a wished-for future. He wished to be married within the month, for he felt certain that *another female,* with whom he wanted nothing to do, would beat him to the altar. Only why was the elegant damsel next to him, to whom he had been engaged for a year and a half, proving so reluctant to become his wife?

Her countenance was exquisite, for she was considered a great beauty, and her temperament one of unruffled calm. Lady Hilary Beaford, eldest daughter of Earl Beaford, was going to make a most appropriate viscountess to grace the halls of his ancestral home. She had considerable breeding and beauty and an exceptional dowry. What more could any man wish or hope for in a wife?

Warm bricks heated the soles of her boots, and a swansdown muff, which seemed to fill nearly the entire interior of the conveyance, kept her delicate fingers in a state of perfect comfort. He watched her remove one of her hands from the muff and begin plucking at a particle of lint from the sleeve of her coal grey woollen pelisse.

He leaned toward her slightly. "Hilary, dearest," he began, "there is something I have been hoping to discuss with you today concerning our future together. Miss Taverstock has declared that she intends to be wed before the end of the month, and though I cannot confirm that the date has actually been set, or even the wedding breakfast arranged, her pronouncement has left me in the gravest fear that I shall lose guardianship of the twins."

He hoped for some acknowledgement of her interest in the subject, but she remained silent as she continued worrying the sleeve of her pelisse. The guardianship of his nieces was shared provisionally at present between himself and Miss Grace Taverstock. The first of them to marry would become the girls' legal guardian. "In view of the sad state of my brother's will, I can only implore you to do me the very great honor of wedding me, oh, let us say, Saturday next, *in the morning?*"

Failing to elicit a response, he felt compelled to add, "Of course you know that I wish more than life itself to make you my wife because my love for you is very great, but in view of the added circumstance of our marriage bringing about the wonderful blessing of Emma and Elizabeth to our home, cannot I persuade you to oblige me? After all, your mother's gout is much improved in the past two months, and even the doctor said your father will unlikely suffer any further discomfort from the arm he broke seven months ago. And . . . we have been betrothed for a year and a half, so—"

"Hen's feathers!" she exclaimed in sudden exasperation.

"I beg your pardon? Hilary, you cannot be that distressed about my wish to see us wed."

"There!" she exclaimed abruptly. "I finally plucked it off my sleeve! You know, Cheriton, I cannot bear even the smallest piece of lint on any of my clothing and especially not on wool or velvet."

"Then, you have not been attending to me?" he asked, chagrined . . . *again*.

She blinked at him. "Of course I have. You were

speaking of my father's injured arm. Do you know that
when it is about to rain, the entire limb, from wrist to
elbow, begins to ache? Whenever we wish to sport the
landau about the countryside, with each of the hoods laid
back, I have but to ask, 'Papa, is your arm giving you
pain? We wish to put the new team through their paces.'
He will tell us yes or no, and then we may be comfortable. Really it is most remarkable. He has become a prog-
nosticator of the weather and all because he fell from
his favorite hack. And it is so kind of you to ask after
his health."

Cheriton frowned slightly. "Though I am as always
eager to learn that your father is well, the content of my
inquiry was directed more toward my hope we could be
married sometime before the end of the decade."

"The end of the decade?" she queried with a laugh.
"Whatever do you mean by that? Oh, I see what it is—
you are funning! Of course we shall be married before
then. Only, I'm 'fraid I have recently received some
rather distressing news. My dear sister will not be able
to journey into Devonshire for at least three, possibly
four months. In her last letter, she informed me of a
matter of extreme delicacy which will keep her *confined*
in Berkshire through the remainder of the winter and into
part of the spring."

He turned this over in his mind and came to a conclusion which he did not hesitate to share with the
woman he meant to make his wife. "She is increasing?"
he asked.

"Cheriton!" she cried, clearly offended. "How can you
be so lacking in subtlety? If I did not know better, I
would think you had not the least appreciation for my
sensibilities. You have guessed correctly, however, which
means the wedding must be put off for a time, at least
until the doctor will allow her to come to us."

"But, dearest!" he exclaimed urgently. "Do you not

understand that if Miss Taverstock marries before I do, she wins whole guardianship of my nieces?"

Lady Hilary pouted. "I suppose now you mean to come the crab, and it is not at all my fault that my sister is, well, you know what I mean!"

She sniffed twice in a meaningful manner. He felt certain a hearty bout of tears would soon follow if he did not take care. "No, of course it is not your fault," he soothed. "If she cannot come, she cannot come."

She smiled faintly. "I know how disappointed you are, but you must understand that I promised Arabella I would not marry except that she was present to grace the nuptials. Only . . ."

He turned to regard her carefully. There was just such a tone in her voice that alarmed him. "Yes?" he queried, frowning at her.

"Well, I could not help but have noticed, my love, that you frequently press the date of our marriage only when Miss Taverstock has set to worrying you by announcing that Mr. Mollant has finally agreed to a date for their wedding. I can only wonder now if she has done so, yet again?"

He was surprised at her comprehension of the situation and dismayed that his own motivations in hurrying up his marriage to her might be so openly understood. "As it happens, they are to be wed Saturday next—*in the afternoon.*"

"I thought as much," she intoned knowingly. "However, I wish to assure you that from my acquaintance with Mr. Mollant I have never known him to act hastily, so I can only wonder if she purposely told you a Banbury Tale merely to frighten you."

"Grace—that is, Miss Taverstock—would never do so."

She did not seem to hear him, for she continued unchecked. "I do not like to mention it, Cheriton, but Miss

Taverstock is quite a spoiled, unruly female. I can scarcely comprehend that you were at one time nearly betrothed to her. Mama was telling me all about it just yesterday. I was never more shocked! You . . . and Grace Taverstock!"

"She is not spoiled," he responded in defense of the woman he had once loved quite passionately. "Merely headstrong."

"And what worse quality can a woman possess than that?" she retorted.

He could think of at least one.

She pressed on. "Which brings me to this—why must we be subjected, yet again, to another play which Miss Taverstock has undoubtedly encouraged your nieces to compose and perform? I vow you ought to consider hiring a governess for them. Surely so much activity, and all under the guidance of Miss Taverstock, is not at all good for the young girls. When I was their age, I practiced my stitches, learned my letters, achieved a fair copperplate, and began perfecting my scales on the pianoforte. All this business, setting pen to paper for the purpose of creating a play, is giving them each a continual brain fever. I am convinced of it, for a noisier pair of girls one never sees."

"I see no harm in their plays," he responded flatly, "so long as they are performed strictly for the family."

"Well, I am not their family nor is Mr. Mollant."

The subject was an old one. Lady Hilary had strict views on just how young ladies should conduct themselves. The putting on of plays in the library of Plymtree Lodge, where the girls resided, was not at all to her sense of propriety, taste or decorum.

For himself, he was less exacting, especially since he was so pleased with Emma and Elizabeth. They were lively, charming, intelligent and quite creative young girls. Grace had seen to that. He did not share Lady

Hilary's views, at least not in their entirety. He wanted to see his nieces embracing all the joys of life, not just one or two carefully regulated activities.

Glancing at the beauty beside him, he could only hope that once they married and he gained complete guardianship of the twins, his bride would be more interested in them generally. Presently, if he had not known better, he would have believed she was postponing their marriage purposely to avoid becoming a mother to them.

"You do wish to marry me, do you not, Hilary?" he asked.

"What manner of question is that?" she cried. "Of course I do. I have been in love with you since I was fourteen, just as I have told you time and again. I have always seen myself living in The Castle." The ancient dwelling known for centuries as Cheriton Castle had for a long time been referred to simply as The Castle. He had resided there year-round from the time he was born. His mother still lived in the great house proper.

"And you do wish to have the twins with us?" he asked, searching her eyes carefully. She averted her gaze and slid her hands deeply into the huge muff. The pause which followed his question made him nervous suddenly.

Whatever her initial response was, he could not know, but after a moment, her entire expression softened. "I am convinced nothing could bring me greater happiness."

"Do you mean that, truly?"

She nodded. "Yes, I do, for I know that having Emma and Elizabeth in your home would afford you an infinite amount of pleasure. You always seem somehow altered in their presence, certainly more content. And, after all, your happiness must be my object."

He was beyond relieved. "You are, indeed, gracious, Hilary. I have often wondered—but never mind, you have reassured me immeasurably."

She was so beautiful of the moment, her rich brown eyes supplicating and warm. He loved her. Truly he did, even if she was inattentive at times and just a mite frosty in her affections. He knew it had been a terrible mistake to allow the betrothal to become prolonged. His beloved had lost the bloom of her excitement at having accepted his hand in marriage and for several months had come to behave toward him with all the dullness of a wife of many years. He felt certain, though, that as soon as they were wed, he could tenderly coax her into loving him once more with at least a measure of the enthusiasm she had shown the first month of their engagement. It was the wait that had driven the joy from her face, surely.

She glanced at him, and her smile became one of utter charm and sweetness. "What are you thinking?" she inquired softly.

"How much I love you," he responded.

"Indeed?" she murmured.

Hope rose in his chest. She smiled somewhat shyly and offered her cheek to him. He leaned toward her, feeling decidedly amorous, only the closer he drew, the muff beside him seemed to rise up and inhibit his advances. So it was he could do little more than brush the air beside her cheek with his lips. With this, however, she appeared to be completely satisfied.

His thoughts suddenly and quite inexplicably became full of *another female*. Grace Taverstock . . . again. She would not have been so satisfied with a mere brushing of the air beside her cheek. When he had been in pursuit of her, so many years ago, she had delighted in being crushed to his chest, her hair pulled from all its ribbons and pins, her lips devoured beneath his own. But that had been so long ago, past seven years now. Still, when he thought of what it had been like kissing her, time seemed insignificant. He could recall the sensations as though he had just now held her in his arms, and only just now released her.

He repressed a sigh.

Lady Hilary seemed to sense his unhappiness. "You must not think that I am unaware of your wish to see this unhappy situation brought to a proper conclusion. The truth is, I still cannot comprehend how your brother could have arranged matters as he did, leaving the guardianship jointly until one or the other of you married. I have never heard of anything so ridiculous."

"He had no thoughts of dying when he did, nor of his wife perishing beside him. At the time, I believe he thought I would soon be wed to Grace."

She clucked her tongue. "What a tragedy it all was, the way he and your father and your sister-in-law perished. I shudder to think on it." She fell silent, and he was left to contemplate the terrible yachting accident which had bereft him of so many loved ones all in one stormy afternoon. He could not think of it still without deep feelings of guilt that he had been unable to do more than save his mother during that wretched, tempestuous day.

Grace had never forgiven him; that much he knew for a certainty. She had experienced strange and dramatic forebodings of the sailing excursion and had asked them all to postpone the outing. He had laughed at her for being silly and histrionic. Later, he had been unable to meet her gaze. Nan Taverstock, his brother's wife, had been Grace's world, for the sisters had been orphaned since Nan was sixteen and Grace two years younger.

Grace had been alone for seven years now, save for her betrothal to the honorable Stephen Mollant, of course. And why the devil she had chosen to take such a mealy-mouthed man to husband, he would never comprehend. Mollant would never be able to manage her.

Not that it was any of his concern, but he truly believed she could never be happy with such a man.

His beloved interrupted his thoughts. "I hope your nieces do not mean to thrust those horrid animals upon me again."

He turned to look at her. What the devil did she mean by *those horrid animals?* He sought about in his mind as he reviewed the creatures to be found on his Uncle Plymtree's estate—the horses for riding, the pair of peacocks in the barn, the cows, the chickens—oh. "You mean the kittens?" he inquired at last, astonished.

"Yes," she said, apparently happy to be so readily understood. "I feel I must tell you that I find them utterly abominable. I but walk into a room and I must greet each by name, cuddle them beneath my chin, before the girls will leave me in peace. And the names they have chosen—completely ridiculous—Faith, Hope, Charity, Prudence, and what is the last one?"

"Angel," he murmured resignedly. "Emma and Elizabeth are inordinately fond of them."

"And I wish them very happy, but must they shove them at me at every turn? I am wearing a gown of dark blue velvet today! Can you imagine the fur I shall be sporting the rest of the evening once I am called upon to fawn over the little beasts? It is unbearable, Cheriton. I tell you I will not do it anymore!"

Though he did not in the least comprehend her dislike of the kittens, he said, "I shall speak to Emma and Elizabeth. I am sure they would not wish you to hold the kittens when you dislike them as you do."

"Also, if they insist on putting on their little plays, I think you ought to give them a hint that the subject is altogether ridiculous for girls of their age. What can they possibly know about love and the dangers of making a *mésalliance!*" She sighed heavily and pressed a hand to her forehead. "I am beginning to feel the pressings of a headache. Dear Cheriton, must we go tonight? It looks as though it means to snow. The air is as cold as frost and see how heavy the sky is become."

"We are nearly arrived as it is, and I certainly do not intend to turn the coach about now. Besides, you need not worry if it should snow so heavily that the roads become impassable—my aunt will be overjoyed to have guests for the night. And were we to stay the night, you and I might be able to steal a little time together."

She sighed and turned to stare out the window. "Yes, I suppose that much would be delightful. However, I do not wish to pass the night at Plymtree Lodge. The chimneys smoke—all of them."

He did not know what to say. The entire journey had not gone as he had planned. Somehow in his mind he had believed he would take his beloved in his arms, kiss her thoroughly a number of times, and finally persuade her to set a wedding date—preferably before Saturday next. Instead, Lady Hilary Beaford was now picking at yet another, nearly invisible particle of lint on her sleeve.

"Where are your nieces?" Mr. Mollant queried.

Grace, who was standing on a ladder and arranging a festoon at the top of the stage curtain, glanced down at her betrothed. "I believe they are fetching the kittens even now."

"Is the hour very late?" he asked, casting his gaze in the direction of the windows. "The sky is darkening even as we speak. Ah, it has begun to snow. I only hope Lady Hilary—and Cheriton, of course—will not become trapped in the storm."

"Cheriton has the finest teams in six counties, and he never travels with less than two pair. Believe me, even if a blizzard should ensue, he will have his bride-to-be here in perfect safety."

"He is in possession of excellent horseflesh, is he not?" Mr. Mollant mused.

Tying another ribbon about the hooks screwed into the valance, she noted Mr. Mollant's bitterness and frowned. Perhaps she had hurried him into the betrothal a year and a half ago. They were not entirely well-matched, for though she was able to bring Broadhem Manor to the marriage, the rent rolls were barely able to sustain the manor's day-to-day expenses, nonetheless add significantly to an expendable income. Her dowry as well, though respectable at three thousand pounds, was hardly an increase to any fortune. Mr. Mollant as heir to Three Ash Manor would one day enjoy a fine inheritance. His good father, however, seemed destined to live a long, long time. Together, therefore, their prospects of a comfortable housekeeping arrangement were not at all what Mr. Mollant had come to expect as his due.

To his credit, however, he never spoke of his dissatisfaction. She only heard of it when he admired Cheriton's horses, or his house, or the number of his servants, or his rent rolls. She only wished he did not admire Cheriton's good fortune so very frequently. She chose, therefore, to change the subject.

"I am so very happy we are to be wed in less than two weeks. We will be able to bring Emma and Elizabeth to Broadhem, and I shall feel as though I have a true family for the first time in many, many years." She smiled at him, hoping he would share in her happiness.

He smiled in response. "You are very fond of the girls."

"Yes," she stated, her heart warming up. "As I am certain you will be once we are all together and they come to look upon you as a father."

"I shall never be that," he stated. "Cheriton would have my head were I to even hint at such a relationship between myself and his nieces."

"Whatever do you mean?" she cried.

"Only that he sees them as his particular property. I vow, sometimes I think the pair of you entered a wager to see who would become their sole guardian. On occasion, I even feel you accepted my hand in marriage simply to beat Cheriton to the altar."

Grace laughed brightly. "How ridiculous you can be, Mr. Mollant! What manner of reason would that be to accept a proposal of marriage? Why, it is too absurd to be contemplated!"

Mr. Mollant eyed her narrowly. "I was funning—nothing more," he returned.

"Of course you were, and what a tease you can be. It is just that for a long time I have been wondering whether you truly intended to marry me or not. After all, a year and a half is an excessively long time."

"My mother's health, you know," he offered stiffly.

"Of course," she returned. She succeeded in securing the festoon of tulle and ribbon to the center of the valance and began descending the ladder. When she had gained the floor, she looked up at her work. "I hope that is what Emma envisioned."

Mr. Mollant cleared his throat. "Miss Taverstock," he began solemnly. "I fear there is something I must tell you."

Grace glanced at him, her heart sinking. "Oh, no," she murmured.

"Yes, I can see that you have guessed at what I must say to you."

"Not your mother . . . again!" she cried.

"A terrible pain has inflicted her left hip. She awoke this morning and immediately summoned her physician. She can barely walk."

"But surely you do not mean to postpone the wedding. She will be well quite soon, I am certain of it."

"Dear Miss Taverstock," he murmured, taking up her

hand in his and covering it with his own. "Always so hopeful and generous. But I fear I cannot relent. My dear mother begged me quite tearfully to postpone, and I simply could not refuse. The doctor told her she must lie abed for several weeks. You would not want me to be the cause of further injury, would you?"

Grace considered the notion of causing further injury to Mrs. Mollant. The lady was always suffering from some manner of ailment, at least at precisely the moment it appeared her eldest son would at last be wrested from her. Grace had suspected as much the last time, when, upon learning that a date had been set, just past All Saints' Day, she took to her bed with a sick headache which did not relieve itself until Mr. Mollant promised to wait until the new year to be married.

How magically she had recovered then!

"I wish you to marry me anyway," she stated with some finality. "I have been kept on tenterhooks these many months and more. It is become clear to me that your mother creates her illnesses with the strict hope of keeping you pinned to her side. You must admit it is true?" Only then, upon posing the question, did the strength of her feelings subside enough for her to become aware of the deeply shocked expression on her betrothed's face.

"Miss Taverstock!" he cried. "I have not known you at all these many years past if this is, indeed, the opinion you have of my dear mother. I cannot credit what you have just said to me. Is this truly what you believe?"

Grace compressed her lips and strove to restrain the tears which seemed very close to erupting from her eyes. "I can see that I have given you a shock, and perhaps I have expressed myself with more vehemence than I ought; but do you not see that her illnesses—every one of them—have occurred at the precise moment you declared yourself ready to be wed? Do you not believe this is too strong a coincidence to be entirely ignored?"

He shook his head. "I believe no such thing and never shall," he responded gravely.

Grace looked into serious brown eyes. She had erred in revealing her opinions to him, yet her disappointment was so severe that she could not be entirely sorry that she had spoken her mind. To have her wedding delayed, for the eighth time, was more than any hopeful bride could bear with even a particle of equanimity.

"Come," he said softly. "Let us not quarrel. I am certain once you have considered the harshness of your words, you will repent of them."

Grace did not think she would. However, she saw in his expression the sweetness of temper that had drawn her to him in the first place. She could not be angry with him for long. She smiled and gave his hand a squeeze. "Perhaps I did speak harshly, but you must admit I have every reason to be vexed."

"Of course you do, yet you must believe me when I say that I am as deeply disappointed as you are. Oh! Do I hear the carriage in the drive? The traces perhaps? Yes, I think so." He hurried to the window. "They are arrived! Ah, I see Cheriton chose to bring the barouche. You would think he might spare my feelings a little and employ the traveling chariot which is not nearly so grand. He has two footmen behind." He sighed heavily.

Grace had moved to join him by the window. Because the library was situated on the first floor, she had an excellent view of the viscount as he stepped down from the carriage and turned to help his bride-to-be descend the precarious steps. Good heavens! Lady Hilary's muff was nearly as large as a ewe. However had it fit inside the coach?

"Well, I see why he felt it necessary to bring the barouche!" she cried. "I have never seen such a large muff."

"It is very cold outside," he said in Hilary's defense.

Cheriton somehow must have divined he was being observed, for he suddenly lifted his head. He caught her gaze, and Grace felt a shock of excitement go through her as familiar as it was unwelcome. From the time she could remember, he had had this effect upon her, as though in merely looking at him she was witnessing the birth of the universe. She withheld a sigh. Faith, but he was a devilishly handsome man, and it seemed to her that the older he grew, the more handsome he became. His hair was a raven's black and his eyes a cool grey that always seemed to be piercing her thoughts. Sometimes—though rarely, mind!—she even wondered if she still loved him. Her musings never lasted long, however, for he had but to speak to her in just that arrogant tone of his and she quickly realized she could never truly love such an ill-tempered, quarrelsome creature.

Movement at the door distracted her from the scene below. "Oh, dear," Mr. Mollant murmured as he, too, turned around and caught sight of the twins just now entering the library. Between them, they carried a deep crate draped with a dark green fabric. "Miss Taverstock, I trust your nieces do not mean to set those wild animals at me again."

She laughed and turned to him. "Wild animals?" she cried. "You mean the kittens?"

He nodded, and in a whisper continued, "My valet spent an entire day removing fur from my brown coat after my last visit when I was asked to share tea with the little darlings. Gervase was miserable for an entire sennight. Must we sit through another play, and this time one with kittens as actors? I vow, I am fatigued with the seemingly endless supply of dramatical stories your nieces contrive."

"Mr. Mollant," she returned quietly. "They are but children, just ten this past autumn. During the winter months they have so little to occupy them. They are very proud of their plays, and though I daresay this might not be a propitious moment to tell you, I feel I ought to warn you that there is not one play but five in all. Pray do not screw up your face in that manner! I assure you each of the plays is very brief."

Mr. Mollant rolled his eyes. "And are we to endure all five tonight?"

"No, no, of course not."

"Well! Thank God for that."

She ignored his discomfiture. "Come," she coaxed, "they will probably be in need of some help."

"Aunt Grace," Emma called to her, "is Uncle Will arrived yet?"

"Indeed he is, just now, this very minute. How are the kittens? Are they prepared to be very good for you during the course of your performances?"

Elizabeth smiled broadly. "All the kittens know their parts to perfection!" she cried. "Mr. Mollant, will you hold Prudence for me? She has been crying fitfully now for several minutes. All she needs is a cuddle."

Grace turned to observe just how her betrothed would conduct himself. He cleared his throat and straightened his spine. "I am very sorry, Miss Westleigh, but I cannot of the moment. I promised Lady Hilary that I would, er, relate to her the most recent nature of my mother's sufferings. She has been ill, you see."

"What, again?" Elizabeth queried, her gaze shifting suddenly to Grace, her eyes brightening. "Does this mean the wedding is put off?"

Grace was a trifle stunned that even young Elizabeth understood the meaning of Mrs. Mollant's numerous illnesses. "Yes, I am afraid it is, dearest. I hope you are not too terribly disappointed."

Elizabeth shook her head, then cried, "Mr. Mollant, I can hear Lady Hilary on the stairs even now. Perhaps you should join her."

Grace was about to interject that Mr. Mollant would surely prefer to remain and lend his assistance, but her betrothed was otherwise inclined and immediately scurried from the chamber as quickly as a mouse after a morsel of cheese.

Elizabeth lifted her gaze to Grace. "Will you hold Prudence, then?"

Grace nodded. "Of course I will." Prudence was a beautiful, grey-striped tabby, long-furred and winsome. She held the kitten up and looked into her face. "As for you, my little darling, are you ready for the play?"

Prudence gave a squeak of a mew as she settled into Grace's shoulder, clinging with her baby claws for safety and protection.

Grace moved away from the stage, allowing Emma and Elizabeth to begin preparing for the first play. Though she offered to help them, the girls were quick to inform her that there was very little in the way of stage dressing and they were ready to begin if only the ladder might be removed.

"The festoon is quite lovely, Aunt Grace," Emma said, staring up at the tulle and ribbon confection.

"Thank you. I hope it is what you wished for."

"Very much so," Emma said with a brisk nod of her head. Whirling suddenly toward the door, she cried, "Here is Uncle Will!"

Grace turned to watch Cheriton, Lady Hilary and Mr.

Mollant enter the library. How quickly her gaze became fixed upon Cheriton, for he moved with the ease and grace of an athlete, and something about the way he smiled crookedly upon her set her heart to beating very fast. "Oh, little Pru," she murmured to the ball of fur presently purring against her shoulder, "have I truly been prudent?"

TWO

Cheriton moved away from his bride-to-be, who was listening quite enthusiastically to Mr. Mollant as he related the nature of his mother's most recent illness. He felt Hilary was exhibiting a great deal of civility in attending to Mr. Mollant's rather intricate descriptions of the good woman's sufferings, though how she could do so, he could not comprehend in the least, for in his opinion the honorable Stephen Mollant was a dead bore.

For himself, he had no intention of enduring the man's absurd ramblings, not when Grace was looking as pretty as a snowdrop in March. She was holding one of the kittens against her shoulder, and something about the portrait she made plucked at his heartstrings. She smiled, holding his gaze, not looking away. He found himself drawn to her, as he always seemed to be whether or not they had brangled on their last meeting, which usually they had. Crossing the chamber, he quickly caught Emma up in his arms and twirled her once in a circle. "And how are you, my darling?" he queried, giving her a hug. "Are you well since last I saw you?"

"Yes," Emma cried, giggling. "You saw me yesterday. How much could have happened in less than a day?"

"A great deal. I do so worry about you, pet."

"Well, you need not," she responded sliding to the floor. "For two years, ever since I had a putrid sore throat, you have been watching me as though I might disappear at any moment. I wish you would not be so anxious. I am made of stern stuff, like my sister."

"So you are," he remarked, glancing at Elizabeth, who was standing on the stage and arranging a chair in anticipation of the first play.

The girls were both healthy in appearance besides promising to outshine their beautiful aunt once they grew up. Each bore long, blond curls and regarded him from expressive blue eyes. The resemblance to Grace was remarkable except that Nan Taverstock, long-deceased mother of the twins and sister to Grace, more than once had been mistaken for her younger sister—beauties, one and all.

His gaze slid to Grace, and he felt his throat constrict strangely. His heart began racing as it always did whenever he would but lay eyes on her. She was exquisite, a diamond of the first water, with her blond hair caught up high on her head and her lovely gaze settled on the kitten now curled up against her shoulder. The kitten was purring so loudly the rumbles could be heard at a distance of several feet. How safe the small, helpless creature appeared in her care, just as Emma and Elizabeth were secure in her guardianship.

He realized that once she was married in a fortnight, he would lose forever the right to be their legal guardian, but in this moment, seeing the kitten snuggled against Grace's shoulder, he knew that the two adorable girls, whom he loved with all his heart, would thrive under her careful eye. With a start, he also realized Grace was just the sort of mother he wished for his children—spontaneous, affectionate, yet firm.

"Uncle Will," Emma said, "will you take hold of Charity? She is climbing up the side of the box, and I fear she might escape."

"Of course," he responded readily. He scooped up the kitten and emulated Grace's coddling pose. He cupped

Charity in the palm of his hand and held her against the well of his shoulder. He found he had to hold her quite firmly else she would wiggle from his grasp and attempt to climb over his shoulder and down his back. Once in position though, and pinned securely by his fingers against the blue superfine of his coat, Charity seemed to relax. He rubbed her ears, as Grace was doing to her furry little charge, and glancing at the grey-and-white-striped kitten, he saw that her eyes were closed. The next moment, a miraculous purr ensued.

He approached Grace. "They are quite responsive, are they not?"

"Indeed," she agreed. "I believe it is because Emma and Elizabeth have cared for them so well these many weeks. They are used to the comfort and support of people."

"Who do you have in your hands?"

"Prudence."

He nodded. "I am holding Charity. You are in excellent looks, Grace. I suppose the bloom on your cheeks is because of your approaching nuptials. I know I have not always been gracious, but I do wish you every happiness and"—here he took a deep breath—"I know Emma and Elizabeth will thrive in your care."

Grace stared at him as though she could not credit what he had just said to her. "Why must you be generous now!" she cried at last.

"Whatever do you mean? I would have thought you would have been pleased that I had finally admitted that without my guardianship the twins will still enjoy every happiness."

She glanced away, rolled her eyes and sighed. "You cannot imagine how long I have waited to hear you say as much, only, if the truth be known, Mr. Mollant and I are not to be married in two weeks after all. His mother, you see."

Cheriton shot a glance at Mollant, who had guided Lady Hilary to the far side of the room, quite at a distance from the *horrid beasts* as Hilary was wont to refer to the kittens, and seemed to be keeping her tolerably well entertained. He could not withhold a snort of disgust. "I cannot like him," he whispered at last. "To treat you in this manner—"

"You astound me!" she cried. "Do you actually tell me that for once you do not mean to gloat over my ill fortune?"

"Possibly because for some inexplicable reason we seem to be sharing the same fate. Only it is not illness this time which is preventing my marriage."

"Ah," she mused. "Lady Hilary has refused to set a date . . . again?"

He nodded. "Another *situation* has arisen."

"So, I have heard," Grace murmured. "Arabella is in the family way. Aunt Plymtree told me only this morning."

He smiled. "You do not seem in the least embarrassed by the subject. Have you no sensibilities at all, no feminine reticence?"

She shook her head. "You know I have not, for you have known me since I was a child."

"Game for any lark," he said approvingly.

"You were not always so kind," she said, frowning at him.

"I never meant to be cruel," he returned, frowning as well.

He watched a faint blush rise on her cheeks. "Perhaps not," she murmured. Her gaze shifted suddenly to the doorway. "Ah, here is my aunt now."

"Hello, my dears," Aunt Plymtree called out. "You are all assembled. Lady Hilary, Cheriton, so pleased you could come for the girls' play. I see it has certainly set on to snow. I daresay if the storm does not cease in an hour, the drifts will be far too deep for the horses to manage with ease, especially at night. I do not wonder if you will have to rest the night here. Do not fret, though. I have ordered the rooms made ready, just in case, mind." At a noise in the hallway, she turned to find her butler in the doorway. "Ah, there you are, Linton. As you can see, we are all assembled—except the admiral. Do send someone to fetch him. He will want to see the play." Upon query from the butler, she continued, "Yes, yes, you may bring the table in now and please see that the ladder is removed."

Cheriton watched as a minor procession of servants arrived with refreshments. In a matter of minutes, a table was made ready, the covers laid, and a host of delicacies presented for their pleasure including a bottle of champagne which Linton popped open in honor of the play.

Just as the champagne had been served in tall glasses, Admiral Plymtree arrived with part of his grey hair sticking up behind. Aunt Plymtree went to him immediately and smoothed it down. "Were you asleep again in the billiard room? No wonder you were unaware Cheriton and the others had arrived."

The admiral, who was missing an eye and wore a black patch to cover the absence of it, moved easily into the chamber, his legs slightly akimbo as would be expected of a man who had marched the length of a ship-of-the-line for nigh on thirty years. He had even seen action with Nelson at Trafalgar, but that was many years ago.

"Hallo Lady Hilary, Mollant," he called out buoyantly. "And you, Cheriton, how is your mother?"

"Quite well, thank you. She is presently in Bath taking the waters and enjoying a good gossip with a friend from school."

"Excellent. Glad to hear it. Any news on how soon you'll be tying the connubial knot?"

Cheriton smiled. "A serious impediment has occurred again."

The admiral frowned and lowered his voice. "Lady Arabella is breeding, is she not? Heard all about it from Connie this morning. Well, well. I suppose Lady Hilary will want her family to attend. Cannot be helped, undoubtedly." He clapped Cheriton on the shoulder and spoke conspiratorially. "Never fear. The day will arrive soon enough, and then you will wish yourself well out of it!" With that, he laughed heartily.

Mrs. Plymtree immediately scolded him. "How can you say so, Horace! These young people will begin to believe you if they do not already, and then where will Emma and Elizabeth be? Residing with an old woman like me until they are so fractious no one will want them. No, no, you must make your apologies for saying something so absurd."

The admiral apologized grandly, though with a wise twinkle in his eye.

Once everyone had sampled the candied fruit, tarts, biscuits, and exotic cheeses, as well as the champagne, the stage was made ready. Two branches of candles, settled to either side of the stage, lit the players in a strong glow. Six chairs were arranged, by habit, in front of the stage, and Elizabeth bid everyone take their seats.

"Our first play is a lesson in faith," she stated, giggling, as she held up the kitten by that name. Faith was yellow-striped and wiggly and had to be returned to a lidded basket on stage. Once secured within, faint meows could be heard through the narrow slits in the golden wicker weave. "I am a genteel lady, whose eldest son is in love with a young lady about to become betrothed to *another*."

She settled the basket on the chair upstage, moved downstage and clasped her hands in the air. "Oh, woe is me! Whatever shall I do? My poor, dear, beloved Captain Beetlehead is not yet returned from the wars. He's been fighting that monster, Bonaparte, these ten years and more." The admiral, upon hearing a reference to an English officer battling Napoleon, gave a single "Huzza!" Both Emma and Elizabeth giggled.

Elizabeth, in the character of Mrs. Beetlehead, continued. "He was an excellent correspondent, my dear husband, but his letters have stopped. I have my fears, but I do not heed them. Instead, I believe with all my heart he will be home soon. Yet, my dear son grows more desperate every day. All I have is my faith that something will happen to set things to rights."

Cheriton was at one end of the row of observers. He glanced down the line and saw that Grace was at the opposite end. Beside her sat Mr. Mollant and Hilary. His bride-to-be was quite intent upon plucking something from off the sleeve of her dark blue velvet gown. He sincerely hoped this would not become a habit with her. Mollant, for his part, sat with his arms folded across his chest and a cold expression in his eye. He obviously took no joy in the play. He wondered if Mollant would be kind to Emma and Elizabeth once he was wed to Grace. His thoughts took another leap—how the devil could Grace have chosen to wed such a milksop?

The play continued. Emma entered and dipped a curtsy to the audience. A round of applause and a faint rumble of laughter ensued, for she was wearing a man's black hat which sat low on her head covering her ears.

"Dear Mama," she began in the character of John Beetlehead, "things have come to such a pass that I greatly fear my beloved Beatrice will become betrothed before Michaelmas."

"My dear John," Mrs. Beetlehead returned. "I am very sorry to hear of it. Very sorry, indeed! But the Smythe's are a dreadfully proud people and will want their daugh-

ter to get a handle to her name if she can. The Duke of
Ogle has been a suitor these three months and more."

"How I detest the Duke of Ogle!"

"You must not say such a thing."

"Of course you are right, Mama, only I do not believe
he can make her happy. Why, all the world knows he
despises cats while dear Beatrice must have two or three
kittens about her to be content. She will be forced to
give them up forever, I am convinced of it. And if she
will be forced to give up her kittens, she will be forced
to give up many other things as well."

Mrs. Beetlehead sighed. "I believe you are right. Oh,
if only my dear Captain Beetlehead was here. He would
know what to do, for he was used to go to Oxford with
Mr. Smythe. He could speak on your behalf."

"But, Mother, what if—I mean, you have not heard
from Papa in so many weeks . . ."

"I have every confidence he will come home to me.
You must have the same, just as you must believe that
somehow Beatrice will one day agree to become your
dear wife."

"If only I could have such faith," John Beetlehead
muttered, dropping into a chair near the golden wicker
basket. Little Faith mewed, and Emma lifted the lid, heft-
ing the small kitten into her arms.

"Hark!" Mrs. Beetlehead cried suddenly. "Do I hear
a song through the window?"

Cheriton found himself charmed by the portrayal of
Emma as a young gentleman. She was perfectly adorable
with the hat bouncing on her head and the kitten in her
arms as she jumped up from her seat and moved to the
makeshift window.

The admiral next to him was chuckling. With the exception of Mollant, who was still frowning his disapproval, everyone seemed to be enjoying the play. Even
Hilary's attention appeared to be caught, for she was sit-

ting forward as though something about the play had struck home.

"I can just make out the words," John Beetlehead said, " 'Tis father's favorite ballad, 'Her hair is like a golden clue.' "

"Oh—oh! Captain Beetlehead has come home from Spain, for he was always used to sing that particular song to me!"

"It is Father," John Beetlehead cried, awestruck. "Your faith has served you well. He has come home and just in time. Do you really think he will be able to dissuade Mr. Smythe from permitting his daughter to enter into this abominable betrothal?"

"I have every faith it will be so," Mrs. Beetlehead said confidently.

The girls held their positions for a long, silent moment, then indicated the play was at an end by joining hands and moving downstage to take a bow. Young Faith regarded the applauding audience with surprising equanimity.

Cheriton joined in the applause, but was struck by the nature of the play, so closely related as it was to his own predicament of a betrothal that did not seem to be reaching a happy conclusion. He glanced at Grace, who also seemed somewhat perplexed. He could not help but wonder at the same time how it was the girls continued to create their plays about a subject that seemed quite sophisticated for girls of ten.

An hour later, Grace sat down to dinner, her thoughts still fixed on the nature of the play the twins had performed earlier. She felt uneasy for some reason, as though the play had some meaning for her yet unrealized.

The group gathered about the table, though affecting very polite greetings to one another, was rather somber.

The weather undoubtedly had affected everyone's spirits, for the snow had not ceased since Cheriton and Lady Hilary's arrival, which meant that no one would be leaving Plymtree Lodge tonight. For herself, Grace was happy to be under the admiral's roof, but such was not the case with Mr. Mollant, who was presently pushing his peas about his plate in a very dull manner.

She pondered her betrothal to him. For many years, since she was in the schoolroom, he had been a friend to her, and once she had enjoyed her come-out ball, he had become a quiet if persistent suitor. He had several times professed his love for her.

After her sister's tragic death, he had been a strong and true support, even then when he was but nineteen, the same age as herself. Over the years she had become accustomed to his presence in her lonely house, and she had come to rely on him, especially since her budding romance with Cheriton had drawn to an abrupt close following the accident.

By four-and-twenty and with so little fortune to recommend her to a great variety of young gentlemen, she had dwindled into a spinster. She had faced the very real possibility that the only children she might ever have the privilege of knowing and loving would be Emma and Elizabeth, whom she had tended since they were three. So it had been, that when Mr. Mollant offered for her a year and a half ago, she had willingly agreed to become his wife, but not until after contemplating his proposal for an entire sennight. In the end, she had joyously consented because she could then finally be able to bring Emma and Elizabeth to live with her. Knowing she was not in love with Mr. Mollant had caused her many qualms of conscience, especially since the betrothal soon became fraught with postponements, one after the next.

As she watched him now, she realized she had convinced herself that the affections she felt for him would certainly blossom during the course of their betrothal, but had they?

When dinner finally drew to a close, she found herself grateful. Conversation had lagged considerably throughout the entire two removes, and not even Cook's fine meal had served to rejuvenate to any significant degree the general spirit of the party.

The three ladies left the gentlemen to their port, adjourning to the drawing room in order to partake of a little tea. Grace would have found the circumstance enlivening except that she had never been particularly fond of Lady Hilary, who she felt was a rather cold, unfeeling female.

The task was left to Mrs. Plymtree to sustain the conversation, which ordinarily she was capable of doing. Tonight, however, Lady Hilary was unusually quiet and once or twice pressed her temples as if in some discomfort. After a quarter of an hour, she excused herself with the confession that she had been nursing a headache throughout dinner. Mrs. Plymtree, the soul of kindness, expressed her sincerest sympathy for her sufferings, then escorted her to her bedchamber.

Grace waited for the gentlemen to arrive, which they did in due course. Mr. Mollant greeted her with a half smile and a faint kiss on her cheek. Learning, however, that Lady Hilary had been taken ill with a headache prompted his brow to grow furrowed. "Indeed? I hope she does not have the ague."

"Nor I," said Grace gently. She might not have been excellent friends with Lady Hilary, but she certainly did not wish to see her condition worsen beyond a slight pain at her temples.

At that moment, Emma and Elizabeth arrived to bid everyone good night. As was befitting their age, they had enjoyed their dinner in the nursery in the accompaniment of two of the youngest serving girls of Plymtree Lodge and the housekeeper, who had become very fond of them. Each of them hugged and kissed the admiral and performed the same display of affection upon Cheriton. They bid Mr. Mollant a polite good night and hugged and kissed Grace with much enthusiasm, which was interrupted quite abruptly by Mr. Mollant suddenly crying out.

"Good God! Get it off me at once!"

Elizabeth turned around. "Hope!" she exclaimed. "Why ever did you leave my pocket?"

Hope, a yellow-striped cat with white markings, was presently sitting on Mr. Mollant's knee and staring up at him quite innocently. Mr. Mollant, for his part, was leaning backward heavily into his chair, his hands tilted up as though warding off an evil spirit.

"Oh, good heavens," Grace cried impatiently, scooping the ball of fur up with both hands. "Mr. Mollant, it is only a kitten. She could not possibly hurt you as small as she is."

She did not wait for him to reply, but hurried the girls along into the hall, returned Hope to Elizabeth and suggested to her that the kittens had gotten far too big to be carted about in the pockets of their gowns.

Elizabeth giggled. "I am sure you are right, but Mr. Mollant looked very funny just now. Did you not think so?"

"I thought no such thing," she said, withholding a smile. "Now, off with you and have the sweetest dreams imaginable tonight."

"We will," they called together gaily. She watched them move briskly down the hall and was not surprised when Emma withdrew a kitten from the pocket of her gown. The last view she had of the twins was of two bewhiskered faces peering back at her, one over the shoulder of each girl.

She reentered the drawing room smiling and was further happy to observe that the whist table had been set up and both Cheriton and his uncle had taken up their places. "Whist!" she cried. "How perfectly delightful. Mr. Mollant, do you not think a round or two the exact tonic we need for a snow-laden evening as this?"

"Yes, of course," he responded dully.

Grace's heart sank. Her betrothed was rather unskilled at card play, and she could not help but wish that her aunt would return swiftly from tending to Lady Hilary in order that she might replace her inept partner.

Her wish was soon answered, for within ten minutes of having to endure Mr. Mollant's inexact play, Mrs. Plymtree entered the drawing room, her eyes lighting up as she saw that the party was at cards.

Within a scant few minutes of standing behind Mr. Mollant and urging him to play this or that card, Mr. Mollant wisely relinquished his seat to her. Once opposite Grace, she winked broadly and suggested that now they might be able to take the wind out of the admiral's sail!

When it was, precisely, that Mr. Mollant retired for the night, Grace could not recall, for she was deeply engrossed in the game. Vaguely, she was able to recollect that he had placed a kiss on her cheek and that he had bid her good night, but her mind was far too intent on the game even now to recall if he had been gone five minutes or fifty. She did so love an excellent game of cards!

The game lasted until ten o'clock, at which time the admiral took up the several hints of his wife and said, "Oh, very well! If you feel we ought to call the evening to an end, though I must say I have not enjoyed myself so much in a very long time. Although, I begin to suspect that you ladies have some secret manner of communicating the contents of your hands, for you win far more often than you ought."

Grace rose from the table laughing. She had been so much a part of the life of Plymtree Lodge because of Emma and Elizabeth that she had come to think of the admiral as near to a father as anyone had ever been in her situation. She did not hesitate, therefore, to embrace him with affection as he took his leave with his wife by his side.

"No, no, Cheriton!" his aunt called to him from the doorway. "Don't bother putting everything away. I shall have Linton see to it in the morning."

"As you wish," he responded.

A moment more and the couple was gone.

Grace watched Cheriton for a moment, wondering at the astonishing circumstance that she was not in the least fatigued nor did Cheriton seem to be either.

"There is something I would say to you, Grace," he said, slapping the deck of cards against the palm of his hand.

She moved toward the fireplace, a shiver of goose bumps suddenly running down her arms. "And what would that be," she cried gaily. "Have you some complaint regarding my conduct this evening?"

"Why do you say that?" he queried, his brow furrowed.

She chuckled. "You always criticize me, Cheriton. You know you do!"

"You are greatly mistaken," he stated firmly, settling the cards back on the table and joining her by the fire.

"I am not," she returned. "Whenever we are in company together, you generally offer some *helpful* remark on the content of my discourse, the cut of my gown, the arrangement of my hair, or upon some other aspect of my person, all to find fault. Admit it is so."

"I will admit no such thing," he returned with a smile.

She turned to face him fully. "Yesterday, when you were here, you told me that the color of my gown, *that particular shade of green,* as I recall, was not at all suitable, for it did not set my complexion to the least advantage."

"Yesterday," he grunted. "I won't allow you to use yesterday as even the smallest example of my conduct. I was in a foul temper if you must know, and it was your fault entirely, for you had just told me Mollant meant to see you to the altar."

"And now that he has rescinded his decision, you mean to be kind?"

"Yes, I suppose I do," he retorted with a chuckle of his own.

She couldn't help but laugh since they both seemed to be enjoying the same difficulty with their respective betrotheds. "So, now, what is it you mean to say to me?"

"Ah, yes," he murmured. "I know I spoke to you earlier about my belief that once you marry, the twins will continue to thrive under your guardianship, but I also wish you to know how grateful I am that you have so nearly involved yourself in their lives these many years and more. Your very great generosity of time and trouble has had the most pleasing effect, for Emma and Elizabeth are lively, charming young girls, everything I truly wish them to be. Nan would undoubtedly be more than pleased by how wonderful they are, and primarily because of your tutelage and love."

Grace was stunned and stared at him for a long moment. "You astound me!" she cried. "After all these years of brangling with me—Cheriton, what has occurred to have altered your opinion so? Yesterday, I vow, you nearly bit off the end of my nose."

"Well, if you hadn't taken such great pleasure in telling me Mollant had agreed to set a date . . ."

Grace chuckled. "I admit it is true. Nothing gave me so much pleasure as telling you we were to be married—at last!"

"You reveled in your triumph, just as you have over and over."

"Not more than you!"

"All right—it is true. But I do not always criticize you, only when you are being particularly aggravating, and my *opinion* of you has not altered in the least. I have held the same opinion of you since times out of mind."

"Indeed," she murmured, her knees feeling a little weak, for he had an odd, almost amorous expression on his face. "That I am on ungovernable female with a fishwife's tongue and a temper to match?"

He chuckled. "Hardly. I have always thought you one of the loveliest ladies of my acquaintance, beautiful of face, elegant of countenance, witty, lively and generous to a fault."

Grace swallowed hard, for he had drawn close to her and his voice had dropped to a whisper. "Is this, indeed, what you think of me?" she murmured.

"Would you permit me to kiss you?" he asked gently.

Her mouth fell agape. "Kiss me?" she responded. "B-but, whatever for?"

He shrugged and smiled softly. "Just a friendly salute as a pledge that I shall never speak crossly to you again."

Grace felt very strange as her gaze fell to his lips. He moved closer still. She felt certain she should put out her hands and prevent him from—too late! She was in his arms, and his lips were on hers.

Oh, what joy, she thought. She had truly forgotten what it was to be kissed by Cheriton. She felt as though summer had suddenly begun to pour in through the windows, for she grew warm all through. Oh, but seven years was a dreadfully long time to have been without his embraces.

For a long moment, because the kiss was so unexpected, she hung limply against him. As his kiss deepened with such sweet familiarity, a fire began to burn brightly in her chest. She slipped her arms about his neck and clung to him. How many times had just such a sensation engulfed her during the summer of their courtship?

She had forgotten entirely how wonderful it could be to be kissed and embraced and held as though the future of the world depended upon it. Mr. Mollant had never kissed her thusly—a mere peck on the lips a time or two, for he was fastidious about such things.

Mr. Mollant!

She drew back slightly, her breath coming in a long gasp. "Cheriton, that was no mere friendly kiss!"

He seemed a little astonished as well. "I meant it to be so, only why did you fling your arms about my neck?"

"I did not!" she exclaimed, a blush burning on her cheeks as she withdrew her arms from about his neck.

"Yes you did!" He appeared to be as horrified as she. "You . . . you became so impassioned!"

"How could I not with you kissing me back so fiercely!"

"I did not . . . at least I did not mean to. Oh, Cheriton, this was very wrong."

He nodded. "Very . . . only . . . oh, the devil take it!" He begged forgiveness, bowed to her and immediately quit the chamber.

From across the room, Grace stared at the door through which he had just disappeared. She found her legs were trembling, and her lips felt bruised oh-so-improperly but in the nicest way. She turned toward a winged chair by the fireplace and dropped onto the cushion as one who could no longer stand.

"Oh, dear," she murmured. "Why did he have to become like the man I once knew . . . now . . . after so many years?"

THREE

On the following morning, as the second play was just about to begin, Cheriton found himself stealing a glance at Grace. His conscience had smitten him wretchedly throughout the night, causing him to sleep fitfully and to awaken with the sure knowledge that he needed to apologize to her again. Why he had ever conceived of the notion of placing a kiss on her lips in the first place—however innocently intended!—he would never know. He had been able to determine several possible causes—that he had enjoyed her presence at the whist table, or perhaps because, for the first time in a long time, so much good-will had flowed between them throughout the evening, or perhaps because he had been frustrated that his own nuptials had been delayed yet again.

He wanted a wife!

As he regarded her lovely face now, however, he knew these were mere excuses. The truth, the truly wretched truth, the reason he had kissed her, was because he had wanted to, not even just a little bit, but with his whole heart. The manner in which they had conversed, so gently and honestly yet with a streak of hearty playfulness which had always appealed to him, had not occurred even once since his brother and father's death seven years ago. To have the flavor of his courtship of Grace return to him last night evoked so many sensations within him that when she had responded to the pressure of his lips upon hers and actually embraced him, he had been overcome with passion.

Thinking of it even now made his chest tighten ominously.

Grace had greeted him this morning with reserve and civility. She had scarcely been able to meet his gaze. Clearly he had overset her by his boorish manners last night, and he had only himself to blame. Yet, somehow, he could not regret having kissed her, not entirely. For the first time in many years he had felt alive, wonderfully alive to the possibilities of life. He would speak with her later, however. He would apologize to her, and he would most definitely promise he would not kiss her again! After all, he was betrothed to Lady Hilary Beaford and nothing would change that.

At last Emma and Elizabeth were ready. This time, Emma took center stage. "Our second play is a lesson in hope." A small table and two chairs graced the stage. Beside the table was a small reed basket through which he could see several kittens stirring about. Elizabeth sat with one of Aunt Plymtree's bonnets on her head and the white-and-yellow-striped kitten, named Hope, curled on her lap.

"Which kitten is this, Mrs. Beetlehead?" Emma began in her low man's voice as she donned the admiral's cumbersome hat.

"Why, Captain, I have named her Hope," Elizabeth said, "for I promised myself that I would never give up hope that you might return from the wars. Tell me, have you, indeed, pushed Boney's army out of Spain?"

"We have, indeed." At this point, since the papers were full of the news that the French army had withdrawn from Spain entirely and Wellington was in dogged pursuit of Napoleon's *Grande Armee,* the admiral clapped loudly and even whistled his approval. The rest of the audience followed suit.

After a moment of celebration, the play continued. "How do our children fare?" Captain Beetlehead asked.

"They have missed their father. They, too, refused to give up hope that their beloved papa would return from the wars. I have come to believe hope is everything—hope that the past can be made better with a little understanding and love. Your absence, so painful to all, was particularly difficult for our eldest son, John."

"So it has been, for he has confided in me. A very sad dilemma, what? If the Smythes, however, are intent on marrying their daughter off to a duke, I do not see how I can be of the least use."

"I wish you might try," Mrs. Beetlehead said, her hands clasped together imploringly. "For our dear John's sake."

Captain Beetlehead rubbed his chin in a thoughtful manner. "Do you say the chit is in love with John?"

"I have a letter from her addressed to our John." Mrs. Beetlehead drew a letter from the pocket of her gown. "I shall read only a portion: *My dearest John, I wish ever so much that something might be done, for I have loved you since I was very young and we was used to play in the fort by the river. Do you remember?*"

Cheriton's thoughts were drawn back instantly to the fort in which he and his brother and the Taverstock sisters—Nan and Grace—used to play. Grace had been very young, and he had been the eldest and strongest and had built much of the fort with his own hands. The memories called forth filled his heart with so much longing that he could not restrain stealing another glance at Grace.

She met his gaze this time, her own expression one of warmth and humor and something more, something which spoke to his own heart—a wish perhaps that the past could be returned to them in the purity and simplicity of childhood.

But their shared childhood was gone, by decades now.

So much had happened to separate them, not least of which was the accident that ripped their families apart so completely.

An uproar on stage snapped his attention back to the play. Emma was suddenly crying out, "Lizzie, I told you they would escape!"

The kittens seemed to be pouring from the shallow reed basket which Emma had opened. Since his attention had wandered, he did not know why his niece had released them.

"Our . . . our children!" Elizabeth cried. "You must keep them from coming to harm!"

"Do stubble it, Lizzie! We cannot continue the play now. Help me catch them!"

Elizabeth scooped up Hope from her lap and disappeared behind the curtain. The next moment, she returned dragging the deep box with her.

Cheriton, seeing that one of the kittens was about to leap off the stage, grabbed it quickly, but not before Faith, the other yellow-striped kitten, succeeded in making his escape. He hit the floor with all four paws flush and was immediately running. He seemed intent on his object and immediately ran toward Lady Hilary and began climbing her skirts of soft midnight blue velvet. The thick fabric was a rather perfect weave for tiny, sharp claws.

Before Faith could reach the safety of her lap, Hilary jumped up and began to shriek, "Get off me! Get off me!" The kitten held on for dear life, its claws sunk deeply into the velvet. Hilary began to whirl in a circle, batting at the air above the kitten's small head. "Get off, you little beast! Get off, I say!" she cried, as the kitten flew, body outstretched, in a circle with her. "Get off at once!"

Emma called out, "Uncle Will! You must save Faith. Lady Hilary is hurting him!"

Cheriton took two strides and drew his spinning betrothed to an abrupt halt. The kitten cried out pitifully.
"Do stop making a cake of yourself, Hilary," he commanded. "Please remain standing just as you are and I
shall remove the kitten. He is only a little frightened. You
might have simply taken him in hand and held him firmly
and avoided this ridiculous display altogether."

With one hand on Faith, he kept the kitten locked in
place on Hilary's skirts. He then handed his own kitten
to Grace, who had come to help. "Thank you," he murmured.

He began gently extricating each of Faith's claws from
the velvet and was soon cuddling the terrified ball of fur
against his coat. Hilary burst into tears. "My gown is all
but ruined!" she wailed, afterward fleeing the chamber.

Mr. Mollant, who was also on his feet, proclaimed, "I
shall go after her. We have been friends for so long, I
daresay I can soothe her distress. Cheriton, see to the
kittens, will you?"

Cheriton stared at Mr. Mollant's disappearing back in
some surprise and not a little irritation. He thought the
fellow had been officious beyond permission ordering
him to *see to the kittens*. At the same time, he was so
out of temper with Hilary's conduct that he was not of
a mind to tend to the exacerbated sensibilities of his
bride-to-be.

Mrs. Plymtree's voice could now be heard. "Horace,
do stop laughing. Your face has turned the color of a
beet. And I do not see what you find the least amusing
about Lady Hilary being attacked by a kitten!"

"She was not attacked, Connie," he said, dragging a
kerchief from the pocket of his coat and mopping his
face. "But by Jove, I am enjoying the play immensely."

"We hardly saw any of it," Mrs. Plymtree complained.

"No, no. You are greatly mistaken. We saw it all,

though I daresay there is more to come of even greater interest."

"Whatever are you about!" his exasperated wife cried. "There are three plays to follow, though I must say if you intend to laugh yourself silly each time, you might wish to excuse yourself. I daresay Emma and Elizabeth are mortified."

Cheriton turned to his nieces and wondered if this much was true. The girls, however, disproved Mrs. Plymtree's notion entirely, for they both ran to the admiral, each settling on a knee and smiling up into his face. "No, we're not!" Emma cried.

"Indeed, not!" Elizabeth added. "I think the play had a wonderful effect."

"There, you see," the admiral said. "What did I tell you!"

Cheriton cocked a head at the trio, watching with some intrigue as the old man gave each a hug and a smile which seemed utterly conspiratorial.

Once the kittens were returned to the deep wooden box, where they soon quieted down, Grace addressed the twins. "Was there more to your play? Shall we regain our seats and begin again?"

Elizabeth shook her golden curls. "Only a few lines more, nothing to signify. I do not suppose it is near to noon, for I find I am suddenly peckish."

Emma's face brightened. "And Cook said we would be having lark pasties for nuncheon!"

Cheriton watched the girls for a moment, noting they did not seem the least overset, neither that their play had been disrupted nor that for a few minutes the entire party had been chasing the kittens. He thought it ironical that they should show a greater degree of composure than his bride-to-be.

This thought dimmed his spirits considerably, a sensation which deepened when Lady Hilary excused herself from nuncheon, once more retiring to her bedchamber, ostensibly because her headache of the night before was still plaguing her. Lady Hilary seemed prone to such headaches, he realized, especially when there were children, or kittens, about.

After nuncheon, the twins announced that later in the afternoon, plays three and four would be combined, and the fifth play would be performed sometime in the early evening following dinner.

Mr. Mollant stated that until such time as plays three and four were to be performed, he intended to spend the afternoon in the library improving his mind, an occupation Cheriton could see did not appeal overly much to Grace. When the admiral suggested a game of billiards, to which he invited both Cheriton and Grace, Cheriton was not surprised that she heaved a sigh of relief and joined the party with alacrity.

Mr. Mollant wished them every enjoyment of the game, words spoken in just such a manner that only a nodcock would have believed sincere.

"It is just that he considers the game rather vulgar," Grace explained. She walked beside the admiral as they headed toward the billiard room with Cheriton following behind.

"And you still intend to marry the man?" the admiral queried bluntly.

"Mr. Plymtree, what an odd question to put to me when I have been betrothed this year and a half and more."

"The only sensible question which ought to be put to you, m'dear. He's not the man for you—just ask Cheriton. He'll not mince words either, I daresay."

Grace felt her cheeks begin to burn. "I would not place him in such an awkward predicament by posing any such question."

The admiral merely chuckled.

The billiard room was tall-ceilinged, finely lit and made quite masculine by the fact that in previous centuries it had served as the armory. The walls were paneled with thick oak, several stag heads hung in stately dignity upon the wall, and numerous swords and implements of war were mounted in between. Two full suits of armor graced the walls to either side of a massive stone fireplace. "Used to be part of the hall, I am told," the admiral said, gesturing with a nod to the deep hearth and blackened stones. "Cannot imagine horses once living in here, but I have been told so it was, and my ancestors above, in the loft. Though I must say it would have been warm at night up there if the fire was kept burning. Quite comfortable, but—good God!—the smell!"

Grace laughed heartily. She enjoyed the admiral's direct manners and cutting humor. He poured them each a glass of sherry before picking up a cue stick and toasted Emma and Elizabeth's cleverness. He then blurted out, "Why ever did not the two of you get buckled? You were courting once, I recall it quite vividly. Smelled of April and May all through the summer. Of course, I expected a brief delay of the posting of banns following that horrible tragedy, but whatever happened to prevent the two of you from coming together again?"

Grace felt the blood drain from her face. She did not want to think of the past, not when Cheriton had been so kind to her last night, not when she had seen something of the return of his good-naturedness and teasing, lost since the accident. She feared he would remember all over again, then set to brangling with her as before.

Cheriton took a sip of sherry and responded succinctly, "We found we did not suit—as simple as that."

"Bah!" he cried. "The pair of you are as right as rain when you're together. But I do not mean to argue with you. Who will be my first challenger?"

Grace took up a seat and let the men clatter the balls about the table until the admiral's proficiency proved Cheriton unequal to his skill. She then possessed herself of her own cue and strove to match his facility, for he had been teaching her himself over the past two years. She nearly beat him, too, which caused her to clap her hands once she made her last play. She turned to Cheriton. "I have only beaten him twice, you know, in all these years!" Turning back to the admiral, she kissed his cheek. "You have taught me well, but make no mistake. I shall get the better of you sooner or later."

"Then, I had best stop teaching you altogether, my dear girl, for I dearly love to win!"

Grace chuckled. "I shan't speak to you again if you refuse to further my instruction, for I vow the time we are together I count as some of the dearest of my poor existence."

"Your existence could never be poor, Grace, for you have a heart as large as the ocean." He kissed her forehead, then addressed Cheriton. "Let Grace give you a lesson or two, Will. I promise you will see an improvement in your shot within a sennight. For now, I intend to seek a quiet corner of the lodge and, er, count a few sheep." He then left the room in his sailor's undulating stride.

Grace began putting the balls back on the table. "Do you care for a game, Cheriton? I find I am not in the least fatigued."

He rose from the wing chair of a faded red damask, settling a half-empty glass of sherry on the mantel. "You only wish to play so that you might trounce me and then boast of it at dinner."

"Well, that was not precisely my present motivation, for I do so enjoy a good game. However, now that you mention it, I am warming to the idea every moment."

He chuckled and took up his cue stick as well. The

game was spirited, quick-paced and lively, but in the end, Cheriton was no match for her improved skill under the auspices of the admiral's excellent guidance. She beat him handily.

"Do not fret," she stated with a smile. "I promise I will not proclaim my victory more than two or three *hundred* times!"

"I knew you would not be able to resist boasting," he responded. He was standing near her and needed to pass in order to return his cue to the rack, but just as he moved, she accidentally shifted sideways with him in an attempt to move out of his way.

"Oh, I am sorry," she said and moved again. But so did he. She fell into a fit of the giggles. "How silly!" she cried. "Shall we try again?"

"I do not know," he murmured, his grey eyes suddenly fixed on her in a way that made her heart leap, "shall we try again?"

The timbre of his voice, so low and resonant, caused her knees to weaken. "Oh," she breathed, trying to right her senses. She found she could not move and that she could not think of why she should move. He took a step toward her, and his thigh brushed up against her skirts. His arm slid about her waist. She dropped her cue stick onto the green felt of the table and settled her hand on his arm. "What do you mean, try again?" she asked.

He shook his head slowly. "I do not know. I wish the admiral had not posed so many questions earlier, for my mind has begun spinning on the subject. Why did we not marry?"

Grace knew the answer and feared that it would suddenly burst upon his mind, for then this moment would be lost, for he would once again be reminded of those terrible days and weeks that followed her sister's death. She had not been kind to him then, nor for months afterward.

Even now as she thought about her terrible conduct, she shuddered. "I do not know," she answered feebly.

"I want to kiss you," he stated. "I promised myself last night that I would not do so again, but God help me, right now, I wish for it more than life itself. Grace, would you let me kiss you?"

She swallowed hard, her heart beating furiously. She knew she should not acquiesce, for to be kissing Cheriton was a betrayal of Mr. Mollant. For some reason, though, she nodded. "Yes, if you please," she breathed. "I should like it above all things."

She leaned into him and tilted her head back. A moment more and his lips settled on hers, so soft and moist. She felt tears spring to her eyes at the sweet gentleness of the kiss. His lips began to drift over hers, and her lips parted. She felt his tongue and received him, remembering again the summer of his courtship. He made gentle, exotic explorations of her mouth, so familiar, so desired. Her hand slid up his arm. She had forgotten how strong he was, relearning as her fingers kneaded the muscles of his arm and shoulder. The tips of her fingers travelled farther and found his neckcloth and then his face.

She heard him groan as she touched his cheek. His kiss became more demanding and his arm tightened around her waist.

He had kissed her a thousand times during that rich, warm, dappled summer of their courtship. He had kissed her softly one moment, wildly the next, and utterly soul-drenched in the dark shadows of night. She could feel all the memories of that wonderful time flow over her in ripples of pleasure and wonder. She had known herself loved. She had given herself to loving him, to opening her heart fully to all the mysteries of a growing attachment. By the beginning of fall she had been completely besotted and so Cupid-struck that rarely did it seem her silk slippers ever touched the earth.

"I had forgotten," she murmured breathlessly, "how it had been with us. Truly, I had forgotten." She met his gaze and saw that he was lost in his feelings for her as well. She fondled the hair at the back of his neck.

"I promised myself I would not kiss you again," he murmured. Yet, he settled his lips upon her once more.

After a moment she drew back slightly, tears stinging her eyes. "Do you remember what happened so long ago?" she whispered, her knees quaking. "Why we could no longer love each other?" She needed him to remember, because for some reason he had forgotten, truly forgotten.

He shook his head. "That time in my life is full of empty places like the coastline between drifts of fog. Figures emerge and disappear, haunting me like ghosts in a nightmare. Why did you have to arouse the memories in me? I do not want to think of them. I do not. Not now, not while I have you in my arms."

She drew back from him a little more. "But we must think of them, both of us. Our love ended the day your father's yacht sank in the Bristol Channel. You know it did."

Her words had a proper effect. He appeared stunned. She had little doubt that one memory after another, of her own hateful words and conduct, began battering his mind. "You hated me," he whispered.

All the same memories began to pile up in her mind. She had lost her sister because he had insisted on sailing that day. She took a step away from him. She had been cruel, yet still she blamed him, even after all these years.

Just as Grace turned to go, Elizabeth came running into the room. "You must come! Lady Hilary is in hysterics—again! She was in the library with Mr. Mollant— he seemed to be comforting her—and Emma and I brought the kittens in, for it was nearly time for the third play to begin. Though I do not see why Mr. Mollant must be angry with me, for he knew very well we would need to arrange the stage for the next two plays!" She drew a deep breath and plunged on. "As it happened, Lady Hilary began to shriek, which upset the kittens very much, and the next moment they were climbing out of the wooden box as though running for their poor little lives.

"Now Lady Hilary is standing on the sofa wailing and shrieking, and Emma and I cannot find half of the kittens!" She took Cheriton's hand. "Please come, Uncle Will! *Please!* We will never find them otherwise!"

"Of course I will come."

Grace followed them, picking up her skirts and joining them in a run to the library which was at the far distant end of the house on the first floor. By the time she reached the doorway, she heard Cheriton angrily suggest to his bride-to-be that she was being a perfect ninnyhammer. The sight that struck her most, however, was not the amusing one of seeing Cheriton crawl beneath a cloth-covered table in order to retrieve one of the kittens, but of Mr. Mollant standing on the sofa beside Lady Hilary, fairly holding the overexcited female in his arms. Lady Hilary, for her part, clung to him.

Her betrothed did not see her, and because she was so completely stunned by the sight of the interesting pair embracing one another, she moved back into the hall where she remained out of sight. Her heart was beating hard and fast. She felt as though it might burst. She leaned her head against the wall. The image of her betrothed holding Lady Hilary so tenderly within the circle of his arms seemed burnt in her mind. She realized Lady Hilary was for some reason freakishly overset by the presence of the kittens, but would that, under any circumstances, give Mr. Mollant the right to hug her at will?

Whatever did it mean?

After a long moment of taking several deep breaths,

Grace left the hallway and boldly entered the library. Cheriton was just emerging from under the table, a mewling kitten in hand which he handed to Emma. Mr. Mollant, however, was still cuddling Lady Hilary.

She moved into the chamber sufficiently for her betrothed to see her and to catch his eye. With due grace, a flush began to crawl up his cheeks past the starched points of his collar and climb to the roots of his brown, curly hair. He began to release Lady Hilary, who reluctantly let him go. She cast her gaze on the hysterical young woman and lifted a mild, questioning brow. Lady Hilary's cheeks began to darken as well, just as they should have.

Grace averted her gaze. "Elizabeth," she called to her niece, who was lifting the drapes in the process of her search. "How many are still missing?"

"Only one," she called back. "Ah, there you are, Hope! Come here, my little love. Come here." Her voice had fallen to a gentle coaxing murmur as she attempted to soothe the kitten's lacerated sensibilities.

At the same time, Mr. Mollant jumped down from the sofa and handed Lady Hilary to the floor quite carefully. Though his color had faded, hers had formed two bright spots, one on each cheek. "I . . . that is," she began, laying the back of her hand across her forehead, "I fear my headache has returned anew. I had wanted to fetch a book to read and had been here only a few minutes when the twins arrived and set the kittens to tormenting me—"

"Oh, surely not!" Cheriton argued, gaining his feet and turning to scowl upon his betrothed. "Surely my nieces did not purposely release the kittens in an attempt to upset you?"

Lady Hilary lifted her chin. "You refuse to believe me?" she cried, her voice breaking. "Then, I beg you to ask your nieces just what happened once they entered the library."

Grace glanced from Elizabeth to Emma and saw a smattering of guilt mar each countenance. She bit her lip to keep from laughing, for in her opinion the entire episode had all the hallmarks of a storm in a teacup.

Lady Hilary turned to Mr. Mollant. "Pray, will you escort me from the library?" she asked.

Mr. Mollant cast only a furtive glance at Grace before nodding his acquiescence.

Cheriton caught Emma by the arm just as she made as if to move away from him. "One moment, miss. I beg to know whether or not, in your opinion, Lady Hilary has spoken the truth."

"N-not precisely," she murmured, chewing on her lip.

"Elizabeth, come to me immediately," he said, commanding the other twin, who was edging toward the doorway. "I want the truth from both of you, this instant."

As the door shut upon Lady Hilary and Mr. Mollant, Elizabeth began hurriedly. "We did not precisely set the kittens at her right away, Uncle Will, you must believe us. It's just that the moment she saw us she began complaining about how noisy we were and how horrid the kittens were and how she had come to detest her visits to Plymtree Lodge because we were such naughty, ill-behaved children. I . . . I could not bear it! One of the kittens climbed out of the box and ran in her direction. She began squealing as though she was being chased by a bear. I am sorry for it, but I could not help myself. I turned the box on its side so that all the kittens began to run toward her. That was when Mr. Mollant leapt on the sofa as well and began hugging her."

Grace met Cheriton's gaze and saw that he was as much at a loss as she was. Though the twins had behaved badly, in her opinion not nearly so badly as Lady Hilary.

Whatever fault lay at the door of the twins, how could a grown woman have said such wretched things to Emma and Elizabeth? She doubted sincerely that had she been ten years old and confronted with the same situation, she would have done very much differently.

Regardless, however, of Cheriton's opinion concerning the girls' misdeed, he had but one recourse which was to lecture them quite severely on their conduct. Believing that neither of the twins needed her reprimands as well, she quietly left the room. Once in the hallway, she found herself contemplating in earnest the image of Lady Hilary receiving without even a morsel of reluctance the comfort of Mr. Mollant's embrace.

She closed the door with a soft snap and ambled in the direction of Lady Hilary's bedchamber. Since the room was fairly close to the library, she was not surprised to find Mr. Mollant standing in the hallway, his gaze distant and pondering.

"Mr. Mollant," she called to him softly. "Is that—oh, dear. Is Lady Hilary weeping?"

"I'm 'fraid so," he murmured. "Ghastly business."

She wanted to take exception to his choice of so strong a phrase, but something within her warned her to remain silent. He gathered up her arm and begged for a word with her, in private.

"Of course," she said. "I daresay no one will be in the drawing room just now. We may speak there, if you wish for it."

"Indeed, I do, for I have something most pressing I wish to say to you."

FOUR

Grace stood near the pianoforte, a weak pool of winter light from the windows behind her barely illuminating the dark chamber. Mr. Mollant had possessed himself of one of her hands and was standing directly in front of her, a frown splitting his brows, his demeanor agitated. He seemed unable to speak.

"Mr. Mollant," she urged him. "We have been friends—and more—for a long time. Please do not hesitate to say anything to me, anything at all." She found her heart was beating strongly, for she suspected that her betrothed meant to unburden himself with regard to his newly discovered sentiments for Lady Hilary. She would release him from the betrothal, of course, especially in view of the fact that she was, herself, caught up in many reawakened sentiments for Cheriton.

When still he did not speak, she added, "I am not unaware of an alteration in your sentiments, if that is what you intend to say to me."

He snapped a blink. "Of course not!" he cried. "Why—? How would you think such a thing were possible! I . . . I asked for your hand in marriage because I am excessively devoted to you."

She chuckled and could not help but tease him a little. "Oh, not *excessively* . . . surely!" she cried.

He smiled at that, though nervously, and released her hand. "You are funning, and though I appreciate your attempt to make light of what you must apprehend is my extreme agitation, I assure you I am in the severest anxiety that you might have misconstrued in recent hours my desire to give some relief to Lady Hilary in her many distresses. She has not been happy here, at Plymtree Lodge, of that you must be aware. The kittens! My God, I wish they had all been drowned at birth, for they have been a constant source of aggravation to all of us!"

"Not all of us," she responded quietly.

He did not seem to hear her, but began to pace. "And these plays to which we have been subjected. Each time ending in some mischief where Hil—that is—where Lady Hilary has suffered an extreme abuse."

"Mr. Mollant," Grace objected. "I hardly consider a kitten clinging to Lady Hilary's garments a circumstance of extreme abuse. Surely, you would concede as much."

He gestured with an arm thrown in the air. "Again, I have used too strong an expression, but I must beg you to believe that one person's suffering is not necessarily another's. We must strive to remember how different each of us is in temperament, learning, and sensibility. I daresay Cheriton has not the least comprehension of how his betrothed suffers, which only makes me wonder if Lady Hilary would not be well out of the match. She has asked for my opinion, but what could I tell her except that she must do her duty, which of course, she shall."

Grace thought of many things he might tell her. For one thing, regardless of her *sensibilities,* she might stop behaving like a peagoose whenever a kitten appeared in a chamber. For another, that she was not at all suited to Cheriton, not by half. Cheriton was a gentleman much given to every manner of sport. He had a brutal wit, enjoyed Society prodigiously, and loved nothing better than an excellent joke. What contentment would such a man ever know with Lady Hilary by his side?

Scarcely a mote of happiness, she concluded gloomily.

With a sigh, she addressed Mr. Mollant's concerns. "I trust you found something to say to her that would aid her in her distress."

"I believe I did," he said at last, becoming calmer moment by moment. "I told her the entire circumstance of finding herself at Plymtree Lodge, being pelted by the twins with the kittens at every turn, was entirely my fault."

"Your fault!" she cried. "How on earth did you arrive at that conclusion?"

"Of course it is my fault," he retorted, finally coming to stand before her once more. "After all, had I done as *you* wished on numerous occasions and set aside my mother's ailments so that you and I might be joined in matrimony and the twins settled in our home, none of her sufferings would have occurred. I know she is not at all fond of Emma and Elizabeth, which has further prompted me to say to you, dear Grace, that I am presently of a mind, regardless of my mother's protests, to marry you Saturday next as we recently agreed. Let us make no further delay in our nuptials." He nodded once firmly as though all was settled as it should have been from the beginning.

Grace stared at Mr. Mollant as though she had never seen him before. Did he so lack in understanding that he did not comprehend the insult he had just given her? Did he truly not realize, after setting aside her many pleas that their marriage might take place, he was now suggesting Lady Hilary's needs were a more proper or more significant motivation for him?

She smiled, albeit faintly, and said, "So, let me understand you, *my love.* You wish to resist your mother's dislike of our marrying in order to spare Lady Hilary further agitation in the presence of Cheriton's nieces?"

He appeared to turn this over in his mind. "N-no," he

responded slowly. "That was not at all what I said, is it?"

"Perhaps you intended something quite different, but I greatly fear that is what I heard."

"You have mistaken me entirely," he explained. "It is just that I have come to understand how our marriage conducted in a timely manner would certainly have created a more peaceful arrangement for everyone."

"But most especially for Lady Hilary?"

"She is but a present example, that is all. Nothing more, I assure you. I am not in any way suggesting she is more significant than other circumstances. It is merely that I have become aware of how the repercussions of postponing our marriage have affected everyone."

"Are you aware of how they have affected me?" she asked bluntly. "For instance, how these many delays have made me unhappy?"

He seemed startled by the suggestion. "When were you ever unhappy?" he queried, staring at her from a stranger's eyes.

She laughed outright. *Every moment of the past seven years,* she thought ruefully. Oh, dear. Where had such an admission come from? Had she truly been discontent all this time?

Of course not. Emma and Elizabeth had brought her great joy. The admiral and his wife had become like a family to her. If she knew of a reason why she might have been unhappy, she did not want to think about it just yet.

Realizing that Mr. Mollant was still watching her, his brow furrowed, she shook her head. "It does not signify. Come. The next play is about to begin."

He frowned even more deeply than before as he offered his arm and continued to observe her closely. Just before they entered the library, he whispered, "I never knew you were unhappy. Truly."

"Perhaps we will speak of this later, then," she murmured.

"Yes, we should," he whispered. "Indeed, we should."

Much to Grace's surprise, Lady Hilary was seated beside Cheriton, ready to view the play as well. Her complexion was quite pale and her eyes red-rimmed, but there was something in her countenance that spoke of determination. For that reason she felt compelled to stay Mr. Mollant near the doorway since a certain, telling suspicion suddenly entered her brain. She asked quietly, "Is Lady Hilary to be married as well?"

He nodded solemnly. "The week following our nuptials," he whispered. "She could never be happy with your nieces in her home, something she confessed to me only a little while past. She believes now that she has been postponing her wedding for that reason all this time."

"She did not know of her dislike of Emma and Elizabeth before today?"

"No, she did not. At least, not until it became clear to her that the girls dislike her equally in turn. Why else would they torment her with the kittens when she has expressed her distaste for them time and again?"

Why, indeed? Grace wondered.

She took up her seat, events of the past few minutes whirling about in her brain like a cyclone. Several times she found her gaze drifting to Cheriton and saw that his expression was nearly as solemn as Lady Hilary's. She then noted, with a sudden jolt, that he was in possession of his bethrothed's hand and was holding it tenderly.

So, all was settled just as Mr. Mollant had suggested.

Grace felt suddenly dizzy, almost ill. A stream of truth began to flow through her so abruptly that she could barely comprehend the magnitude of the thoughts which began pelting her one after the other. She loved Cheriton and she did not want him to marry Lady Hilary or any other female. She wanted to be his wife, to be the light in his eye, and the dessert for his soul. She wanted to be held against his broad chest, to feel the beating of his heart beneath her cheek and to wrap her arms about the breadth of his shoulders. She wanted to hear his warm, resonant laughter flow through the halls of her home. She wanted to raise Emma and Elizabeth not under the cold tutelage of Mr. Mollant, but beneath the affectionate, amused eye of *Uncle Will*.

Tears sprang to her eyes which she quickly blinked away as Emma and Elizabeth took the stage once more. Elizabeth walked downstage—the entire distance of two feet—and spoke in a clear voice. "We have combined plays three and four because the snow is beginning to melt and you will probably all be gone by tomorrow morning. Later this evening, we shall present our fifth and final play. For now, we are in a coach and four."

On the stage was the impression of a coach cleverly constructed with wooden slats, tacked with heavy paper and painted yellow like the posting coaches which passed through the village of Bidleigh once every fortnight. Each of the girls took up chairs within the coach. The effect was surprisingly realistic.

"My dear Captain Beetlehead," Elizabeth began, sliding on her feathered bonnet, "have you spoken to our dear son John yet about his beloved Beatrice?"

"I'm 'fraid not," Captain Beetlehead responded. "I have not found the time yet to address his difficulty. I am sorry."

"You must not forget how distressed he is." Mrs. Beetlehead sighed heartily, her bonnet bobbing. "Do you recall our courtship?"

"Of course I do. How could I forget the sweetest days of my life?"

"How you do talk!" Mrs. Beetlehead exclaimed. "You

were very gentle with me and forgave me every nonsense. Do you recall the kittens?"

"Ah, yes, the kittens!" Mr. Beetlehead intoned. "Quite fond of them you were, my dear little Mincy."

Mrs. Beetlehead giggled. "You have not called me that since I was a schoolgirl."

"Ah, Mincy, where have all the years gone? See how our children are almost grown, especially dear John. I am so grateful the war is almost over at last!"

The admiral could not help but cheer. Grace chuckled and, since she was sitting beside him, slipped her arm about his.

"Mr. Beetlehead, do you recall the suitor I set aside for you?"

"How could I forget Mr. Staghound?"

"You even recall his name."

"Of course I remember his name, for I disliked the fellow from the first. He was a good friend of yours, but that is all he should have been—a friend. Besides, I believe he detested your kittens."

"It was the very reason I rejected his suit. Not everyone must like kittens, but my husband should."

"Well, I did not care for them above half," he retorted gruffly.

Mrs. Beetlehead chuckled. "You let dear little Charity, the sweetest kitten of them all, fall asleep on your chest every evening when you were courting me. I decided to marry you then and there, for I always knew you would love our children equally as well."

"Dear Mincy," he responded. He glanced out the window of the coach. "There! That is Staghound's house now. Let us call on him and see how he and his wife fare."

"An excellent notion."

"You there, coachman!" Mr. Beetlehead cried. "Away to the house on the hill!"

Grace felt her cheeks tingling and turned toward Mr. Mollant, who was sitting on the other side of her. She regarded him solemnly. He would never have let a kitten fall asleep on his chest even were his life to depend upon it, of that she was utterly convinced. She wondered what he had thought of the play, and then she wondered just what manner of father he would be to his own children.

Mr. Mollant leaned toward her. "I am beginning to believe someone else wrote these plays. The language is far too advanced, though I do think the subject of the kittens rather redundant."

"Whom do you suspect?" she asked, thinking he was being ridiculous.

"Cheriton's uncle, of course," he whispered. "All this business about the war, always showing up in the middle of the play. Of course he helped them write it."

Grace leaned toward him and whispered, "What about the content concerning the kittens? What do you think of that?"

"It is all nonsense, of course," he scoffed.

"Of course," Grace murmured, unconvinced. She glanced toward the admiral and met his gaze. So much laughter brimmed in his eyes, the general good humor of a man who dearly loved an excellent joke, that she could not help but smile in return. To him, she whispered, "Have you been trimming your pens of late, good Mr. Plymtree?"

"Only to the most excellent of purposes, m'dear," he responded enigmatically. Then he winked at her.

Lord Cheriton sat in stunned silence beside the woman he had chosen to make his wife. She had told him only a few minutes prior to the third play that she had decided to marry him in three weeks' time. He should have been overjoyed, but since she informed him that Mr. Mollant had already expressed his intention of renewing his promise to Miss Taverstock to wed her Saturday next, not only his hopes of becoming Emma and Elizabeth's guardian were dashed, but something more as well. He was unable for the present to put into words why her announcement had given his heart a leaded sensation, but he strongly suspected it had something to do with Grace and with the kisses he had shared with her so recently. He felt oddly as though his life was ending.

And the play. His nieces were relentless concerning their beloved kittens and how everyone was supposed to feel about them and how the treatment of a cat could reflect a proper spouse.

Oh, God, a proper spouse.

His betrothed, now sitting beside him with her spine in a state of determined poise and her complexion the color of faded ivory, seemed as joyous as a stone. "Do you wish to marry me?" he queried in a soft voice as the girls struggled to turn their makeshift coach in the opposite direction.

"What?" she asked, obviously startled.

"Do you, indeed, desire to marry me, Hilary?"

"Are you posing this rather absurd question because I cannot abide kittens?" she asked, obviously offended.

"No." He shook his head. "Well, yes. I mean, I have not been tolerant of your dislike of them. We see so differently about the kittens and about many other things."

"I am sure we do not," she stated with some finality. "Besides, you are taking your nieces' play far too seriously."

"It is not the play," he said. "You truly seem unhappy in your choice of husband."

At that, she fell silent, unable to give him an answer. Since at the same time the fourth play began, he did not pursue the subject.

Mrs. Beetlehead began, "I was never more shocked!" she cried.

"Nor I! To think their eldest daughter eloped to Gretna

Green and all because she tumbled in love with someone else." Emma, as Captain Beetlehead, was now holding a long-haired grey-and-white-striped tabby kitten in her arms.

"Would you have eloped with me?" Mrs. Beetlehead asked.

"On no account," Captain Beetlehead stated.

"What if I had been forced into a betrothal against my will? Would you have been happy seeing me married to someone else? Would you not have tried to stop the wedding or in any other way hinder it?"

"I do not know," he responded. "I do not like to think about it. After all, we are married and nothing will ever change that."

"I know, dear, I know. But I think had I been desperate, I would have agreed to an elopement no matter the consequences. If one's happiness is at stake, would not even a scandal be worth the risk in order to secure that happiness?"

"I think you are speaking nonsense."

"Perhaps, but I must say I do not blame their daughter, not one bit, for making a push to be happy. Is our littlest one becoming restless? Give her to me."

The kitten, undoubtedly exhausted from the earlier travail in escaping the large wooden box, was a limp rag over Mrs. Beetlehead's shoulder. The small whiskers twitched, the legs stretched out for a brief moment, and the paws curled and uncurled. The audience fell silent. Cheriton heard Grace murmur an appreciative, "Oh, how sweet."

"Sweet, indeed," Lady Hilary muttered bitterly.

Cheriton's heart sank farther still.

Captain Beetlehead said, "You were always the best of mothers, Mincy."

"And you, the best of fathers. Only tell me, will you speak to John and tell him he must make a push before his beautiful Beatrice becomes betrothed to the Duke of Ogle, else they might take it into their heads to make a dash for the border themselves!"

"I will speak to John. And now tell me, what is the name of the kitten on your shoulder, dear little thing?"

"Prudence," Mrs. Beetlehead responded promptly.

The twins remained silent for a moment, then broke the spell of the play by rising and taking their bows. The admiral cheered quite enthusiastically, though his lady finally adjured him to cease whistling, for it was most unbecoming in him.

"Ah, Mincy," he teased, turning to her and catching up her hand in his.

"I have been suspecting you have had a hand in these plays," she stated with a laugh. "I was sure of it when I heard that ridiculous pet name."

Cheriton saw that though his aunt was chiding her husband, she was blushing with a great deal of pleasure, even more so when the admiral placed a kiss on the back of her hand.

"Trying to turn me up sweet?" she inquired playfully. "Well, it will not do by half, and what is all this nonsense about kittens and spouses? You will give our guests a complete fright of matrimony if you have not done so already."

The admiral lowered his voice. "The very thing I am hoping to achieve, for a worse-matched group I have never encountered before."

Cheriton heard him clearly and felt that the moral was aimed his direction. His betrothed had already left his side and was now waiting by the door. Mr. Mollant joined her shortly afterward. He regarded the pair for a moment and thought never had he seen two such long faces. They were not conversing at all, a circumstance he realized was quite unusual for them. Mr. Mollant and Lady Hilary always seemed to have something to say to one another.

When he approached his bride-to-be, intending to do better by her, she expressed her desire to rest before dinner. He felt he should say something to her, but no words rose to his lips other than an apology that the stay at his aunt's house had made her so unhappy. She merely smiled faintly in return.

After watching her leave the chamber, he would have turned away from Mr. Mollant, but the good fellow was inclined to speak. "A word with you, Cheriton, in private?"

Cheriton had no desire to speak with Mr. Mollant. Given his present irritable temper, he knew he could little abide Mollant's self-righteous tone, nonetheless his hints on how he ought to conduct himself. He begged to be excused, but Mollant was adamant.

"I feel I must speak with you, m'lord, if you will but oblige me with a few minutes of your time. What I have to say concerns your betrothed, something she has confided in me which I feel you ought to know."

"If she has confided in you," Cheriton returned icily, "then you ought not to speak a word of it to me, regardless of the subject."

Mr. Mollant was not to be so easily deterred. "As her friend, and yours, I have no compunction whatsoever in giving voice to her concerns. Will you please afford me the few minutes necessary to speak with you?"

Cheriton felt as though a puppy had him by the sleeve of his coat and would not be shaken off. He nodded abruptly. "Follow me, then, if you insist on it."

"I do."

A few minutes later, Cheriton stood in a weak pool of winter sunlight near the pianoforte in the drawing room. He was watching Mr. Mollant pace up and down the chamber in an agitated and ridiculous fashion, for his curly brown hair, kept long *a la Cherubim,* was bouncing with each step. The fellow was making a cake of himself with no one to stop him. Cheriton crossed his arms over his chest and only barely repressed a sneer. He could feel his upper lip curl, however, as he pondered the man before him. And this fellow thought he would make Grace a proper husband! What a gudgeon!

"I have weighed the matter in my mind again and again, but I feel I must speak for Lady Hilary's sake. If she is to be happy as your wife—"

"Her happiness will be my first concern," Cheriton stated flatly.

Mr. Mollant stopped his pacing, snapped his brows together, and exclaimed, "I beg your pardon, but I must take issue with you on that score. She has been tormented for the past several weeks, everytime she is forced to journey to Plymtree Lodge, by your nieces and their penchant to thrust these horrid kittens upon her. If I did not believe in the complete innocence of youth, I might suppose that the girls had designed to bring Lady Hilary to tears. Since I refuse to countenance any such notion, I can only conclude that the occurrences are random and unfortunate. However, your conduct in the matter cannot be construed as anything but that which has arisen from a profound disinterest in her happiness."

Cheriton narrowed his eyes. He could not credit Mr. Mollant's impertinence. His fingers ached, suddenly, with the desire to plant the whipster in front of him a hard facer, draw claret, and let him run to Lady Hilary for succor. "My conduct?" he returned through grinding teeth. "My disinterest?"

"You seem to be absolutely indifferent to your betrothed's sufferings. I have noted it myself on a score of occasions and have kept silent, for I felt it was not my place to interfere. However, now I must speak. I will say again, I have seen nothing but indifference in your conduct toward your bride-to-be. You have even gone so far as to give her a dressing down in public because she was

overset by a vicious cat clinging to the skirts of her gown.
I must say, Cheriton, I have always thought you a gentleman, but my opinion is quickly altering. Have you
nothing to say for yourself?"

So many thoughts rose to mind, each desirous of finding the tip of his tongue, that Cheriton could do little
more for the present than stare at the man before him,
his mouth agape. In the course of his career, the viscount
had had occasion to fight two duels, each of them forced
upon him with far less venom and insult than what was
being thrown at him now by a man he considered to be
little worthier than a toad. He felt the ire of the situation
rise within him slowly and evenly, causing his flesh to
tingle with the anticipation of striking the first blow. He
was a head taller than Mollant and weighed considerably
more. He would make a flush hit that would send the
ridiculous fop flying backward, perhaps never to regain
consciousness. He felt the muscles in his right arm begin
to harden, then bristle. His elbow flexed. His fingers
knotted up into a fine fist. "Mollant, I have always
thought you an absurd little man, but now—"

"There you are!" Grace cried, bursting into the chamber with lightning speed. Cheriton had the strongest impression she had been listening just outside the door.
"Mr. Mollant, you are wanted in the morning room. I
believe Mrs. Plymtree wishes to speak with you on a
matter of some urgency. Yes, yes, please go to her at
once. It would not do by half to keep your hostess waiting, now would it?"

These last words had a proper effect. Mollant quickly
expressed his hope of continuing the discussion with
Cheriton, then bowed to Grace. He moved briskly into
the hall and was gone. Grace followed after, but only to
close the doors upon the hallway and to stand before
them as one keeping guard.

Cheriton was upon her in a trice. "Step aside. You had

no right, no business to interfere, and I am not at all finished with that absurd puppy."

"Oh, but you are finished, Cheriton," Grace stated firmly. "Whatever you may think of my betrothed, I will not permit you to thrash him while under Mrs. Plymtree's roof. He may have offended you, and I heard enough to know his offenses were deeply drawn, but I beg you to consider your aunt as well as your nieces. Emma and Elizabeth will be distraught were we all to quarrel now— now, when everything is nearly settled."

Cheriton opened his mouth, then closed it. He clenched his fists and his jaw. He ground his teeth. "How dare that man tell me how to conduct myself when he has been all but hugging my bride-to-be in the presence of my nieces!"

He watched Grace repress a smile. "I could not credit he was actually telling you how to properly love Lady Hilary. But I did fear for him. I know your temper—you are a beast when you are angered. I was afraid you might slay him with a nattily thrown fist."

"I might have!" he cried. "The Lord knows I wanted to!"

"And you would have had I not entered the chamber as I did."

"Of course, only what did my aunt want with him?"

Grace wrinkled up her nose. "I'm 'fraid that was a whisker. I daresay Mrs. Plymtree is dressing for dinner at present, which I should be doing as well. Only, Cheriton, promise me you will leave well enough alone. I daresay tomorrow morning we shall all be returning to our homes, and in a very short time, we shall be married and busy about many other matters."

At that, he grabbed her arms. "You cannot marry that deuced fellow!" he cried. "You cannot! You will make mincemeat of him before the first twelve-month, you know you will! Admit it is so!"

Grace felt her chin quiver. "Yes, I believe you are right, only—"

He leaned his forehead against hers. "Break off the engagement. He is not the man for you."

"I cannot. I have for so long wanted the girls to be as my daughters. I would do anything for them."

"Then, I shall relinquish my claim as their guardian. You can break off the engagement, and I shall postpone my marriage until you find a new husband, someone more properly suited to your temperament and your sweetness and your . . . oh, God." His lips were suddenly on hers. He pulled her away from the door and enveloped her in his arms. She flung her arms about his neck and returned kiss for kiss, wildly and passionately. He held her tightly to him, crushing her against him. "Grace, Grace! I have missed you so much—all these years. My darling, my darling! Please tell me you will not have Mollant."

She drew back, her breath coming in odd bursts and fits. She pushed him away and placed her hand on her stomach. "You should not be kissing me, Cheriton. Not like this! I cannot think and I must think."

She turned and opened the door behind her. Before Cheriton could reach for her, she had slid through, and the door snapped shut just shy of his nose.

Cheriton knew Grace was right about one thing—he should not be kissing her, not when he was to be married so very soon.

FIVE

An hour later, Grace decided she would not join the others for dinner after all. Her mind was in such a wretched state of turmoil that she could scarcely put two thoughts together, nonetheless sustain her part in a conversation. If only Cheriton had not overset the ordered nature of her life by telling her that he would give up his right to the guardianship of Emma and Elizabeth if she would but break off her engagement.

But she had to marry Mr. Mollant. How could she do otherwise? She had been betrothed to him forever, and she had been promising Emma and Elizabeth for years that they would one day come to live with her. Now that Mr. Mollant meant to keep the most recent wedding date, she had but a few days before she could actually call the girls her own.

How happy they would all be!

Oh, how very miserable she was!

Grace instructed Mrs. Plymtree's maid, Angela, to brush out her long hair. She wanted the gentle, soothing rhythm of the servant's ministrations to calm her overwrought nerves. Over the past two days, Cheriton had done the unthinkable—he had kissed her three times and not just gentle, friendly salutes but wild, stirring assaults which had affected her ability to reason.

She closed her eyes and drew in a deep breath as the bristles gently flowed through her hair. If only she could stop thinking about Cheriton's manly embrace and his insistence she not wed Mr. Mollant.

She propped her elbows on the dressing table and dropped her head into her waiting hands. She moaned faintly.

"Have I hurt you, Miss Taverstock? I do beg yer pardon."

"No, no, you have not hurt me at all. I am merely suffering some distress of mind, and your brushing is the precise balm I need. Pray continue."

The maid seemed reluctant to begin again. Grace glanced at her in the looking glass and saw that she was quite agitated. She felt compelled to add, "I beg to assure you that you in no way harmed me."

" 'Tis not that, miss. I only feel so badly fer ye, I do, an that. 'Tis because Mr. Mollant has left, is it not?"

Grace blinked at her. *Mr. Mollant left? To go where? And why had he said nothing to her?*

"I'm that sure he'll be back, miss," Angela rushed on. "Lady Hilary was quite distressed, and I'm sure he meant nothing by it, taking her up in his carriage as he did."

"Do you mean to say he left with Lady Hilary?"

"Indeed, miss. Do ye mean, ye didna know?"

Grace shook her head.

"O-o-oh! Mrs. Plymtree will be that angry with me. But I thought ye knew! Indeed, I thought that's why ye were so unhappy. I never meant—"

Grace rose to her feet. "Hush," she said gently and patted the maid on her shoulder. "I am grateful beyond words that you told me, and I promise that I will say nothing of our conversation to your mistress. So, they are gone, without a word! How very odd."

She thought of the last play the twins had performed. Oh, could it be true? Had something of the fourth play spoken to Mr. Mollant and Hilary, warning them away from two hapless marriages?

Without considering her appearance, that her hair was dangling past her shoulders and that she was wearing her aunt's red velvet dressing gown, she went in search of Cheriton. She found him three doors down the hall in his bedchamber. When he bid her enter, he was seated in a chair by the fireplace, in his shirtsleeves, and holding a missive in his hand. He appeared as though he had suffered a shock.

"Tell me!" she cried, crossing the room quickly to him. "Is it true? I have just learned they left together! Does this—I mean—I cannot credit it! What does your missive say? Is Mr. Mollant merely escorting Lady Hilary home? To her parents?"

He said nothing, but held the letter up to her. She snatched it from him, took a deep breath and prepared to read it, but found her hands were shaking fiercely. She forced herself to become more composed as she moved slowly to the window.

Cheriton joined her. "You must read it. I am not sure it is entirely unwelcome news."

"Are you sure?" she queried, glancing up at him.

He nodded. She took another deep breath, and after noting that the missive was from Lady Hilary, she began reading aloud. " 'Lord Cheriton, I am sorry to inform you that our betrothal is at an end, but you have proven your indifference to my comfort at every turn, and I have become convinced we no longer suit. I have tumbled deeply in love with Mr. Mollant, whose conduct toward me has been all that is solicitous, kind and considerate. He has become a constant watch upon my happiness, has begged me to accompany him to Gretna Green, and I have agreed to go with him, knowing only too well that Papa would forbid our nuptials otherwise. If you must know, my father wished me to marry a Peer, and I fear his desire in this regard led me to accept of your hand in marriage when in truth I now believe I did not love you. For this I express my deepest remorse and hope you will one day find it in your heart to forgive me. However, I beg you will allow us to depart in peace. Please know that Mr. Mollant will fight you to the death, if need be, so if you do come in pursuit of me, expect to be challenged. Yours, etc., Lady Hilary Beaford.' "

A short postscript read, "Mr. Mollant wishes you to inform Miss Taverstock that he is very sorry, but that he is convinced she will understand the pressing need for our elopement. He wishes her to be happy and believes with all his heart that her true contentment must lie elsewhere than in marriage to him."

"Dear God," Grace murmured, fully shocked by the incredible nature of the blunt communication.

He shook his head. "Did she, or either of them, think me such a brute that I would not have released Hilary from the engagement?"

"I do not know," Grace breathed. She was so stunned, she could not think. "What an odd day this has been. Yesterday, as well. To think it has ended in this peculiar fashion. And I do not think I care to be dismissed so readily."

She heard Cheriton's low chuckle. "As if you truly give a fig for any of it."

"Well, I daresay no lady cares to be jilted, especially in such an offhand manner as a postscript to another's letter of dismissal. Of the two of us, I believe I have suffered the worse offense."

Suddenly, she felt fingers gliding down the length of her hair. "I will not allow there to be an offense of any kind," he murmured against her hair. The missive slipped from her hand. "You are in your dressing gown," he stated.

"Your aunt's dressing gown," she corrected rather breathlessly. She felt his fingers on the soft velvet.

"Come, Grace," he whispered. "Turn around and look at me."

She whirled within the circle of his arms and met his gaze which was warm with feeling. "I am free," he stated simply. "As are you. Grace, I have been a fool."

"No more than I," she responded. "Only, Cheriton, there is something I think you have forgotten." Tears came unbidden to her eyes.

"Grace, please do not tell me you are saddened by Mr. Mollant's decision. Please tell me you were never in love with him, that you are not in love with him now, for I will not believe it."

She shook her head. "I am not in love with him. I think I must have convinced myself that I could love him when we first became engaged. We were good friends once upon a time. I—I do not think so harshly of him as you do."

"I only thought badly of him because he was to wed you. He was no match for you."

"Cheriton, have you not considered? I know you have kissed me several times, today and yesterday, but it is as though you have somehow forgotten why it was we quarreled so irrevocably seven years ago. If you have forgotten, you must strive to remember, for until you do I will not believe myself forgiven."

Cheriton was caught up in the strong sensation of loving Grace Taverstock and did not want to heed her warning. He was in his shirtsleeves, and she was before him dressed scandalously in but a thin, velvet dressing gown. He wanted to kiss her as he had an hour past in the drawing room. He wanted to feel her hands kneading his arms through the thin fabric of his shirt. He wanted to touch her, to hold her, to love her.

"Cheriton, no," Grace protested. "You must not do this. We must talk. There is so much we must—"

He kissed her again and tasted the soft, compelling

sweetness of her lips. He found he was starved for her, even more so now, knowing that his betrothal was at an end, as well as hers, and he was at liberty to kiss her without restraint. He lifted her off her feet and had all the delight of feeling her fling her arms about his neck and return the pressure of his lips with maddening desire. Her hunger seemed equal to his, as it always had been. Why had they wasted so many years? How foolish to have let time become an enemy to the happiness that awaited them even now.

He let her feet touch the floor again and cupped her face in his hands. He drifted his lips over hers in a manner that set her to cooing from deep within her throat. She leaned sideways against his shoulder, and he encircled her with his arm, supporting her and letting his thumb touch her lips. She opened her eyes and looked deeply into his own, her expression love-drenched.

She blinked, and suddenly he could see that a ray of sorrow had entered her eye. "Cheriton, you took my sister from me. Do you not remember?"

The words hardly moved the air so softly were they spoken. He drew in a long, deep breath, and his memory, which he seemed to have set aside during the past two days, returned in full. He stared at her, into her, into the pain of their shared loss. A wave of torment flooded him, of the terrible yachting accident, of watching those he loved slip into the sea and not return, of coming back to Bidleigh Village with only his mother safely in his care.

He released Grace abruptly. She bumped against the windows, causing them to rattle slightly. "My God," he murmured, turning away from her. "How could I have forgotten? How could I have kissed you as I did when you were so cruel and unrelenting in your hatred of me?"

Grace looked at his back and felt all her misery return anew. He had spoken truly. She had been unrelenting, if not in her hatred of him, then in her blame. She wanted to say something to him, to beg his forgiveness, but there was a part of her that still believed him at fault.

When he said nothing more, she moved past him and disappeared from the room.

Cheriton stared after her, a terrible hollowness replacing all the former passion. Since the time of his betrothal to Lady Hilary, he had gradually been in the habit of forgetting and forgiving Grace for her many past cruelties. Lady Hilary had served, for the duration of his courtship of her as well as throughout the engagement, to soften the terrible rupture with Grace. He had come to believe, even until now, that he had finally forgiven her, that he had finally grown at peace with the loss of his father and his brother as well as Nan Taverstock, with whom he had grown up.

You took my sister from me.

There it was—nothing was yet healed between them.

Grace sobbed into her pillow for an hour and sent a note to Mrs. Plymtree begging to be excused from dinner. Her hostess and good friend, the woman who had become like a mother to her, brought her a tray of food and at first assumed she was unhappy because Mr. Mollant had jilted her.

Grace turned over and faced her, wiping her eyes and blowing her nose. "How could I be unhappy when I never loved him!" she cried.

"I see," she murmured, her expressive face full of compassion. "Is this about Cheriton, then, my dear?"

Grace nodded. "Oh, I am a wretched person, a terrible creature! I should have perished at sea, not my sister. Dear Nan would have forgiven him, but not I! I had to carry the weight of my loss like a sword. Dear Mrs. Plymtree, once Nan was gone I did not rest until I had ruined Cheriton's love for me. I . . . I blamed him over and over for not calling off the yachting excursion. I told him so a hundred times. I told him he had killed my sister and that I hated him for it. And I told him not once but each time I saw him, for weeks on end, until he grew to despise me."

"You had lost the remnant of your entire family," Mrs. Plymtree said. "I am certain he understood even then how horrible your loss was."

"Yet, why was I so cruel to the man I loved—and I did love Cheriton, I still do—with my whole heart? Why did I turn all my grief against him, for he was innocent? I am a terrible creature, terrible I say."

"Do you know how much he blamed himself for what happened?"

Grace blew her nose and shook her head. "How could I know anything when I was so sunk in my own grief? I did not see that he had lost a father and a brother. I saw only that I was orphaned completely, without even a sister to support me."

Mrs. Plymtree patted her hand, but remained holding it firmly. "That first year he used to come to me, to see his nieces, to help them in their loss, but also to talk to me about the pain he was enduring. He wept once, on my knees. He said you would never forgive him and that he doubted he could ever forgive you for blaming him as you did."

Grace wiped her eyes, though more tears followed. "He was so sweet at first, after the accident, but I was merciless. I would not listen to reason; I could not be consoled. And the worst of it is, I think I still blame him. Oh, what a wretched creature I am!"

Mrs. Plymtree chuckled. "No more wretched than any of us. Yet, have you considered, my dear, that so long as you keep blaming him you will never have to risk loving him and losing him as you did your dear sister, and your parents as well in years gone by. For that reason, I believe you are more afraid of loving him than of anything else in the world."

"Whatever do you mean?" she cried, astonished.

"If you love him, he might perish one day and leave you alone as so many others have upon whom you have depended so deeply."

Grace stared at Mrs. Plymtree and blew her nose soundly once more. "Do you think it truly possible?"

"Perhaps. It is merely a notion of mine. However, you might wish to think on it a little."

Grace searched back over the years. "Cheriton is not a mild man. He takes many risks. Even when we were courting I remember fearing his jaunts to Tiverton with the other members of the Four-in-Hand Club. They would pay the coachman of the mails for the privilege of handling the ribbons! I can still hear the sound of his boot striking the floorboard of the coach as he signaled the horses to start."

"Do not put me in mind of those dreadful days!" Mrs. Plymtree cried. "I can recall most specifically living in such suspense each time he and his friends would go out, driving neck or nothing! I had suffered my own losses—a dear brother and my nephew, as well as your sister, whom I had come to know and love as dearly as my own. I remember begging Cheriton once to cease his trips to Tiverton and, oh, that horrid trip to Plymouth! Good God, I am covered in gooseflesh just remembering the fear of it, for that was the time the coach overturned when his friend was taking a corner too fast, but thank God no one was hurt. We have endured some sad days, all of us." She took a deep breath before adding in a calmer voice, "Only, what will you do now?"

She shook her head. "I do not know. I wish that he would forgive me, but how can he? I was so unjust, so unkind. I even told him I could not love a man like him . . . ever." She burst into tears anew.

Mrs. Plymtree gathered her up in her arms and let her cry. Grace clung to her, grateful to be understood and not condemned. After a time, the tears subsided, and Mrs. Plymtree left her to go in search of the twins in hopes of postponing the final play until the morrow.

However, a half hour later, the admiral scratched on her door. Grace was seated in a chair by her dressing table, quietly reading a volume of verse, when she bid him enter.

"Poetry," he stated in his gruff voice.

Grace grimaced slightly. " 'Ode to Solitude.' I am not of a mind with Pope. I ought to be, but somehow . . ."

"He is not Byron, is he?"

Grace could not help but blush. "Now, there is a poet who possesses a fire more suited to me."

"Not unlike Cheriton, I would suppose."

"Not unlike Cheriton," she agreed, smiling faintly.

"Are you feeling much better?" he queried, laying a hand on her shoulder.

"A little. I can only suppose by your presence here that Mrs. Plymtree told you of our conversation."

"And of your very sad feelings," he added. "Only, you are much too hard on yourself regardless of the past. To a landsman, I suppose there is nothing worse than losing someone to the sea. But when you've lived on the ocean as I have, the experience is wholly different. So very many friends pass in just that way that eventually you make a sort of peace with the inevitable. Old age also gives a certain distance and proper feeling to the horrific events of life. You were, however, most unfortunate to be left so very much alone."

"But you and Mrs. Plymtree helped me enormously."

"We were not without a great deal of compassion for your sufferings, but you must make a clean breast of it to Cheriton. Tell him everything, even that you still blame him. I am convinced you can come to an understanding of some kind. Just remember that there is not a man, in Cheriton's circumstances, who would not believe he had failed you that day, even though it was a sheer miracle he kept his mother alive during those wretched hours of the storm. A miracle, indeed. But a man grows up feeling he must protect those he loves. When he cannot, believe me there is no greater torment.

"But come, I did not mean to give you a lecture on the subject. Indeed, I meant only to persuade you to let the girls have their last play. They have been rehearsing for days and days, and I believe the knowledge that some of our guests have since quit Plymtree Lodge has increased their desire to take to the stage. Will you not join us in the library for their sakes?"

Grace might have refused except that the admiral had become something of a father to her, and with his single blue eye, and the furrows of his sympathetic brow, beckoning her to do his bidding, how could she do otherwise? "Of course I shall attend. I am feeling much better, only, are my eyes as red and as puffy as I believe them to be?"

"Not a bit," he responded a trifle too enthusiastically. "Come, I will escort you to the library myself."

Cheriton could see at once that Grace had been crying. His own heart had been wrung heartily since he had last held her in his arms. She had reminded him of the truth, of what had happened between them seven years ago to separate them so completely. She despised him; she blamed him, nearly as much as he blamed himself. Within the scope of his reason, he knew he had done all he could that day to save his family, but his heart and his conscience still wrestled within him. Part of him yet believed that there must have been some manner in which he could have prevented the accident or, once the yacht overturned, to bring everyone to safety.

For one thing, he had foolishly believed his brother and Nan were safe, else he might have made an effort to pursue them once they drifted away on a small piece of wreckage. Surely, he was to blame for assuming they would not need his assistance.

How he longed to leave Plymtree Lodge. He wished to be anywhere of the moment than in the presence of his brother and Nan's children. He was reliving the nightmare all because Grace had spoken the same words she had spoken more than once following the three funerals, that he had taken Nan from her. The girls looked just like Nan, particularly now that they were growing into young ladies. They looked like Grace, as well, which further deepened his grief.

Grace did not meet his gaze as she took up a chair beside the admiral. Mrs. Plymtree came up behind Cheriton and whispered, "I cannot believe the admiral coaxed her from her bedchamber but you can see she has been in tears, poor thing. You must speak to her, Cheriton, indeed you must, for I believe she has something she wishes to say to you, but not until the play is over, mind."

At that moment, Emma stepped downstage. She wore a black coat over her pale pink gown, and the admiral's black hat atop her blond curls. In her arms was the white kitten called Angel.

"Our final play begins on the steps of the church."

Mrs. Beetlehead, wearing an ancient bonnet of Mrs. Plymtree's, covered in a profusion of lace and ribbons, joined her downstage, dabbing at her eyes with a kerchief. She waved the kerchief at an unseen object. "Goodbye, my dear John," she called out. "Goodbye, dear Beatrice. Oh, Captain, do you not think that our John made a handsome groom, and was there a prettier bride than lovely Beatrice?"

"Not in all of England," Emma proclaimed as Captain Beetlehead, her voice low and commanding.

Grace smiled. The trio on stage was perfectly charming.

Mrs. Beetlehead sighed dramatically. "We owe this wedding to you, dear Captain. You spoke so eloquently on Beatrice's behalf to the Smythes. Mrs. Smythe cried a bucket of tears when Beatrice proclaimed her steadfast love for our John."

"Indeed," Captain Beetlehead responded. "But Ogle gave me the cut direct on the green only this morning."

"What a bad fellow he is, after all."

"A terrible sport, what?"

"Well, I cannot be sad in the least, for our dear John deserves such a fine lady as Beatrice to be his wife, for he will love her all his life, just as he has loved her these seven years and more."

"You have spoken truly."

"I know that I have." She then glanced down at the kitten in Emma's arms and continued. "Our beloved Angel will be the next to be married, do you not think so?"

"Our dear Angel. So she shall."

Both Captain and Mrs. Beetlehead, standing side by side, stared down at the white kitten. Angel, as though on cue, looked up at each in turn.

Mrs. Plymtree murmured a warm, "Oh, what a darling. I have always loved kittens, have you not, Cheriton?"

He chuckled. "Not precisely, but this one could soften anyone's heart."

Captain Beetlehead said, "Angel, you will make a lovely bride, the finest in three counties." Angel cocked her head at Emma as though trying to make her out. "Are you not happy that your brother is married to Beatrice?"

Angel, again as if on cue, released a delicate *meow.*

"Oh-h-h," Mrs. Plymtree sighed.

Mrs. Beetlehead interjected, "I am so grateful you intervened, husband. For surely our beloved son would have been miserable all his days had you not."

"Indeed, I know you are right, but 'All's well that ends well,' what?"

"Indeed! I could not have said it better myself."

The girls paused for a long moment, for the play had come to an end. They moved downstage together and bowed solemnly, an action which, because it forced Elizabeth's bonnet to drape several lace streamers over Angel's whiskers, immediately set the kitten to batting at the intriguing strands.

The girls lifted their heads laughing.

Cheriton sighed deeply as he offered his applause for their joint efforts. He could not help but feel that in their charming way, with the undoubted aid of the admiral, his nieces had been lecturing him, and perhaps Grace as well, on the state of their relationship and the need for a proper conclusion.

He glanced at Grace, who turned to meet his gaze, and saw in her red-rimmed eyes a desire for conversation. He felt her thoughts touch his mind, perhaps because they were his thoughts as well. Time for the past to be set aside, at least he hoped it was possible.

For the moment, however, he turned his attention to his nieces. He kissed their cheeks, complimented them on their ability to both create and memorize so much dialogue, admitted Angel was a fine creature even if she was a cat, and then asked if either of them was saddened by the news that Lady Hilary would not be his wife.

"No!" was the quick, unanimous response.

"Oh, Uncle Will, I never could like her!" Elizabeth cried. "Though I did try, but she was forever putting up a caterwaul when we would but enter the room—with or without the kittens! I did not want her to be my mother."

"Nor I," Emma agreed. "She did not like me, Uncle Will. Of that I am certain."

He nodded and decided to speak plainly. "I did not comprehend her feelings until Mr. Mollant spoke of them to me. For your sakes, then, I am happy she is no longer to be my wife."

"Are you sad?" Emma queried softly, laying her hand in gentle understanding on his sleeve. She still held Angel cradled in her arm, and the admiral's hat was sitting low on her ears.

"No, I suppose I am not, at least not very much. We were not a match." He gently removed the hat.

"Oh, thank you! It was ever so heavy! Would you like to hold Angel?"

How could he resist the supplicating look in her eye. "Of course I would. Come, Angel." He took the kitten in his hand and settled her as he had seen Grace do the night before, into the well of his shoulder, and held her fast with both hands. She struggled only a little at first, then relaxed into a hearty purr. He had no doubt that when he released her, his coat of blue superfine would be riddled with white hairs. The pleasure of seeing the look on Emma's face, however, who had only wanted to share her joy in the kitten with him, was worth the minor inconvenience of a coat that would afterward need a good brushing.

Grace approached the girls and embraced each in turn, exclaiming over their numerous accomplishments. "I am so very proud of you both, you have no idea!"

"Yes, we do, Aunt Grace," Elizabeth cried. "For you tell us so, every day."

"I do, do I not?" she responded with a smile.

"Have you been crying?" Emma queried. Elizabeth shot a foot toward her sister. "Ow! Lizzie! Oh! That is . . . I hope you enjoyed all our plays, Aunt Grace."

"Every one of them," Grace declared, "and I thought

the kittens, on the whole, behaved beautifully throughout. Especially Angel, of course. She is certainly well-named."

She turned toward Cheriton, and as she lifted her gaze to him, Cheriton felt his heart turn over in his chest. He loved her so very much. She stroked Angel's head with the tip of her finger. "Such a clever girl you are," she said softly. Angel turned her head and emitted a cross between a purr and a meow. Everyone chuckled.

"She is clever, I will give her that," Cheriton said.

Grace nodded, but seemed very conscious.

Mrs. Plymtree bustled forth and bid the girls say good night, for it was long past their bedtime. With only a few good-natured complaints, the twins gave another round of hugs and kisses before departing the chamber. Angel, of course, accompanied the twins with Mrs. Plymtree bustling into the hallway after them.

The admiral called out to Cheriton and Grace, "I will be in the billiard room if anyone should care for a game or two. Otherwise, have a toast to the future on my behalf." He gestured to the table near the door where he had poured out two small goblets of the amber-colored wine. He, too, disappeared into the hallway.

When the door snapped shut, Grace turned and smiled falteringly upon Cheriton.

"Come," he said softly, offering his arm to her. "Let us toast the future as my uncle has suggested."

"Very well," Grace murmured, her voice barely audible.

When she slipped her arm about his, he guided her to the table upon which the glasses of sherry rested. He gave one to Grace and took the other in hand. He watched her carefully, his heart on fire. Perhaps the admiral intended for him to tell Grace of the strength of his love for her; indeed the admiral, it would seem, had arranged everything to a nicety. However, how could things be truly resolved between himself and the woman he so adored?

He smiled crookedly. "To the admiral and to the kittens—Faith, Hope, Charity, and what was the fourth one?"

"Prudence," Grace murmured, a smile touching her lips.

"Ah, yes, we cannot forget Prudence. And to Angel. May our lessons be as simple to learn as those presented in the plays we have witnessed over the past two days."

"Cheriton—" Grace began, in a voice dark with worry.

"Drink first, Grace, please."

She nodded. "Of course." She tilted her head back and swallowed the small portion of wine.

"Cheriton—" she began again.

He took her glass and settled it on the table beside his. "No, I will not allow you to speak," he said. "At least, not just yet."

"But—"

"No, Grace. You have had your say these many years and more; but I have never had mine, and I mean to have it now. Come, it is cold in this corner of the chamber. Stand with me in front of the fire."

She nodded in agreement.

Once situated before the crackling log fire, Cheriton said, "I have loved you since we were children, when we were all used to play together as we did—you and Nan, Charles and I. The highest point of any occasion was the moment you walked into the room, and it has always been so, ever since I can remember.

"I can also recall that one of the things I admired most about you was that you always spoke your mind, no matter what the subject. You never let me play the lord which I was wont to do. You kept me thinking, and if ever I preened in front of you—I was maggot-food for days."

"Maggot-food? Oh, Cheriton, how could you bring

that up now," she cried. "I had the worst, most unladylike tongue!"

"You remember, then, the terrible things you used to say to me when we played in the oak and ash woods at the edge of the moors? Or in our fort by the river?"

"I was incorrigible. I have always been so."

"In the most wonderful, adorable way. I want to marry you, Grace, now, more than even seven years ago during that glorious summer we shared. I never stopped loving you. Never."

Grace lowered her head. "I spoke so shamefully to you after the accident."

"It does not matter, not anymore."

"But it does!" she cried. "I blamed you—again and again! I think I still do!"

He offered a half smile. "You were never restrained, even in your grief. Had I been able to comprehend as much, perhaps these seven years would not have passed us by, but I was too lost in my own grief to do more than leave you in peace."

"You cannot say you are forgiving me, for I do not believe it is possible. How could anyone be so generous?"

"I am not being generous, nor even forgiving. I just want you to be my wife more than anything else in the world. If I could have prevented Nan's death, I would have; but I could not, and I daresay there will be a hundred more times in the course of our life together that you will look upon me with blame and I will bear it because I love you, Grace. I want you to be my wife, to be a mother to Emma and Elizabeth while I am a father to them. I want you to bear my children, to walk by my side for as many years as will be given to either of us.

"If I could undo the past, I would. If I could take the advice you gave me on the day of the accident, and *not* insist on going to Plymouth, I would do so now with all

my heart, but I cannot. I cannot undo that dreadful day.
I can only profess the depths of my love to you now and
trust that as the years unfold, my adoration for you will
suffice. Will you have me, dear Grace Taverstock, even
with so much sadness between us. Will you be my wife?"

Grace did not know when the tears had begun to fall,
but presently they were streaming down her face. She
swiped at them, but more followed. "You are too good
and too generous," she cried.

"No," he argued. "I am being selfish and considering
only my feelings in this situation. I want you for my wife
regardless of whether you blame me or not for what happened in the past. I do not even care if you love me in
return. I want you. I want you with all your blame and
anything else that comes with you." He had the good
sense to take her abruptly into his arms. "I want you,
Grace. On that day, that terrible day, the only reason I
lived was because I knew I was coming back to you.
Thoughts of you gave me the strength to survive that
storm, even the strength to save my mother. Tell me you
will have me, Grace. Tell me now."

A light of understanding poured into Grace's mind so
keenly that she began to tremble. "You came back for
me?" she queried, breathlessly.

"Yes," he murmured. "You were in my thoughts every
moment of that terrible ordeal."

"I . . . I could have lost you all, then."

"But you did not," he stated.

Grace saw him through a shimmering of tears. "Of
course I will have you," she assented, gently stroking his
cheek with the back of her fingers. "You have always
had me, heart and soul."

"I love you so much, Grace."

"As I love you," she responded.

He covered her lips gently, holding her fast. He kissed

her tenderly again and again, nearly as many times as he had just now professed his love for her.

"There, you see," Grace whispered to the admiral. "Just as I told you. He is fast asleep, and Charity is curled upon his chest." Lord Cheriton was stretched out upon the sofa in the drawing room, the short-haired tabby sleeping peacefully atop him.

Admiral Plymtree chuckled softly. "So, it is all settled, then? You really are to marry after these many years of brangling?"

"Indeed, we are. As soon as the banns may be posted and the wedding breakfast arranged, but not before his mother returns from Bath."

"She will be so happy to hear of his plans to wed you."

"Is this so?" she inquired softly, considerably surprised.

"Very much," he responded, closing the door upon Cheriton. "She came to believe she had lost you in the accident as well. You were quite a favorite of hers."

"I did not know," she said.

He gathered up her arm in his and patted her hand. "I am so happy for you. Indeed, I am, though I must say I was a little shocked that Mr. Mollant would actually take his fair Hilary to Gretna."

"No more shocked than I," she responded. "Mr. Mollant is so careful, about everything, that never would I have thought—not in a thousand years that he would deign to elope as he has."

"There is no accounting for what one may do when one has tumbled silently in love.

Grace regarded him thoughtfully for a moment as together they made their way to the library. "He is very much in love with her, is he not?"

"Very much so, but did you not have even the smallest suspicion on that score?"

She chuckled. "I'm 'fraid in this regard I was a bit of a slowtop. I only began to suspect his affections had been engaged when he was hugging Lady Hilary while standing next to her on the sofa."

He grunted. "How I dearly would have loved to have seen the sight for myself! Boots and all, eh? On the sofa? Not next to it?"

"On the sofa," she returned.

"And Cheriton did not pay the least heed?"

At that she laughed. "Cheriton was far too busy being angry that his betrothed had yet again fallen into a fit of hysterics over the kittens."

"As well he should have!" he cried, not mincing words. "What a ninnyhammer Hilary Beaford has become. I was never used to think much of her as a child, and now that she is grown up I believe I think even less of her! Well, I daresay she will make Mollant a tolerable wife, for he is as ridiculous as she is absurd. As for you and Cheriton, I say, 'All's well that ends well.' "

"I could not agree with you more."

As she entered the library, she found the twins reading their favorite books with the kittens scattered about them on pillows and blankets.

Emma looked up and held her finger to her lips. "You must be quiet," she whispered solemnly. "All the children are sleeping."

"We shan't disturb them," the admiral returned softly. He turned slightly toward Elizabeth, who was sitting on a chair next to the sofa. "And how do you think our plays fared, Lizzie?"

Elizabeth giggled. "Perfectly, for they had precisely the effect you predicted. You are very wise, Uncle Plymtree."

He smiled broadly.

Grace pinched his arm. "Then, the substance of them was your idea, after all."

"Of course," he retorted. "And a great deal of the writing as well. Now, now! Do not stare at me in that manner, m'dear. Good God, child! Something had to be done when the four of you had made such a mull of it."

She held his arm tightly, tears springing to her eyes once more. "Thank you, *Uncle* Plymtree. Thank you ever so much, for you have saved us all."

"What nonsense is this, now," he responded gruffly. "You do not mean to become a watering pot like that other female, do you?"

"Of course not."

"Good, for I have had all of Lady Hilary I can bear for the winter. I hope I shan't see her face 'til springtime, and even then!" He shuddered eloquently.

Since Grace saw that both the girls were listening to their great-uncle's indiscreet remarks concerning Lady Hilary, she cleared her throat and turned the subject as she drew him toward the windows which overlooked a snowbound creek. Overhead, the sky was a remarkable blue. "I never thought to know such happiness again," she said. "How will I ever thank you?"

"By bearing my nephew several sons and naming at least one of them after me."

"I should like a son named Horace, though I daresay, when he is toddling about, with his stride resembling yours, I shall take to calling him 'The Little Admiral.' "

"What do you mean, with a stride resembling mine?"

Grace smiled. "Oh, nothing to signify."

He chuckled heartily. "Ah, Grace, how you do warm my heart. You are like a daughter to me and a very great comfort. My children are established too far away from Devonshire for my contentment. Your presence in my life, in our home, along with the twins, has been exactly what both my wife and I have needed in these our waning years."

"We have become a family of sorts, have we not?"

"Indeed, we have. The loss of those we loved brought us all together, and for that I cannot be sad."

"Nor can I," she murmured, her gaze again drifting to the snow-packed hills and the blue sky beyond. "Nor can I."